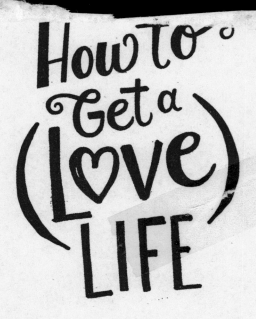

How to Get a (Love) LIFE

Rosie Blake spent her university years writing pantomimes based on old classics, including 'The Wizard of Odd: Search for the Ruby Strippers' and 'Harry Potter: The Musical' (complete with moving opening number, 'In My Cupboard I Will Stay'). Rosie went on to write a winning short story in the La Senza/Little Black Dress Short Story Competition, and features for *Cosmopolitan* magazine, before turning to books.

Rosie likes baked items, taking long walks by the river and speaking about herself in the third person. She can be found at www.r̶

How to Get a (Love) Life

Rosie Blake

CORVUS

First published in 2014 by Novelicious Books,
an imprint of Novelicious Books Ltd.

Published in e-book in Great Britain in 2015 by Corvus,
an imprint of Atlantic Books Ltd.

This paperback edition published in Great Britain in 2017 by Corvus.

10 9 8 7 6 5 4 3 2 1

A CIP catalogue record for this book is available from the British Library.

Paperback ISBN: 978 1 78239 864 6
E-book ISBN: 978 1 78239 865 3

Printed in Great Britain by CPI Group (UK) Ltd, Croydon CR0 4YY

Corvus
An imprint of Atlantic Books Ltd
Ormond House
26–27 Boswell Street
London
WC1N 3JZ

www.corvus-books.co.uk

All the characters in this book are fictitious and any resemblance to actual persons, living or dead, is purely coincidental. Except for Chris, who is as big a knob in real life as he is in this book.

PROLOGUE

STARING UP at the departures desk, I scanned the list of destinations. In just two hours the flight to Greece would be leaving and I would be on it. My compact grey suitcase, hastily packed that morning, stood to attention by my side. I was ready to go.

All around me, loved-up couples held hands and giggled sickeningly over one another. Giddy children gazed up at the illuminated flight boards, their faces full of wonder and excitement. A young mother cooed at her perfect and adorable baby. One daddy clutched his youngest boy to him as his eldest attempted to clamber onto his back.

Everyone is in a unit.

A sad, single tear sloped down my cheek. I wiped it away fiercely. What was I doing? Why was I here? How had things gone *this* wrong?

As I rolled my suitcase over to the check-in queue, I felt a firm tap on my shoulder.

'You going too, eh?'

The voice belonged to a woman dressed as if she was about to strut out on stage at *The X Factor*. Her neon orange vest-top failed to restrain a roll of pasty flesh and her enormous round earrings looked like weird green moons orbiting her head. Her clothes shouted 'teenager!' but the fine lines around her eyes suggested that she was in her early thirties.

'Um, yes.'

'Sick! Me too!' She laughed – revealing a lipstick mark on her front tooth – and pointed a coral-painted false nail at her luggage. 'Packing light as ever. Ha ha.'

The unfeasibly high pitch of her laugh sliced right through me.

'Oh, yeah,' I nodded, trying my best to be polite, while every sinew of my body screamed: *Leave me alone, Overly Bright Airport Girl! Can't you see I want to curl up into a ball and crrrryyyy?*

Remaining firmly at my side, she manoeuvred her suitcase next to mine and held out a stick of gum.

I shook my head. 'No, thanks.'

She popped it into her mouth and talked through it. 'You know, I've been on three of these holidays and I've *always* pulled.' She paused to stretch a bit of the gum out before rolling it back in her mouth. 'Shagged one guy for the whole week last time and then he got picked up at the airport by his *wife*. Awks.'

She smiled at me. It was my line.

'That's *terrible*,' I said.

'Yeah, whatevs. I 'spose it just wasn't meant to be. Better than the 2011 guy who was super clingy. I had to be all, like, "Hellooo, back off, I am totes not into back hair."'

Me again: 'Er...'

'Soooo, you hoping to meet a fella?'

I opened my mouth to speak, but the words stuck in my throat. I wondered again what I was doing in this queue of people: how had my life come to this?

'Your first time?' Her head cocked to one side.

'Yes,' I confirmed, as the gorgeously tanned woman behind the check-in desk beckoned me over. I approached and slid my passport over the counter. Overly Bright Airport Girl stayed fixed at my shoulder. I waited for Check-In Woman to shoo her back into the queue, but it was clearly assumed we were travelling together because Check-In Woman took her passport too. I turned to Overly Bright Airport Girl and said with a gulp: 'It's... my first singles holiday.'

She squeaked at my announcement, her glossy pink mouth a big 'Ooh' of pleasure. A tall man in the queue next door sniggered.

I coughed and continued. 'Yes. I am a single woman who is deliberately going on this holiday with the hope of meeting someone who will love me.'

Check-In Woman looped a sticker through the handle of my suitcase and raised one neatly pencilled eyebrow. Arms wide, I turned to the rest of the airport. 'It is my first ever, *ever* time on a singles holiday,' I cried. 'I booked it last night because it seemed like the right thing to do. I just needed to... I wanted to, you know... um...' I trailed off idiotically, watching as my suitcase juddered along the luggage belt and out of sight.

In the distance I thought I heard someone calling my

name and in that moment my heart soared. I whipped round – hair flicking across my face in my haste – and scanned the crowds hopefully...

Nope.

Nothing.

I'd imagined it. My stomach lurched.

Overly Bright Airport Girl slung her meaty arm round my shoulders.

'We should totes sit together on the flight. I'll show you my holiday pictures from last year. I've got them all on my phone. All of them.'

I sniffed, nodded once, resigned. 'Great.'

Nicola Brown, how the hell did you end up here?

CHAPTER ONE

Single, white, female, 29,
GSOH, N/S. Definitely not
interested in meeting nice
man for friendship or more.

Contact: Box No. 235

IT ALWAYS made me feel itchy when things were out of place. I couldn't seem to settle unless everything around me was completely ordered. For instance: I'd just aimed a screwed-up piece of paper at the bin and missed. It had sailed beautifully over the room, hit the rim and fallen to the floor, where it now lay. And I couldn't stop thinking about it. I knew I should leave it there – others would leave it – it really was no big deal...

Caroline sat across the way, head of wild auburn curls bent over her desk, engrossed in her current task. She was surrounded by a fort of sweet wrappers, invoices, brochures and photographs. She hadn't noticed anything was wrong. Of course she hadn't. To anyone else there *was* nothing wrong.

I stared resolutely at the actor's headshot I was holding until the image swam before my eyes and it became a blur of a face, like a child's watercolour. My eyes flicked back to the paper on the floor.

I drummed my biro against the desk.

Just leave it there, Nicola.

It was no use. With a heavy sigh, I stood up, walked across the office, picked up the piece of paper and dropped it in the bin, exactly where it belonged. I tried to convince myself I was just stretching my legs. Who was I kidding?

Caroline looked up as I passed her, nudged out of concentration.

'Lunchtime?' she asked hopefully.

I gave her a wry smile. 'It's only eleven-twenty, Caroline.'

She pulled a face and returned to typing, though how she did it, I had no clue; her keyboard always seemed to be half-submerged under a sea of paper and neon Post-it notes. How she *ever* managed to get anything done was beyond me. Important documents were nestled under other piles of documents (also important), yet she always managed to produce exactly what we needed, and laughed at my disbelief when she did. 'Organized Chaos' she called it. I called it Black Magic. The notion that anyone could live like that was bewildering to me, but Caroline Harper's desk was a perfect reflection of how she lived her life. At least her mess no longer annoyed me, which was testament to how much I'd grown to like her. I envied her easy manner; people's eyes lit up when they came in to see Caroline, knowing they would be greeted with a hot cup of coffee and some kind words. Desperate actresses, bored and out of work, always left smiling, hope re-born inside them. On the phone, she laughed with potential clients, giggling at their stories. I was more suited to bookings, searching out new talent and ensuring the office ran smoothly. Caroline often said I was the cogs to her clock, which made more sense than most of her phrases (yesterday's front-runner: *He's all talk and no pyjamas* – more information than I really needed about her husband).

We made a great team, Caroline and I, which was extraordinary, considering the rocky first impression I'd made at my interview four years ago...

The Sullivan Agency, Bristol's largest actors' agency, was on the second floor of a Georgian building at the top of Park Street. Below, the street thrummed with the hustle and bustle of city life; busy bookshops, cafes with colourful canopies and beautiful vintage clothing stores lined both sides of the street and curved round the corner at the bottom of the hill. Initially impressed with the entrance to the office – a heavy oak door leading to a staircase lined with black-and-white photographs of the actors on their books – I'd felt nervous as I walked up. I paused on the landing, momentarily distracted by muddy footprints on a carpet the colour of clotted cream, fingerprints on the large sash windows and a dying yucca plant (could you even kill a yucca plant?) wilting in the corner. I'd breathed in, and then out even more slowly, attempting to steady myself. The glass lettering on the door to the office announced *The Sullivan Agency*. I knocked tentatively, palms damp. Clutching my black leather satchel in one hand, I waited. My outline was reflected in the cloudy glass. I patted at my bobbed hair, trimmed that week.

'Come in, come in,' called a bright female voice.

Fixing what I hoped was a relaxed and confident smile on my face, I pushed open the door.

'Arrrrrrrrrr,' screamed a small boy dressed as a pirate. He brandished a cutlass sword at my stomach. His eyepatch meant I could only make out one menacing eye.

I jumped backwards, one hand to my chest, and let out a yelp.

'Who be you, arrrrrrrrrr?' he asked, waving his sword from side to side.

A woman, about ten years older than me, with a mass of red curls, kind eyes, and a small girl on her lap, looked up. 'Ben – don't scare the lady. Be nice.'

Ben pivoted back round, *Arrr'ed* at the woman, who I assumed was his mother, ran over to a swivel chair, threw himself into it, and started bashing the keyboard with both hands.

'Welcome, hi, I'm Caroline,' said the woman, with a grin. 'I would get up and shake your hand, but...' she nodded her head towards the young girl in her arms and re-adjusted the green ribbon in her hair. 'Alice, Ben, say hello to, um...' she paused and looked down at her sheet.

'Nicola.'

'Of course, Nicola! I'm sorry, I've got baby brain, or children brain... actually, to be honest, I'm useless with names most of the time.'

'It's fine,' I said, looking surreptitiously around the room for somewhere to sit and wait. Pirate Ben had moved on to picking up the telephone and screaming 'Arrrrrrr' into it before slamming it back in its cradle. I smiled at him but he was far too involved in his world of pirate destruction to notice.

'... I've had to bring these two to work because my child-minder just let me down. She normally does Thursdays, but – *oh no, Alice!*'

Alice flung her apple juice carton down on to Caroline's desk, where its contents seeped into the computer keyboard.

'Oh Christ.' Caroline swung her daughter across her body, seized a filthy-looking wet wipe and dabbed at the juice. She was wearing some sort of colourful poncho and as she cleared up the mess it jingled with the sound of little bells sewn into the hem.

Ben, sensing new commotion, jumped down off his swivel chair, swished his sword around again and told me to, 'Walk the plank, walk the plank.'

I was seriously considering whether to about-turn and run far, far away from this nightmare of mess and madness when a man burst out from a side office, filling the cramped space with his tall frame and wide shoulders.

Raking a hand through his dark hair, he said, 'Caroline, I've got bloody Chris on the phone asking for the details of his voiceover on Monday. What did Suzy do with the info from the compu...' He trailed off as he caught me hovering by the doorway. He looked momentarily puzzled before realization lit up his eyes. Walking across the room in three big strides, he held out his hand. 'I'm so sorry, you must be Nicola, here for the interview. I'm James, James Sullivan.

We spoke on the phone last week.' I leaned towards him and took his hand in my best firm grasp. I'd recently read a book about successful interviewing and it said that the handshake could potentially decide *everything*. I was so busy thinking about whether I was doing a good handshake, I'd forgotten to actually let go of his hand. I swiftly removed it.

'That's me!' I said in a strangled voice.

'Brilliant. And you're early.' He glanced at the clock above the doorway. 'Ah, no, you're right on time. Wonderful, great, well, do come on in, and apologies for the bad language earlier, and the, er, carnage, it's been a busy day, week.'

'Month,' Caroline muttered, just loud enough for me to hear.

Ben tugged on the bottom of James' navy jumper.

James immediately stood to attention. 'What is it, my Capt'n?'

Ben proffered a bundle of papers, which, judging from James' relieved expression, contained the information he'd just been after.

James thanked him with an 'Arrrrrr, my matey!' and turned to me. 'It seems you have some competition, Nicola,' he laughed, ruffling Ben's hair. Before I could say anything in return, Ben suddenly decided to become a helicopter (since being a PA was obviously not exciting enough). Rotating his arms, he started running round the room, causing his sister Alice to gleefully clap her hands and drop the apple-juice carton once more. Caroline simply sat there laughing as the juice ran across a notepad and dripped rhythmically on to the office floor.

CHAPTER TWO

STEPPING OVER three abandoned toy cars, Helicopter Ben, and a Thomas the Tank Engine colouring-in book, I'd followed James into his office.

As he closed the door, I could make out the soothing murmur of Classic FM filtering through his radio, the children's voices now an indistinguishable haze. James indicated a worn brown leather chair by the fireplace. 'Do take a seat. I'm sorry to have kept you.'

'Not at all,' I said, sitting down carefully, one leg tucked behind the other, back straight.

'Well, you've had quite an introduction.' He grinned, unearthing my CV from a desk strewn with pieces of paper, rogue stationery and, oddly, some gold coins. 'Pirate money,' he explained, before catching my polite 'work' smile and coughing. 'So, Nicola, your CV is excellent. I see you've got a lot of experience working in busy offices?' He scanned my credentials. 'You worked as a PA for a head-hunting firm. I'll bet that was busy?'

'Yes. Very busy.' I answered stiffly.

'So, why do you want to work as a PA in a small agency like

this?' His grey eyes examined my face. I shifted in my seat.

'I... wanted a change of job. I thought that working for an actors' agent would be a new challenge, a fresh start, a step towards, um, a step towards, to, to...'

I floundered. I was pretty sure that *because I'm really desperate* or *because I won't be able to pay my rent this month if I don't work* wouldn't cut it as appropriate answers. I felt hot. It was really hot in here. My hands hovered over my skirt, wanting to smooth it down again, wanting to do *something*.

'Don't worry, Nicola,' James said kindly. 'The truth is, I just need a good PA. Someone who doesn't mind working hard. Of course, you'll occasionally have to be able to deal with egos, field calls from exasperated actors, difficult clients, although,' he glanced back down at my CV, 'with your experience, I doubt you'll find that a problem.' He smiled, showing off a row of perfectly straight white teeth. 'So, when can you start?'

I blinked in surprise. *That was it?* 'I, well, um, I...'

'Oh, sorry to just blurt that out. Would you like me to make an offer in writing? It's just we are so bogged down at the minute and you seem perfect for the job. Do you think you could work here?' I examined his face a little more closely. A pulse throbbed in his neck, his eyes were slightly bloodshot. I felt an urge to say yes, to rescue him. But I didn't like to make quick decisions. Ever.

I pictured my neatly handwritten list of other interviews I had lined up. Each job had a blank box beside it ready to be ticked when I had been. My heart thumped quickly in my chest. This was my first interview; what if this office was wrong for me? What if Caroline and I hated each other? What if James was a nightmare boss? What if...?

Then I looked up at him again, saw his strained smile, those bloodshot eyes, and found myself nodding at him.

James leapt up from his chair with a delighted smile and shook me enthusiastically by the hand. 'That is excellent, very good.'

I couldn't help but laugh.

'So, when *can* you start?' he asked.

Without pausing to think about it as seriously as I usually thought these things through, I heard myself reply: 'Today.'

'Caroline, get in here,' James called in the direction of the outer office. 'Quickly! Before the spell is broken and she changes her mind!'

Caroline appeared in the doorway, her daughter dangling from one leg, her arms in surrender as Ben stood behind her with what looked like a stapler-cum-gun.

'Tell me good news, please,' she said, shifting her daughter from one leg to the other.

'Nicola here has kindly agreed to start work today.'

Caroline moved – as fast as a woman with a toddler attached to one limb could – towards me. 'That is fantastic news! I like you already,' she said, her poncho and necklace jangling along with her words.

'Well, arrrrr,' James said. 'I think the good ship here is in safe hands and someone can take their little pirates home for fish fingers and chips. What say you, tiny pirate?' He peered at Ben who, thankfully, had lowered the stapler/gun.

'That would be incredibly kind of you,' Caroline said. 'But perhaps I should stay, show Nicola the ropes...' She stifled a yawn as Alice attempted to climb further up her leg.

I felt a spark of sympathy towards her. She looked shattered. 'Really, go, I'll be fine,' I said in my brightest, most 'can-do' voice.

She didn't need any more encouragement.

'Are you sure? Thank you! I owe you! See you tomorrow!' And, with that, she gathered up her handbag, coat and unruly offspring and dashed out of the office. James raced off soon after for an important lunch meeting and I was left standing alone on the blue carpeted floor. I blinked. I did not expect to be left on my own in the office within twenty minutes of being hired. It was highly unorthodox and oddly trusting. How did they know I wasn't a burglar? An office stationery-stealing burglar. Looking around at my new workplace, I exhaled slowly. Before I could even sit down at my desk, I spotted a thick layer of dust on the top of the filing cabinet, old coffee cups ringed with brown, and a scattering of pirate money across the carpet. I cracked my knuckles and moved towards the kitchen to find cleaning equipment. There was work to do.

The sound of the downstairs door opening pulled me back to the present and I straightened in anticipation of James' imminent arrival. Whereas I knew every intimate detail of Caroline's personal life (she was a sharer), I knew very little about James', although I *did* know that he had lots of girlfriends. His latest – Tahlula or Tuilie or Tinkerbell, one of those exotic names – did something arty with clothes. She often swept glamorously into the office in search of James, chatting overly loudly with the actors and demanding coffee espresso, which Caroline always went out and got her from the cafe next door.

In a whirlwind of energy, James Sullivan burst through the door and made a beeline for his office, wrestling himself out of his caramel-coloured woollen coat. 'Caroline, can you do me a favour? Get me Pamela's PA on the phone and tell her—'

'*Morning*,' Caroline smiled at him, waving a pen.

He blinked. 'Oh yes, morning. And, Nicola, will you tell Chris that he really needs to make a decision about that camera ad? Can you also chase Prince Productions for the repeat fees from that police TV series? Thanks.' He dived into his office and closed the door. A few seconds later it opened again and he popped his head back round. 'You're both darlings.'

'And you're welcome,' Caroline laughed as he re-closed his office door. She turned to me and shook her head. 'That man needs to slow down or he'll have heart failure by the age of thirty-five.'

'I concur.' I nodded, as I reluctantly dialled Chris's number.

Chris was one of our agency's most successful actors. Which was good. But he was a complete nightmare to deal with. Which was bad. He liked me, though, which made him marginally less irritating to deal with. When I'd first met him he'd been sitting at James' desk laughing uproariously, beautiful head thrown back, perfect bleached teeth flashing dangerously as a deep growl of a laugh reverberated around the room. It was rare that any man made an impression on me, but even I had to (begrudgingly) admit that Chris was very, very good-looking. He had the lazy confidence of a man who was used to being looked at by women. He'd landed a ton of commercials playing the smouldering hero and was now a main character in a soap. He'd recently been requested for a digital camera ad. The ad agency creatives wanted Chris to play a smouldering hero who meets a smouldering woman for plenty of smouldering looks, etc. He'd known about the advert for a week but still hadn't confirmed if he could do it. Other actors would visit the office weekly, ask what we'd put them up for, update their CV, ring us back the second they picked up our messages. But not Chris. Oh no. I sighed as his answerphone kicked in and his smooth drawl announced: 'You've reached Christopher Sheldon-Wade's phone... you know the drill.'

I cringed at the message. 'Chris, it's Nicola calling from The Sullivan Agency. We need an answer on the camera commercial so we can set it up with the client. Could you please call us back when you pick up this message. Thank you.' I replaced the receiver, careful to straighten the phone so that it was in line with my notepad.

Caroline didn't look up from her work. 'He won't call you back, you know, Nic. He'll make you chase.'

'I know,' I muttered grumpily.

'He's just sitting there, Nic, looking at his phone as it rings, laughing at us!'

I tucked a strand of hair behind my ear. 'I'm sure he's not!'

'I bet he is. That boy needs a good… a good…' She waved her pen around again, struggling to find a suitable phrase. 'A good smash round the ear,' she finished triumphantly.

'Er…' *Smash?*

'Honestly, Nic,' she continued, warming to her topic. 'He swaggers about, flicking his hair and refusing to say yes or no to anything, never has the decency to tell us when he becomes "ill".' She put her pen down so that she could mime the quotation marks. 'Never cares if we secure him a job or get him an audition, and he never calls back, never, never, never, nev—'

The ringing of the phone silenced her rant. I smirked at her as I lifted the receiver to my ear.

'Well, it won't be him,' she said, crossing her arms.

I poked my tongue out at her and smiled smugly as I replied into the phone receiver, 'Ahhh, Chris, how *nice* of you to phone back so quickly.'

Caroline rolled her eyes at me. The grin was soon wiped off my face, however, when Chris purred down the line 'Niccccccola… will I ever see your kniccccccckers?'

Instantly flustered, I ignored his question and instead replied with a formal, 'Right, okay, so this camera ad wants you to confirm—'

'Your voice is so sexy on the telephone, Nicola,' he whispered laughingly.

As always, I tried to remain professional. Chris was used to having women fall at his feet and he'd been pretty put out that I never had. Consequently, he now seemed determined to make me agree to go out with him. It was tricky because he was one of our biggest clients and I had to keep him on side, meaning I'd spent four years making up feeble excuses and dreading his every phone call.

'Um, Chris, I just want an answer one way or another so I can call the people back.'

'Nicola, you never play with me. Always work, work, work.' He sighed. I pictured his peachy lips in a childish pout.

'Yes, well, it is my job,' I reminded him, reaching out to put my pencil back in its place, on the right of the keyboard. 'So, Chris...'

'So, Nicola,' he teased, not at all put off by my clearly unenthusiastic tone.

'Chris.' I repeated.

Caroline gave me another quizzical look; I shifted a little under her gaze.

'*Nicola.*'

'Yes.'

'Nicola, Nicola, Nicola,' he went on, 'my answer is...' He paused, and I waited, refusing to give him any new distraction.

'It's a...'

I waited some more.

'A... yes!' he exclaimed grandly.

I exhaled quickly and swung into action. 'Wonderful, that is wonderful. So, I'll just book that in and let you know when you need to be there.'

'You do that, Nicolllllla.'

'I will. Okay, well, that's everything!' I said briskly, the end of the phone call in sight.

'Oh, and Nicolllllla,' he drawled in an irritating sing-song voice.

'Yes, Chris?' I gritted my teeth.

'I'll be seeing you soooon,' he whispered. Then, with a roar of laughter, he hung up. I stared blankly at the receiver.

Caroline didn't look up from her work. 'Prick,' she muttered and I gave a snort of laughter in reply.

CHAPTER THREE

AS USUAL, the morning swept by, the phone rang off the hook and I barely even had time to sip at my eleven o'clock glass of chilled mineral water. At five to one, I swivelled round in my chair. Caroline looked up.

'It must be five to one,' she smirked.

'Ha ha ha, yes, you win.'

'You are as regular as a watch.'

I shrugged. I liked routine! Caroline teased me about it but I didn't get what was so bad about wanting to do things on time. I took out a cellophane sandwich bag from the top drawer of my desk.

'Ooh, what are you splurging on today then?' taunted Caroline, accustomed to my weekly meal plan. 'Let me guess.' She put both hands to the side of her head and massaged her temples in the manner of a psychic. 'It's... avocado salad with pine nuts?'

I silently produced my avocado salad with pine nuts from the container in the bag. I only glanced up when she cackled and yelled 'Bingo!' My cheeks flushed with heat. I lifted out my cutlery, getting up to wash it carefully in our miniscule kitchen, before popping a tea towel on my desk so nothing could spill. I sat back down and started eating my salad. As I chewed, my mouth watered at the thought of my chocolate mini roll, not to be eaten until one-fifteen. I fantasized about the smooth case of chocolate, giving way to the succulent sponge underneath, made complete by the spiral of cream piped through it. I stared longingly at it over my lettuce.

Caroline giggled. 'I dare you to leave it till half past one,' she said, pointing at the mini roll.

I laughed casually, in an attempt to pretend that I was unbothered. But I would not be leaving it until half past one. I liked to eat my mini roll at *quarter* past one. There was nothing weird about that.

'Go on, Nicola,' she teased, 'leave it till half past, I double-dare you.'

Caroline often dared me to do things. She often double-dared me. Sometimes she even double-dared me with no returns. Of course, I never took her up on them.

'Go away,' I said, chomping decisively down on a carrot stick and eyeing my mini roll with concern. Would she take my mini roll to prove a point? Would she ruin my one pleasurable lunchtime treat? I bit my lip.

I nibbled at the lettuce, enjoying the taste of the avocado and wishing for a moment that I'd added some dressing. But the moment passed and the voice of my super-thin mother echoed around the office space: 'Little pickers wear bigger knickers.'

I took another look at the mini roll.

Caroline sighed mournfully as she watched me delicately

21

picking through my first course. 'I wish I could limit myself to salad,' she said, polishing off an enormous baguette that contained so much cheese and meat the sight was almost indecent. She grabbed what she could; always far more concerned with her kids or her husband David's eating habits. As she carefully wiped a crumb from her top lip, I realized she'd managed to finish the thing in less than four minutes.

'I'm impressed,' I laughed.

'I'm going for the world record,' she said solemnly. 'You just wait, Nicola, one day when there is a universal food crisis, all the people with lots of flesh are going to last a lot longer than you skinny belinkies. Right, I'm popping next door for a Snickers, do you...' The question died on her lips and she sighed again. 'I'll bring you back some Tic Tacs.'

The rain outside was persistent and the heavy drops on the window next to me made their unpredictable routes downwards. I looked out and onto the street below. A woman battled with an umbrella and a child, scolding one and then the other as they both refused to do her bidding. I was pleased to be inside, in the comfort of our office, heating always turned up to near tropical, prints on the walls depicting calming oceans and rolling sand dunes.

Caroline, having returned from her Snickers run, was sitting quietly at her desk, systematically binning junk mail and opening the day's post. It was calm, easy, comfortable. And yet, as ever, I had a nagging feeling of something forgotten, a hole. As I glanced back out at the grey skies, a face swam into my mind's eye. Thick blonde hair, cheeks red from the cold. He was tenderly wrapping a black scarf around my neck and the look in his eyes made me shiver. He held out one gloved hand to me, inviting me onto the ice. I took it, feeling a surge of love for him.

I shook the thought away, looked down and mentally scolded myself for failing to pay attention to my work. I'd almost put all the 'W' contacts into the 'P' column.

Focus, Nicola.

I heard a low whistle and glanced up. Caroline was looking at the CV of another aspiring young thesp seeking an agent. She inhaled sharply and followed it up with 'Oooooh. He's lurvely!' She held up a black-and-white headshot of a brooding hunk. 'Nicola, look at him!'

'Thanks, Caroline, but I'm still digesting my lunch.'

'Isn't he wonderful? A face that could get lots of ships to sail.'

'*Divine*. But I think that prize goes to Helen.'

'He's wonderful, but...' She paused. 'He's still not quite up to Patrick's standard, is he?'

'Hmmm,' I replied non-committally.

Please don't bring out Patrick's picture again, please don't, please don't, please... But Caroline was already carefully taking Patrick out of her desk drawer. She sat in a familiar pose; eyes glassy, face focused on the piece of card she was now holding carefully in both hands, lest she bend it.

'Look at him,' she sighed.

'Oh God,' I giggled, leaning back in my chair. 'Let him *go*, Caroline.'

'Just... *look* at him,' she repeated, standing up abruptly and clutching his face to her substantial bosom.

'*Caroline!*' I laughed as she walked towards me with the picture of Patrick: her favourite on the agency's books, her Number One, her 10/10.

'It's like he's looking right at you, isn't it?' she crooned, thrusting the photo of the brooding young actor – all toothy smiles, deep pools of loveliness for eyes and lustrous dark hair – under my nose.

'Yes, yes, he's very nice.' I nodded. I knew what would come next.

'Nice?' she spluttered. 'Is that the best you can do, girl? Look at those eyes, look at those cheekbones, look at the sculpted face and hair you could rake your fingers through of an evening. Look at those long eyelashes and the haunted expression that says *lie with me, come hither, I want you...*' She sighed dreamily and stroked the photograph.

'Hmm, I agree he's very attractive.' I nodded, trying not to giggle. Caroline could get quite cross if I wasn't suitably appreciative of the sculpted face of Patrick.

'God, Nicola, say it like you mean it. Would you even care if he walked into this office right now?' She gestured dramatically to the empty doorway.

'Er.' I followed the direction of her arm uncertainly, almost expecting to see Patrick standing there. 'Sure, yes,' I said, trying to bury this conversation quickly.

Caroline continued, 'If he swept in and said—' she held his photo in front of her face so it looked like he was talking to me – 'Nicola, Nicola *Beautiful* Brown, come away with me to Paris

24

tonight, for dinner, you and me. Come away with me under the stars and let me *woo* you.' Then she made kissy noises and waggled his photo at me. I started to giggle as this weird puppet with a pretty boy's head and Caroline's enormous flowered breasts bobbed up and down in front of me.

'Stop it, Caroline,' I squeaked.

She carried on with the kissy noises, making them even more amorous.

'Stop it,' I insisted more firmly.

She pulled the picture away from her face. 'And what are you doing tonight anyway? What if someone *did* ask you to Paris?'

'I've got a nice quiet night in planned.'

'No hot date lined up?'

'No.'

'No boyfriend cooking you a meal?'

'No, you know I don't have a boyfriend.'

She put the photo onto her desk and looked at me seriously. 'I know that, but it's madness, Nic. You're beautiful and lovely, you could get anyone.'

'Don't start that rubbish.'

'It's not rubbish. You're rubbish!'

We both stared at each other a little stonily, and then I started to laugh. James put his head round the door. 'What's so funny?'

'Nothing. Nothing's funny,' I said quickly, before Caroline could say anything to embarrass me.

Caroline looked directly at me and, mouth downturned into a sad smile, said, 'No, it really isn't.'

CHAPTER FOUR

I **LIVED ALONE.** In many ways I would make an excellent room-mate: I am meticulously tidy due to an obsession with cleaning that borders on OCD, I like to catalogue my DVDs and label all foodstuffs neatly and clearly. After seven years of living like this – three in London, four in Bristol – it had become a welcome habit. Just me, in my house, with my things. No hassles, no fighting over the remote, no petty things to fall out over, no seemingly innocuous comment that plunges you straight into a hideous row you never wanted.

Nobody to break your heart.

Considering my preference for living alone, when I returned to my flat that evening I should have been surprised to find the lights already on. I should have been surprised to smell the pleasant aroma of a dinner in the air, to hear the television blaring out. I should have been doubly surprised to see my older brother Mark lounging casually on my cream -leather corner sofa. But I wasn't.

'How the hell did you get in... *again*?' Tiredness made my voice grumpy.

'Ah, sister, what a greeting,' Mark said, jumping up and pressing mute. 'Your loopy Spanish landlord waved me in and kindly lent me the spare key.' He dangled said key from his finger.

'He's Portuguese,' I corrected.

My brother shrugged. 'Still loopy, though.'

I made a mental note to tackle the landlord again but knew in my heart I wouldn't summon the guts required. I'd always nodded politely at him when I'd first moved in, thanked him quietly when he picked up the previous occupant's post. Then he'd got a bit more personal, asking me questions about myself. He'd started calling me 'Neecola' and leaving me presents at my door (biscuits, cards, flowers, a porcelain rabbit). I hadn't the nerve to ask him to stop and assumed he'd thought my silence signified his passion was not so requited. The final crunch had been when I'd come home to discover two towels on my bed rolled into the image of two swans kissing. I'd got my brother round to have some strong words with him and the two of them had hit it off. Bloody typical. The landlord had promised Mark that he would never enter my flat without my permission again, or sculpt any of my linen into any shape of any kind of animal, and the matter had been dropped without the need to pursue a restraining order. Sadly, this meant the landlord and my brother were now so bonded he clearly thought nothing of letting him into my flat at the drop of a hat.

Mark was what people described as *a real character* which, roughly translated, meant that at times he bordered on the socially unacceptable. He had a wild mop of dark brown hair, lived in a battered leather jacket and drove a moped which he treated like a motorbike (and therefore considered an acceptable mode of transportation). He worked at the planetarium – a sort of enormous silver football right in the centre of town – spending his days pointing out the various constellations of stars to eager youths, and sending his science show reel to various production companies in the hope of becoming a hugely successful science presenter. He resented the fact that I had been unable to secure him a presenting job and thought that I was deliberately keeping my science-producer/BBC-documentary-makers-contacts firmly to myself. Mark loved all things science and was absolutely obsessed with bats. Bats were Mark's one true love. *'Wouldn't you be obsessed if you knew there are over eleven hundred species of bat and that they make up twenty per cent of the world's mammal population?'* Quite.

He rarely took an interest in the opposite sex, preferring the safety of a lab and a bunch of coloured test tubes for company. I once asked him where he would go on a honeymoon and he'd answered, in a perfectly serious voice, that he would spend seven days in a cave photographing and studying the nocturnal habits of the Townsend's long-eared bat. When I'd pointed out that his beloved might not be so keen on the idea of resting her head on an inflatable pillow, curled up in a sleeping bag as small rodents dive-bombed overhead, my brother had looked at me blankly. 'We would never be able to carry all that equipment. Inflatable pillows are an enormous waste of backpack space.'

Recently, however, he'd been taking more of an active

interest in females. He was approaching his thirty-fifth birthday and had decided that this was an appropriate age for him to 'settle down'. He had made the misguided assumption that, as his little sister, I was surely a great way to meet women of a similar age. So every now and again he would descend on me for the night just in case I was suddenly spending my Wednesday evenings surrounded by a team of supple, yet intelligent, female netballers or a book club of sexy, bespectacled young ladies.

'Tell me. To what do I owe this wonderful pleasure?' I asked, gesturing at him lounging all over the furniture. 'No plans tonight, brother dear? No spectacular date lined up? Or have you just come over specifically to damage my coffee table with your ugly boots.' I stared deliberately at them (does anyone else wear Doc Martens in the twenty-first century?).

'You need tea, sis,' Mark said, removing the boots and ambling into the kitchen. 'Or wine,' he called. 'Where's the wine?'

'In the fridge,' I called back as I frantically wiped at the table where his boots had been. I had some glass polisher under the sink... *Should I wait until he's gone to work at the smears? Oh, what does it matter? I'll get the polish now, otherwise I won't relax at all.*

Mark didn't look in the least surprised as I pushed past him while he waited for the kettle and returned to the living room with a cloth and a spray can to hand. By the time he emerged, the coffee table looked brand new. I thanked him for my glass of wine and fetched two coasters.

'Just wanted to see you, sister dearest. I went on a date last night.' He perched on the arm of the sofa.

'Oh, really,' I said with interest. 'How did it go?'

'Go?' He looked up in surprise. 'I suppose it went well... Yes, as dates go, it could be rated positively.'

'What was she like?'

'Oh, hopeless,' he said, with a dismissive wave of his hand.

'But you just said it went well?'

'The date did. She, however, was all wrong.'

'Oh. Well, what was wrong with her?' I asked. 'Boring?'

'No.'

'Ugly?' I ventured.

'No.'

'Crazy?'

'No.'

'Too loud?'

'No.'

'Too quiet?' I asked, tiring of this game rapidly.

'No.'

'Too... uninterested in bats?'

'No. Too old,' Mark said matter-of-factly.

'Charming. How old is she?'

'Thirty-three.'

'Thirty-three isn't old.'

'Doesn't matter anyway,' he said brightly. 'I've got another date tomorrow night.'

'Fast work, brother dear.' I nodded. 'So, how's life at the planetarium?'

'Fine...' he said.

Oh God. I was going to have to ask. 'And, er, how's the search for a bat TV show?' I tried to sound breezy and light-hearted.

He exhaled dramatically, the wine glass wobbling precariously in his hand. 'I'm brilliant, but I'm undiscovered and I'm running out of time.'

'Rubbish...' I said, and then after a pause, 'you're not brilliant.'

He looked aghast.

'That was a *joke*,' I said hurriedly. 'You've just got to keep sending your stuff in and build up some contacts. What happened to Snake Man?'

Snake Man had been a particular stooge at the BBC who had managed to get my brother a five-minute segment on a wildlife programme for the Natural History Channel. They'd paid Mark £250 for two days of filming and he'd spent the rest of that year behaving like David Attenborough, often at unexpected, and usually inappropriate moments (one particularly memorable moment being at the dinner table after Aunt Hilda's funeral when Mark's impression had set my uncle off into a fresh round of tears – 'Hilda loved nature programmes.'). Since this triumph, however, there had been no work forthcoming and no more phone calls from Snake Man.

'You must know of some jobs going in the presenting world,' he said huffily, before taking a sip from his glass.

'Look, as I've told you a million times, we are an *actors'* agency. We don't specialize in the niche of science presenting jobs.'

'Oh come on, sis, you're all in on it together,' he grumbled. 'You guys are always hobnobbing at these awards and things.'

'What awards?' I laughed.

He still thought my job involved going to the BAFTAs to watch our clients accept little gold statues and make emotional speeches about their *wonderful* agents.

'Today I got one of our clients an advert for a digital camera. There aren't too many award ceremony invites flooding our post,' I insisted.

'Well, surely you see each other at agent things,' he huffed, determined not to give it up.

I sighed. 'I will try to make more enquiries into production companies looking for ageing science presenters who have an unhealthy and unnatural obsession with bats,' I droned.

'Thanks, sis,' he said, his face lighting up, brain seemingly unable to register my sarcastic tone.

The timer pinged in the kitchen. 'Dinner,' he announced with a grin.

'Great, what have you made?' I asked, instantly planning to eschew his dinner in favour of my own regular Wednesday evening meal of grilled salmon, baby potatoes and mange tout.

'Pizza.'

He scooted into the kitchen and after an unusual amount of noise for someone simply finding a plate, he re-entered holding the pizza aloft on a wooden chopping board. 'Grub's up, sis!' He lowered the chopping board reverentially onto the table. I cringed as I watched the stray crumbs scatter themselves over the clean surface.

'I'm fine, thanks. I'll make myself something in a bit,' I said with a grimace.

'Oh, come on, Nicola, there's loads.' He crammed a large slice into his mouth. 'Don't be so uptight! You're skin and bones anyway. Relax, have a bit of pizza, it'll sort you right out.'

I looked at it slavishly. The melted cheese, peppers, pieces of meat and other delights were chopped into its gooey topping. The crust looked lightly browned and delicious, the scent of it like a bakery in the morning. *What would it matter if I had some pizza?* I mused for a brief moment before pushing the thought away. I'd already bought the salmon for tonight and Thursdays were chicken risotto, so if I didn't make the salmon now, then it would go to waste.

I shook my head. 'No, no, truly I am going to make myself a little something now. I'm, um, not in the mood for pizza.' I stood up, practically drooling on my India silk-wool carpet.

'You've got issues, sis,' said Mark through a mouthful, a tiny string of cheese dangling from his lip.

My stomach dropped. 'What?'

He sighed. 'Nothing, sis. Go and make your... salmon isn't it?' he said, giving me a weak smile. 'Always salmon on a Wednesday.'

I sloped off to the kitchen, feeling odd and foolish.

CHAPTER FIVE

MY THOUGHTS festered throughout the next morning. Mark's 'You've got issues' comment had really stirred me up. I wanted to ask Caroline if she thought the same thing about me, but every time I opened my mouth to ask her, I bottled it. I tried to concentrate on my work, I really did, but before I knew it I was shouting out:

'You know, I bungee-jumped in Australia when I was nineteen!'

Caroline stopped typing and looked at me, eyes wide. 'I didn't know that.'

'Forty-five metres, all by myself.'

'Well, that sounds like fun.'

'And once, Caroline, I hitch-hiked,' I went on, jabbering now. 'Do you remember there was that petrol crisis? Well, I was in Wiltshire and I needed to be in London because I was watching Take That in concert that night with Natalie, who had a squint but had got money off the tickets, and I flagged this car down and jumped in.'

'That's brave,' Caroline said, eyebrows meeting as she looked at me.

'It was.' I paused for a moment and pleated the soft fabric of my grey wool dress. 'Do you think I'm unadventurous?' I blurted at her.

'Unadventurous?' she repeated.

'You know, sort of stuck in my ways? Uptight?' I carried on, tripping over the words now to get the question out.

'Well, you like things...'

'Like I like them?' I finished for her.

'Exactly,' she said, then fell silent for a moment. 'Um, it wouldn't be so bad to loosen up a little on some of the, er... *habits*.'

'*Habits*?'

'You know the, er, timing of things and the food, the keeping yourself to yourself. You *could* ease up a little,' she said lightly. 'I mean, don't you get horribly lonely at home?'

'No, no,' I said brightly. 'I'm used to being on my own.'

She looked at me in a way that could only be described as 'sympathetic'.

'I mean, I *like* being on my own,' I corrected.

'But you're so *young*.' I rolled my eyes, recognizing the familiar lecture that was about to begin. 'You just seem so frightened of letting—'

I gushed over her. 'Sorry, I shouldn't have said anything, I was just thinking out loud, don't wor—'

'No, listen, Nic, you asked me, remember!' The pitch of her voice rose an octave. 'Now, I want you to hear this.' Caroline never raised her voice. I stared at the keyboard of my desk, not seeing any of the letters, only hearing her words. 'You should be getting out there and living your life, not worrying about whether your carrot stick is exactly five centimetres long. You should be meeting people, you should be out with friends, you should be dating, seeing people, having *fun*.'

'Okay, Caroline.' I held up my hands to signal the diatribe could stop.

'No, Nic, you *asked* me,' she stressed. 'And so I'm *telling* you.'

'Fine, thanks. I get it. Can we drop it now?' I pleaded.

I heard a door open. Caroline paused, mouth agape, her fresh attack momentarily suspended.

'Nicola,' came James' voice.

I jumped and spun round on my chair to face him.

'Nicola, I need you to pop to Alexandra Street and pick up the proof for our new poster.'

I looked at him blankly for a moment, then registered his request. 'Oh, right, yes, of course, James,' I said, flustered.

'Everything okay in here?' he asked, smiling round at us both, an eyebrow raised.

'Absolutely fine,' we chorused at him.

He gave us one last funny look and then returned to his office.

I sighed, picked up my handbag and, looking anywhere but at Caroline, went out to the printers.

I brought Caroline a Twirl from my trip out and things went straight back to normal. The power of chocolate. I was relieved to see Caroline bustling about as if the horrid conversation had never happened. She was arranging the diary for next year and kept muttering things like, 'I can't *believe* it's only seven weeks till Christmas' and 'Where on earth does the time *go*?'

'Nic,' she said, 'I'm sorting out holidays for next year. I'm taking a week off in January to get the kids ready for school. When do you need your time off?'

'Oh, um, I haven't really thought about it.' I shrugged.

'All right, well let me know whenever you know.'

'Bet you've already booked Valentine's Day,' I chuckled.

Last year David had flown Caroline to Rome on a friend's private jet for the weekend. 'Completely extravagant,' Caroline had fussed. Secretly she'd been delighted and I'd spent the year wondering how David was ever going to top that.

'Nope, I've actually booked the fifteenth off.' She smiled wickedly. 'I won't want to work the day *after* Valentine's Day. To have and to hold and all that.'

'Eugh.' I clapped my hands to my ears in mock horror. 'Stop talking like that, I'm only young.'

'What about you, Nic? Why don't you take Valentine's Day off, keep it free for... someone?'

'I don't think so, Caroline. I've never had a date on Valentine's Day.'

'*What*, ever?' she frowned.

'Never,' I confirmed, smiling ruefully at her.

'But you *have* been asked out on a date on Valentine's Day before?' she checked.

'Er, no,' I mumbled, suddenly deeply embarrassed by this confession.

'That's awful,' she said, looking aghast. 'Just awful.'

'It's not awful,' I protested, trying my best to brush off her reaction.

'But didn't you date a man for three years, didn't he—?'

'Don't, Caroline,' I warned.

'But... but...'

'Just forget it. It's fine!'

'Of course, I, well, it's just...' She tried to recover herself and clearly couldn't. 'Actually no, that's awful.' She shook her head and we lapsed into an awkward silence.

A few uncomfortable moments passed and then, all of a sudden, she launched herself out of her chair and marched over to my desk.

'Right,' she said, reaching above my head. I cowered for a brief second in case she was here to *smash* me round the ear. She wasn't. Instead, Caroline took down the faded wall calendar that hung behind me (an Impressionist calendar from 2006 that was always on April because everyone liked the Degas ballerina picture on it). She flipped through to February and took out her big red marker. She circled the fourteenth. Then she placed it on top of the work I'd been doing and stood before me. I looked at the new picture, Renoir's *The Theatre Box*, and looked back up at her, baffled.

'You, Nicola Brown,' she said, pointing at me with an unsteady hand, 'are going to listen up.'

I gulped.

'By that day,' she pointed at the circled fourteen, 'you will have been asked out on a Valentine's date by someone wonderful.'

'Caroli—'

'Shush! By Valentine's Day, you are going to make certain that you have tried *everything* in your power to secure yourself this fabulous date and then, and only then, will I, Caroline Harper, agree to never again hassle you about your love life. Or lack thereof. Ever, ever again.'

I raised an eyebrow. She wasn't finished.

'In short,' she announced grandly, her eyes gleaming, 'I dare you to get a love life.'

What?

'Well? Do you accept?'

'No!' I spluttered instantly. 'You're being ridiculous.'

'I double dare you.'

'Stop it, Caroline.' I squirmed under the intensity of her gaze.

'I double dare you, no returns!'

'Caroline, I can't, I won't, it's...' My voice trailed off as I looked down at February the fourteenth circled in bright rose-red.

She'd thrown down the gauntlet. I stared at it, mesmerized. I couldn't do this. It was a silly, daft idea. *Wasn't it?*

'No, I can't,' I said, pushing the calendar away. 'I'm sorry, Caroline, I won't.'

CHAPTER SIX

I **ARRIVED BACK** at my flat that evening with a heavy heart. The apartment, which usually looked so spacious and light, tonight just seemed too big for me. I got the chicken for tonight's dinner out of the fridge and started chopping it into neat slices. I had a sort of empty feeling in my chest and I couldn't shrug it off. Almost as if everything seemed a little bit pointless. I mentally scolded myself, walked purposefully through to the living room and put on the most upbeat music I had to hand. But even playing *Musical Theatre's Greatest Hits* at full volume couldn't lift me out of the gloom. When 'Close Every Door' from *Joseph* sounded out through the speakers, I felt my mood slip further. Clutching the tea towel I was holding to my chest, I looked dramatically into the half-distance and started to sing about shutting out the light. Caroline was right. I was alone. Utterly alone, and no one could do anything about that but me.

I thought back to her dare, what it represented, what it might give me the chance to do. I sighed; I didn't have the nerve to go through with it. Look how things had ended before. Trusting him had led to so much pain. It was too messy. I was better off this way. I turned the music off and flopped down onto the sofa, aimlessly flicking through the television channels. It seemed as if the universe was highlighting my sense of isolation: *Coupling* was on a BBC repeat, *Friends* was on E4 and *Love in a Cold Climate* was on ITV2. Thanks for the pick-me-up, World. With a grunt, I settled for *Saw* on Film 4. Maybe watching people trying to decide whether to remove keys from inside their heads or let themselves explode would scare me into distraction.

Halfway through a particularly vicious death involving a spanner, the telephone rang and I answered it in a dull voice. On hearing who my caller was, my heart sank a little more: this was *not* going to improve my mood.

'Hi, Mum.'

'Please don't call me that, it's so common.'

'What would you rather I called you?' I asked, my tongue pushing against my teeth.

'Have you heard from your father recently?' she asked, ignoring my question.

'Which one?' I quipped.

'Don't be cheeky.'

My mother was on her third marriage. The latest was a high-flying investment banker who dyed his hair and drove a Porsche convertible. He was the polar opposite of my father – a struggling artist with straggly hair, whose bold canvases looked the same, whichever way up they were hung.

'No, I haven't heard from Dad,' I sighed.

'Fine. If you do, will you please tell him to call me. Guy and I are going to buy a holiday home in Menorca and for some strange reason Guy wants to decorate the place with your father's art. Must be mad, but he's adamant.'

'I don't know how to contact him, Mother, he always calls me. You know what he's like.'

'Yes, I do,' she said resignedly. 'Well, I thought I would check on the off chance,' she said, ready to hang up. 'Life fine with you?'

'Yes,' I replied automatically.

'Good. Okay. Bye, Nicola, I'll see you at the fair.'

'Oh yeah, twenty-first, isn't it?' I rolled my eyes, mouthing an 'Oh God' at the ceiling.

'I knew you would have forgotten.'

'No, I haven't forgotten, I'm *really* excited about it.'

'There is no need to be sarcastic,' she sniffed. 'Must be off then.'

She hung up before I could properly say goodbye.

Switching off the horror film, I walked through to the kitchen to find my half bottle of Emergency Merlot. I poured myself a large glass, barely tasting it as it passed my lips. The silence of the flat weighed heavy in the air and I took another gulp. I felt utterly hopeless. The oven timer blinked at me. It was only 9:30 p.m. but I'd had enough of today. The thought of my king-size bed with its creamy Egyptian cotton sheets, crisp and inviting, won out. It would all look a lot better in the morning.

I'd only just rested my head on the pillow when my mobile sprang back into life. Damn! Why hadn't I remembered to turn it off? I answered it blearily.

'Mum, I'm—'

'Sister!' Mark sang down the phone. 'You're in, thank God.'

I struggled up into a sitting position, 'Oh, Mark. Hi, I thought you were on a date?'

'I was.'

'Bad?' I rubbed my eyes.

'Dreadful. I'm outside your door. Julio let me in, hold on...'

What!

I heard a key turning in the door to my flat, and my brother saying 'Thanks, Julio!' Then a Portuguese voice: 'No problem. Tell Neecola I say hello.'

'Are you in *bed*, Nic?' Mark asked, his eyebrows raised as he appeared unsteadily in the doorway to my bedroom.

'No.' I frowned, wrapping the duvet around me protectively. 'I'm... I... was... reading.' I gestured to my book on the chest of drawers ten feet away.

'Hmm. You're lying.'

I rolled my eyes at him. 'I bow to your superior powers of observation.'

'I'm making tea, want one?'

'Tea? No, Mark, I don't want tea, I want answers. Why are you here, for one, and when are you going, for another?'

'I was going home after my date and my motorbike packed in. I couldn't afford a taxi so here I am!' He did a 'Ta-da' for good measure and advanced on me in a wobbly line. '*Plus*, I wanted to see my little sis. Yes, I did, yes, I did.' He waggled my cheek like I was a baby. He smelt of stale cider and cheese and onion crisps. He was clearly still drunk.

'Fine,' I said, slapping his hand away. 'I'll make up the spare room, you get the tea.'

'Excellent.' He skipped through to the kitchen and I tried to block out the noise of one man making two cups of tea. Soon enough, we were both settled on the sofa, tea was warming me out of my sleep and Mark seemed a little more sober. Although he was cracking himself up by making shadow puppets have sex with each other on the wall, so not *entirely* sober. I wiggled my toes out in front of me and felt relaxed for the first time that evening. Mark was, at the very least, a distraction from my own tightly wound brain.

'Who were you on a date with?' I asked him.

'Carole,' he replied.

I sat up, the sudden movement causing my tea to slosh perilously close to the edge of the cup. 'Carol, as in THE Carol?' I asked.

'No, *Carole*,' he said. 'I met her earlier this week. Carole with an *E*.'

'Earole?' I giggled.

Mark stared at me. I fell silent.

'So what about THE Carol? How is that little um... *difficulty*?' I ventured.

'He is still very much around.'

'Oh.'

Mark nodded miserably. He'd been in love with Carol, a girl who worked at the planetarium with him, for nearly two years now. She had long flame-red hair, a tiny waist, enormous tits and an interest in natural history. It had been the latter fact that, of course, had my brother drooling.

'We had a fight the other day about what was the best mammal, living or extinct, and she said,' he chuckled quietly to himself, 'she said the lemur.' He scoffed, as if I was meant to shake my head and cry *OUTRAGEOUS*! Smiling, he dreamily repeated, *'The lemur.'* He was lost in his little rodent world. His happy place. 'It's probably because the females are socially dominant,' he mused. Then he looked up sharply, his expression insistent. 'I will marry her.'

'Okay, that's Plan A but, just for argument's sake, let's say that falls through, what is Plan B, Mark? Is there anyone else?'

'No.'

'Oh, come on, there must be someone. What about this date tonight?' I persisted.

'She was awful.' He shivered, not offering any details. Then he added thoughtfully, 'And she is too old.'

'Again? You have a thing about age, Mark.'

'She is too old,' he insisted.

'How old is this one?' I asked.

'Thirty-three'

This rang a bell.

'Brother, do you have a problem with the number thirty three in general, or is it just with women who happen to be that age? Why is thirty-three such a problem?'

'It's highly probable she'll be infertile,' he said with a casual shrug.

'What! At thirty-three?'

'Well, no, but by the time I've taken her on dates, wooed her, courted her, gone on holiday with her, proposed to her, married her and then knocked her up, she'll be of an infertile age. So I really need to meet someone younger to do all that and then I can fertilize her and get on with things.'

I sat through this entire exchange with my mouth wide open.

'What?' Mark asked innocently. 'What is it?'

Lying in bed an hour later I couldn't sleep. My mind drifted over the day's conversations and I tossed and turned, trying to block them all out. I was shaken by my brother's charming announcement about thirty-three-year-old women. Of course, I didn't take it seriously, but it had unsettled me. Should I be worried? When I was younger I'd never imagined I'd be lying in a bed alone at twenty-nine with little prospect of a relationship anywhere on the horizon. I hadn't imagined that life would ever not be what life was always supposed to be. You get a job, you meet a man, you fall in love, you marry him, you buy a house with a garden, you have children, you buy a bigger house with a swing set for the garden, you bring up your family, you retire and take up watercolour classes. That was how I'd always assumed my life would pan out. But how many people really did end up with this reality? Wasn't my own mother on her third marriage? Wasn't my brother thirty-four and single? Hadn't things veered completely off course for me?

I didn't like these thoughts. I threw off the duvet in frustration and focused on the breeze brushing past me. Kicking myself out of bed, I stepped quietly through to the bathroom, being careful not to wake my brother, who was no doubt in the middle of his favourite dream: 'I wake, yeah, and I'm a fruit bat, right...'

I examined myself critically in the mirror. My heart-shaped face peered back from the glass, the bobbed hair exaggerating my long neck. I leaned closer. My grey-blue eyes were perhaps a little red-rimmed, a few faint lines could be seen when I smiled at the mirror. My lips seemed marginally thinner these days. Was my jawline as defined as it once was? Was *I* running out of time? It suited me to be alone right now, but soon I would be thirty-three, then thirty-six, then thirty-nine. What if I changed my mind? Would it be too late?

I tucked a strand of hair behind my ear and stared deep into my own eyes. Maybe Caroline was right and I did need to take a chance for once, to get *out there*. Maybe I *could* stand to go on a date or two. Maybe I *did* need to move on from the past.

I rested my head against the cool glass and closed my eyes. Something had shifted. I knew I wasn't happy. Not really. I took a long breath. Perhaps I *could* be brave enough to take a risk. Because I knew, in my heart, that I didn't want to live like this forever.

'I'll do it,' I whispered to Caroline the next day.

'Hmmm?' She looked up from her computer keyboard.

'Your dare. Tell me what to do. I'll do it.' I held out my hand. 'You're on. I'll get a date for Valentine's Day.'

Caroline didn't laugh as I expected she would. Instead, she took my hand, shook it and broke into an enormous grin.

'Excellent.'

CHAPTER SEVEN

Single girl with good
prospects and nice eyes,
seeks man who wants to stare
into them.

Contact: Box No. 367

MY WEEKEND began with a continuous humming noise.
The humming was coming from the sitting room and,
unless it was a seriously happy and very indiscreet burglar, I
figured it was Basia's weekly clean. Being a teensy bit careful
with regards to cleanliness (fine, bordering on obsessive),
I paid a Polish lady, Basia, to come in every Saturday to go
over surfaces and make sure that the kitchen and bathroom
were left sparkling. She was pathologically cheerful and
had an absurdly energetic way with a bottle of Dettol and a
scrubbing brush. Today, as I entered the kitchen, Basia was
in her usual perky mood, pausing to laugh inexplicably at
her reflection in a saucepan.

'Ah, Mees Brown, I wake you?' she asked, trying to look sorry but failing miserably as her light-beam smile hit me full in the face.

'No, no, I was just resting my eyes.'

Basia frowned at this so I mimed my eyes shut. She threw her head back and laughed. I clicked the kettle on and wished that some of Basia's enthusiasm would rub off on me. I thought dolefully back to yesterday and the moment I'd signed my life away (quite literally, ten minutes after agreeing, Caroline had made me sign an actual oath).

'I, Nicola Brown of Flat C, 26 Hewston Gardens – is that really necessary? –' I'd argued, 'do hereby promise to do everything in my power to find and secure a date for Valentine's Day next year. I promise to seek love, not hide from it.'

I'd rolled my eyes at that point, forcing Caroline to bark, 'Continue, Nicola Brown of Flat C.'

'I promise to meet new people and see who's *out there*. And I promise to take risks when before I might have said "No".'

So I'd signed, and as I was doing it, I felt a sense of relief to be giving power and control over to The Dare, ready to take on the new challenges it would bring. But today was a whole other day. *What had I been thinking?* As the kettle boiled, it occurred to me that all my soul-searching yesterday had probably just been because I'd had a bit of a low day. I'd *obviously* been a little depressed after the whole hideous 'fertilization' speech from Mark. That, combined with Caroline's comments about my being unadventurous, meant I'd acted too hastily.

I jumped as the kettle clicked off, cracking Basia up as she cleaned the hob. Pouring myself a coffee, I offered Basia one too. She looked as if she might burst with happiness at the offer. 'Mees Brown, thank you, I would yes to honestly love one.'

I set about making two coffees. 'Milk?' I checked, moving to the fridge.

'Oh yes, thank you, yes,' she said, flinging her Marigolds down in glee.

I poured in the milk, daring to ask, 'Sugar? One?'

I waited for an answer, spoon hovering over her mug. She clasped her hands together. 'One fantastic, yes.'

'Here you go.' I handed her a mug and scuttled out of the kitchen before she could embrace me or light a candle in my honour.

Walking through to the sitting room with its painted white walls and tan curtains, I plunged gratefully into my squashy cream sofa and continued to mull over yesterday's turn of events. It had taken me less than an hour to change my mind. I didn't want to go through with it. But before I'd had the chance to pipe up and tell Caroline it had all been a ghastly mistake, that I was absolutely fine and that the dare was so *not* necessary, she had already swung into action. By lunch she'd emailed me the names of six men she knew who might be suitable date material, and had sent me a link to a website called *findmeamate.com* with two hippos kissing on the homepage. By each name on her list of potential men, Caroline had been kind enough to list a few reasons as to why they had made the shortlist. For example, in at Number Four, Brian apparently owned a boat (she didn't specify yacht or rowing) and had a holiday home. Number Six liked to go wine tasting in France (I assumed she'd included this as a positive and it was not her cunning way of telling me he was an alcoholic. 'Yes, I like to wine taste in France, England, hic... Iceland, Mexico, hic... anywhere really...'). Number Two was self-employed and *had only been married once before*. I'd examined her list and wondered if I would ever contact them. It would just be so... *awkward*, wouldn't it? Still, I was touched she'd thrown herself into the task and I'd spent an uncomfortable hour wondering how I was going to break it to her that, if I was going to do this at all, I wanted to tackle the challenge in my own way. Never one to rush into things, I'd already formulated a rough outline of a plan. I would go through my old address book and underline the men I knew were single and I would cross out those I knew were married/in long-term relationships or were family (even distant – I shivered to think of second cousin Hugh who had once letched on me on Remembrance Sunday). I then planned to draw up a chart using Microsoft Excel. I'd type the potential men's names out in alphabetical order, in a separate column I would enter the reasons *to* date them, and in a third column the reasons to *not* date them. I would then draw up a fourth column with a potential score out of 20, which I would decipher from a number of bar charts detailing all the potential dates' qualities, both positive and negative, in order to work out our compatibility. I'd been at my desk thinking about what colours to make the various sections in my bar charts when a piece of paper in the form of a paper dart bounced off my forehead and landed in my lap. I'd bent down to scoop up the childish missive. It read: '7 p.m. Café Rouge, next Tuesday.' I looked up at Caroline to ask what the heck this was, but maddeningly, she was on the phone, so instead I mimed angry gestures in her direction. She just smiled and gave me an enthusiastic thumbs up. When she put down the phone, she swivelled her chair in my direction.

'Sooo I set you up,' she said.

'Who with?' I frowned.

She pointed to the phone. 'Him.'

'Who is "Him"?' I wailed, waving my hands around. 'The telephone operator? The BT man?'

'No, no. Him.' She pointed at the telephone again. 'Him, the man I was just speaking to!'

'WHAT? Who were you just on the phone to?' I was aghast. 'This is not a Thai Bride Takeaway service, Caroline; you can't just sell me over the phone to some stranger. He could be anyone.'

'No, I KNOW him, idiot child,' she giggled. 'I didn't just randomly dial a number, hear a male voice and think Bingo. Although... that's not a bad plan,' she muttered, looking round for the phone book.

'So which one is he? Brian? Richard?' I asked, picking up her list from my desk.

'Oh, he's not on the list.' She waved a hand dismissively.

'Why not?'

She paused and frowned slightly. 'Hmm... that's a good

question. I didn't think of him.'

'Why not?' I persisted. 'He can't be that wonderful if you managed to forget him completely and include, and I quote "Number Five: George – very funny, a *brief* stint in prison in 2010 but might have been a miscarriage of justice like in *Shawshank Redemption*". So you were setting me up with some guy who has done jail-time before What's-his-name-Mr-Eligible-Phone -Bachelor-2013?' I asked, pointing at the phone and panting a little with exasperation.

'He's called Andrew. Oh, but he's lovely,' she said insistently.

'I'm sure he is, but I'm not going.'

'Oh, you must, Nic. He's very excited about it.'

'He can't be that excited – he's never met me,' I pointed out, turning back to my desk.

'He's *seen* you,' Caroline said in a voice that made me think that Andrew had, at some point, been sitting outside my flat, clutching his night-vision goggles.

'Seen me where?' I asked, spinning back round to her and willing my stalker suspicions to be laid to rest.

'Around,' she said, confirming the worst.

So that had been yesterday. Date Number One was planned. Tuesday night. With this Andrew. Caroline had outright refused to call him back to cancel and had then spent the next five minutes solemnly reading me the oath that I had signed only minutes before. So, assuming Tuesday's date wasn't the answer, and assuming I didn't want to leave all my plans for future happiness in the hands of Caroline who could barely remember the names of her children, I knew I'd better start work on a Plan of Action. I decided to start with some research, and soon enough I was ensconced in the local library, a pile of books to my left and some hastily scribbled notes on an A4 pad to my right. I was on a fact-finding mission. I was here to seek answers. I was here to make my search for a Valentine's Day Date, my search to get a love life, a little bit easier. So far I had read chapters from seven dating and relationships books and two articles. I had learnt the following lessons:

~ If a man calls a woman she should end the conversation first to leave him wanting more.

~ If a man calls a woman she should let him direct the conversation: that shows he's in charge!

~ When a woman likes a man she should try to mirror his body language.

~ A man likes a woman who knows her own mind.

~ When a man likes a woman he will find ways to touch her during their conversation.

~ When a man likes a woman he can sometimes appear distant in her company.

~ If a man calls a woman she should not return his call until he makes the third attempt to contact her.

~ If a man calls a woman she should return his message within the hour. This will show that she is keen!

~ A woman should be clear in her signals to ensure the man is confident she returns his interest.

~ A woman should keep her cards close to her chest to ensure the man retains his interest.

~ A woman should be distant and cold, he will find this intriguing.

~ A woman should be warm and welcoming; no man wants to date a sourpuss!

~ A man will always make the first move if he is interested.

~ A man likes a woman to instigate the first move.

I placed my head in my hands and decided to return home.

CHAPTER EIGHT

Single girl seeks man who
hasn't read 'The Rules',
doesn't know that 'Men are
From Mars and Women are from
Venus' and calls women back
after an appropriate length
of time. Oh, and who doesn't
look into what it means if
there are no kisses on a text
message. Or if there are 3.

Contact: Box No. 78511

THE WEEKEND might have proved a dead loss for my research into 'How to Win a Man' but it had clearly not dampened Caroline's enthusiasm for what she insisted on calling her *project*.

'Did you see that episode of *Time Team* last night?' she asked before I had barely rested my buttocks onto the chair.

'Er... no. I'm not an avid fan of *Time Team*,' I admitted, sipping at my echinacea tea and flicking through my diary.

'Aren't you?' She raised her eyebrow as if this was a fairly sensational statement. 'So you didn't see the bit where they were making ale in the old brewery?'

'Nope.'

'Well, there was this brewer,' she explained, 'who was quite tall with a lovely build...'

'That's... nice,' I said.

'Yes. He was sort of a Christian Bale meets Ed Norton size.'

'Er... right,' I said, trying to work out how her Christian–Ed mix might morph into a real person. 'That's just great.'

'Yes, not too big, but you know, not... insubstantial.'

'Good for him.'

'So, do you like the sound of that, er, kind of build?'

'Build?' I furrowed my brow.

'Yes – in a man. It might be defined as *Muscular* or *Around Average* for a man.'

'I'm sure it suited him.' I smiled. Caroline had clearly developed quite a crush on this *Time Team* extra.

'Good. So that's a yes,' she said, suddenly tapping something out on her keyboard.

'Er... what's a yes?' I asked.

She paused. 'That you like average, muscular sort of men.'

'Right,' I repeated, narrowing my eyes.

Caroline nodded happily and went back to her work.

Later, as I ate Monday's snack of choice: uniform sticks of celery with a bottle of Goji Juice health drink, Caroline suddenly piped up.

'Eyes.'

She'd been so unusually quiet in the past hour that I'd practically forgotten she was there.

'Hmm?' I looked up.

'Eyes. Are you bothered?' she asked, finger hovering above her keyboard.

'Bothered by *eyes*? What?'

'Do you like men's eyes?'

'Well, I usually prefer men to have eyes, Caroline, but I still don't really get why you're asking…'

'Oh, sorry, I just mean do you care what colour people's eyes are, um, usually. Like, in general.'

'No, Caroline.' I exhaled slowly. 'I am a fan of all eye colours. They are all equal in my book. I don't dislike one type of eye. I am not eyeist.'

'So people can have any colour eyes, in your book?' she added.

'Yes, they can go mad and buy coloured contacts for all I care. It's a free country, after all.' I shook my head. Caroline was quirky, but she'd really been excelling herself in the last few hours.

'Right. Good. So you don't mind people having any coloured eyes… and that includes men, does it?'

'Yes, women, men, children. Are you regularly in contact with people who have issues with eye colour?' I asked in an exasperated tone.

'No, no, no,' she said breezily, tapping at her keyboard. 'I'm just curious. I prefer blue myself, but I just wanted to see what, you know, other people liked.'

'Right,' I said, distracted by the ringing of the telephone.

I answered with the usual patter. 'The Sullivan Agency, Nicola speaking.' Moments later I was rifling through my out tray for a contract that should have been signed first thing that morning. I gulped and jumped up. James was, thank goodness, in the vicinity so all I needed to do was ensure he signed it and then I could courier it over. How had I forgotten this? I scolded myself. I'd allowed all this personal commotion to distract me from my work.

I knocked timidly on the door to James' office and waited. He was probably doing something horribly important and I hated rushing in and imposing administrative duties on him. I could hear him talking on the other side of the door. He didn't have a meeting so I assumed he must be on the telephone. I looked at the contract in my hand. I had to have it signed and sent out in the next half an hour. There was just no time to wait. I took a breath and knocked again a little louder. I heard a quick, 'Come in', and pushed open the door. James was pacing up and down the room, talking into a blue vase that he had looped around his neck with some kind of frayed ribbon. My brow creased in panic. He was saying things like, 'Well, just order something in suede then' and 'Peter Jones is a great idea' into the vase. I hesitated. What was happening? Why was my boss speaking rapidly into a piece of handblown glass that was precariously balanced around his neck? I knew he was stressed and busy but had he finally tipped over the edge? *Should I run for help? Maybe I should get Caroline, at least? Oh God. Caroline is useless in a crisis*. There was nothing in the office guidelines to cover a moment like this. I knew this because I'd written them.

'Yes, yes, no, it's just Nicola. Okay, fine,' he was saying to the vase. 'Yes, go ahead then. Okay. Bye.'

He signed off with the vase and I gaped at him. 'Er, Mr Sulli, James, I wanted to... I needed to...' Now I had *completely* forgotten why I was there. My eyes flicked back to the vase around his neck.

'Nicola, this must look a little strange.'

I sighed with relief. He had at least noticed that he was coming across *unusually*.

'Well, I didn't want to say but I... you see... um... CONTRACT,' I eventually shouted, brandishing the bunch of paper before him. 'I wanted you to sign this,' I said, finally remembering the original reason for my visit to his office.

'You have small hands, don't you, Nicola?' he stated.

'Er...'

WHAT was going on today?

'Um, yes. I suppose they are fairly small,' I said in a barely-there voice.

'Well, you're a woman so they must be smaller,' he muttered, unlooping the vase from around his neck.

'Smaller than what?' *Children? Hobbits? What was he on about?*

'You see, Nicola, I have managed to, er, drop my mobile phone in this vase and I can't get it out because of all these stupid blue baubles that keep sliding out and getting in the way. I don't want to smash it because it is a present from Thalia and she is bound to ask me to produce it at some point and I don't—'

'Fine.' I put up my hand to stop his explanation. Then I smiled at him. The relief in my face must have been apparent because he started laughing.

'Probably looks like I've lost the plot, eh?' he hazarded a guess. 'Talking to the vase?'

'Something like that.'

He placed the vase on the desk and I peered inside. I could make out the mobile phone but knew my hands weren't that small. I had a go. James looked at me hopefully as I plunged my hand in, face scrunched in concentration, fingers wriggling around to see if they could clasp at anything. Every time we tipped the vase, the blue baubles slid over the phone.

'I'm sorry.' I gave up after a good five minutes of digging around.

'Hammer it is.' James sighed, realizing there was little chance of seeing his mobile again otherwise. 'Thanks anyway, Nicola.'

'Not at all.' I shrugged. A few awkward seconds passed before I remembered again why I was there. 'Contract! I need you to sign it!' I explained, holding out a pen and the pieces of paper. He quickly scrawled his name on them and before he could say anything else I bolted back towards the main office. Curiosity overwhelming me, I paused in the doorway. 'So how did you answer the...'

I was cut off by his mobile ringing again and watched as he produced a biro, leant over the vase and jabbed at the mobile. Then he grinned at me. 'Hello,' he answered. 'Hi, Thalia, you're on loudspeaker.'

I smiled back and nodded at him. He shrugged his shoulders and put the vase back around his neck.

I was still smiling as I returned to my desk.

'Oh good, Nicola,' Caroline began the moment I'd taken my seat.

Oh God.

'Yes,' I sighed.

'I'm just sitting here thinking of all the latest films at the cinema and I'm wondering what your favourite film is.'

'Um... I can't think. I don't have a favourite.'

'Oh.' Her shoulders slumped. She looked crestfallen. *Wow. She must be really interested in films.*

'I like a good drama,' I said, trying to buck her up a little.

'Oh goody! Any one in particular? Say, *Legends of the Fall*? Or *The English Patient*? *Last of the—*'

'Yes, yes, *The English Patient*, that's my favourite,' I said quickly, before she continued her list of movies.

'Righto.' She beamed at me and clicked her mouse. She was a strange one.

The morning passed by in a similar vein. By 2 p.m. Caroline had asked if I played any unusual sports, had enquired as to whether I was a Christian, a Hindu, an atheist, a Sikh, an agnostic or 'other' and had wanted to double-check I was definitely the youngest child in my family. I'd been desperately busy doing paperwork and had answered her questions quickly without wondering why she was suddenly so concerned about my religious well-being and sporting hobbies.

Then at around 2.11 p.m. she said, 'Um... Nicola...'

'Yes, Caroline,' I said, anticipating a question on the type of books I read or my preferred choice for a city break, or the regularity of my bowel movements.

'Um... Do you like children?' she asked casually.

'Like them? Um...'

I didn't know. The truth was, I was a little bit afraid of children. They were fragile, stamped 'Handle with Care', utterly reliant on you. And then there was all the poo and smells and germs. But I could hardly say that to Caroline when she doted on her own two little treasures.

'Do you want them some day? Children?' Caroline pressed.

'Yes, of course, um... with the right person,' I said vaguely. Caroline dropped her head to type something and then looked up at me.

'And how about smokers?' she asked. 'You don't seem the type to like smokers, but I'm just curious...'

'Children smokers or smokers in general?' I quipped.

'Smokers as a group. Forget children, just smokers, smoking, how do you feel about them on the whole?'

'Look, Caroline, I have no idea why you want to discover every little thing about me on this dreary Monday morning, but I know you are up to something. With regards to smoking, *I* don't like it, but I don't mind if others want to partake of a cigarette or two. Happy?' I finished, scowling at her.

'In your home?'

'Sorry?'

'Do you mind if they smoke in your home?' she went on. I sighed.

'Caroline, are you organizing some kind of Smokers Anonymous get together in my home? Because, yes. I do mind. I don't want smokers in my flat.'

'Right, phew, good, thought so.' She tapped at her keyboard once more.

'Okay.' I frowned. 'What do you keep typing?'

'Nothing,' Caroline replied, eyes darting left then right.

'You're lying!'

'It's a...' She clicked on her mouse again. 'A...'

'Yeeeeesss?'

'A press release.'

'A press release for what?'

'Oh, um...' She closed her eyes. 'A press release for a new... a new... Oh, fine.' She crumpled. 'Fine. It's not a press release, Poirot, it's a little something I am doing for you. A *favour* if you must know. It was supposed to be a surprise.'

'What favour?' I asked, reckoning that this favour might not be favourable at all.

We both jumped as James wordlessly swept past us and out of the office. I shook my head and turned my attention back to Caroline. 'Explain yourself?' I hissed.

Caroline tutted. 'All right, all right! I might have signed you up to that dating website I showed you.'

'Nooo.' I put my head in my hands.

'Look, Nic, you don't have to do anything about it, but take a look, see who's on there. Some of the fellas are gorgeous.'

'Hmm...' I groaned, unconvinced.

'Honestly, if I was ten years younger...' She sighed

dreamily. 'Look, I'll send you the link and you can just have a little look at who is out there. I've made you sound great. Not that you're not, but well, you sound great, because you are great. Oh, Nic, just look at it.'

'Fine, fine, fine, fine,' I said, lifting my hands in surrender. 'I will look at it, but—'

Before I could finish my sentence, James erupted back through the office door, a determined expression on his face and clutching a hammer in his right hand.

'Everything all right in here?' he asked, seeing our startled faces.

'Er... yes. Lovely,' Caroline said.

'Great, just great,' I added, the two of us worriedly eyeing the hammer.

'Good, good,' James said, stalking through to his office and slamming the door behind him. A sudden flash of light went off to my right.

'Smile!' Caroline said, springing up by my desk. 'It's for your profile on the site.'

I blinked rapidly, trying to clear the bright light from where it had imprinted on my retinas. A few moments later Caroline said, 'Sent!'

I slumped into my chair. So, Nicola Brown was now on the internet. On a dating website. This whole process was frightening. Was it weird to be so blatant about my quest to find a date? The fact that millions of other people did it every day didn't really make me feel any better.

My email pinged as a new message popped up. 'Welcome to Find Me A Mate! Nicola Brown.'

The two hippos were kissing. I put my head back in my hands. Oh God.

From James' office, I heard the sound of a vase smashing.

CHAPTER NINE

Single girl WLTM real man
in the flesh. Not internet
weirdo who says he is
athletic and 30 and is,
in fact, 55 and medically
obese.

Contact: Box No. 90002

I **GOT HOME** that evening feeling ready to tackle the
task ahead: find me a mate *my* way. Caroline's efforts
had prompted me into further action. I needed to continue
with my plans, claw back some control. I settled myself
onto my lovely squishy sofa and forced my mind back to
past relationships. I reached into the shoebox of letters
I'd retrieved earlier from the top shelf of my wardrobe.
Squirreling through the pile of papers, I pulled out one
particularly dog-eared photo from my last year of university.
There we were. The two of us. Even without the photograph, I
was able to recall every detail in my mind. I remembered the
day it was taken. His arm was slung over my shoulders, his

warm smile directed towards the camera. I was beside him, blissfully content, relaxed, my body melting into his. He'd just asked me to move in with him after graduation. Exactly a month later he'd left me. I was distraught. To make matters worse I'd only just scraped a third-class degree after three years of studying and having always been top in my year. It was then that I vowed not to ever let another man mess up my life. Of course I'd had the odd evening out, the odd date, but nothing that ever came to anything. I was completely closed off. Protecting myself from hurt had been my grand plan. And it had worked. It had worked so well that now, seven years later, I was sitting alone in my flat wondering where the girl in the picture had gone; the girl brimming with confidence, with a wide grin and glowing skin, shiny dark hair flowing over her shoulders, the girl completely at home amidst the buzz of university life, surrounded by friends. My throat felt thick as I traced her outline with my finger. She had been me. She was still me. I felt determined to find her again.

With renewed energy, I got up and rummaged through the drawer of my desk, pulled out my address book, practically blew the cobwebs from its surface and took a deep breath. This was it. The summary of past relationships, friendships, people that had fallen by the wayside. People I'd let go. I smoothed my hand over the cover. Right. I flipped to A, pen poised. There was Suzie Allen at the top, a friend from university who used to sleepwalk, then there was Bob Arkman, a handy electrician who'd moved away from the area and, oh, there was Jon Allen who I'd once gone out with for the weekend to learn clay pigeon shooting. Taking the highlighter I'd purchased for this exact job, I highlighted Jon Allen. The first possibility. Aside from the clay pigeon shooting I remembered little about Jon. I'd worked with him briefly in London and he had once sent me a Christmas card with penguins kissing. Now that I came to think of it – a promising start.

But I had twenty-five other letters of the alphabet to check through. I opened a chilled bottle of Sauvignon Blanc and got to work.

The entire bottle of wine, three raspberry yoghurts, and a peach later, I had my list.

NICOLA'S LIST

Jon Allen – Clay pigeon guy, 1 Christmas card (penguins kissing – suggestive?)

Fred Davies – Think he lives in Liverpool. (Consider long-distance relationships at later date?)

Edward Gough – One kiss circa 1995, possibly his parents' address (double-check this).

Paul Kleiner – German, so would need to rely a lot on mime, but might have better grasp of English language by now?

Clive Reegan – Had long-term girlfriend, but once laughed at a joke I made in a seminar, a good guy.

Steve Thompson – Played in jazz band of old firm. Hot. Wore a Swatch.

Jake Young – Old university flatmate. Have seen him use sink as toilet, not sure can move on from that.

By the end of the list I reckoned Jon Allen was not a bad bet at all, but I was encouraged to see a couple of other possibilities there too. Step One, tick.

CHAPTER TEN

TUESDAY IN the office was unbearable. In the morning Caroline spent hours staring at me, denying she was staring at me, or staring at me from behind other objects. In the afternoon when I finally told her to PLEASE STOP STARING AT ME, she asked me numerous questions: what was I going to wear for the date that night? Was I nervous? Wasn't I glad I was getting *out there*? The last phrase was delivered with a very gung-ho voice and when we left the office at the end of the day she gave me a hearty slap on the back, as if she were sending me to the front line.

I scuttled out into the cold, wet night and headed to the coffee shop opposite our office until it was time for the date. I was meeting Andrew in the Café Rouge at the top of Park Street. It would only take me two minutes to walk there, so I had plenty of time to compose myself beforehand. Most of the shops were shut for the night, though the glow of their window displays were a warming contrast to the darkness outside. I pushed open the coffee-shop door, headed straight to the counter and ordered an espresso, before taking a seat in the corner.

I was particularly dreading the start of the date; did we hug, kiss or shake hands? Then how long would we have to spend lumbering through the inevitable small talk and coping with lengthy awkward pauses? How early on would I be forced to comment on the decor of the restaurant, him on the general ambience? And what was the right food for the occasion? I'd been on one date at university and ordered the spaghetti Bolognese – student budget – and had spent the entire evening unwittingly talking through a little moustache of tomato sauce. I started to panic. Dinner was quite a commitment. What if we decided we didn't like the look of each other on sight? What if, over the starter, we discovered we had conflicting world views and there was simply no hope of compatibility? Did we then throw down our soup spoons, split the bill and wander off into the night?

I spent five minutes in the loo of the coffee shop, which earned me a raised eyebrow from the owner. I wondered if they had CCTV... I hoped not; I must have looked ridiculous, doing those five minutes of deep-breathing exercises while intently staring at my own reflection in the mirror. I checked my make-up, straightened my crisp pale-pink shirt, paid the bill and headed to Café Rouge. My stomach plunged as I saw Andrew already sitting at a table in the window of the restaurant. Well, I assumed it was Andrew, simply due to the fact that he was the only lone man waiting in there. He was studying a newspaper with a slight frown on his face. I couldn't get a good look at him. He glanced up as I pushed open the door, cast aside the paper and stood up to greet me – I noticed he was a tad on the short side, but at least he was punctual. I liked that.

Stooping a fraction, I held out my hand. 'Andrew?'

'Nicola,' he said, shaking it. 'You look just like your photo. Actually, better.' Then he smiled. I felt relief sweep through me. He seemed relatively normal, his handshake was an appropriate pressure, he'd demonstrated an ability to make eye contact and pronounce my name: all positives. 'I reserved us a table,' he said, indicating a small, candlelit table on the left-hand side of the room.

'Great!' I smiled, as a skinny waiter appeared and took my coat. 'Thanks!'

Okay. Phew. *This is all going to be fine.*

I unrolled the napkin and placed it carefully on my lap. Andrew sat down, handed me a menu and we both scanned it, wondering who was going to get the conversation going. Andrew did the honours with a polite, 'This looks good.'

I nodded my head and agreed with a hearty, 'Doesn't it?'

Then we lapsed into silence once more.

Fortunately, the waiter appeared and after a vague pretence at perusing the wine list, Andrew ordered the House White.

'Very good, sir.' I just knew that he wanted to roll his eyes.

When the waiter departed, Andrew turned his attention to me. 'So, Nicola, this is a little strange but I'm glad we're both here.' He chuckled. 'I'm not exactly a serial dater.'

'Me neither,' I said, pleased that he'd broken the ice.

We chatted fairly amiably for the next few minutes and sank easily into a few of our favourite Caroline-related anecdotes. The story about her family's week in France camping in torrential rain, ha ha ha, a friend's wedding in Manchester where Caroline had fallen into a fountain taking their photo, ha ha ha. This wasn't too difficult. It was actually going well!

Andrew seemed to find my stories interesting. He wasn't checking his fingernails, looking over my shoulder, examining his reflection in a spoon – so I couldn't be doing too dreadfully. I started to relax into it.

We moved into fresh conversational terrain: where we both lived, where we were brought up, our hobbies, and what we would do with a million pounds (I'd panicked and plumped for establishing a turtle sanctuary). Andrew worked as a teacher at a local secondary school that I'd heard of, and I even managed to comment on some maths genius that had left there with ten A*'s last August and had appeared in *The Telegraph*.

'So, what made you become a teacher?' I asked, resting my elbows on the table.

'Oh, I had a horrible passion for my subject – I teach geography. I was always nose-deep in an encyclopaedia when I was younger – obsessed with volcanoes and earthquakes. I suppose teaching seemed the natural course for me.'

'Why not a PHD or, I don't know, a lecturer?'

'That's a great question, Nicola,' Andrew said, sipping his wine. I smiled to myself, imagining just what he was like in the classroom. 'I was pretty unsure about becoming a school teacher initially – I'm not particularly confident – but I knew I wanted a good excuse to talk about all the things that had fascinated me as a child, and a teacher seemed the obvious choice. I figured the pupils would be sweet little smaller versions of me.'

'Oh, I couldn't do it,' I said, shaking my head at him. 'I'd hate having to stand up and talk to a whole class of teenagers about, well, anything.'

The waiter appeared before Andrew could reply. He placed a mushroom risotto in front of me and my mouth watered at the smell. *I could get used to dating in nice restaurants.* Andrew had ordered chicken with a cheese sauce and a creamy-looking mashed potato. He ordered some more wine, and after my first bite of delicious risotto, I picked up our conversation.

'I remember being horrible to some of my teachers,' I said, which was kind of a little white lie. The other, way cooler, kids in my class had been horrible to the teachers. I'd actually been the one at the front paying attention, making notes, keeping my head down and my grades up.

'Yeah, usual kid's stuff, I suspect,' Andrew chortled at me, cutting into his chicken. 'The kids always know how to wind us up.'

'What are the pupils like then? Any hideous beasts?' I asked, realizing I'd started to enjoy myself.

'A few in year ten,' he nodded, laughing a little at my question.

'Year ten?'

'Fourteen- to fifteen-year-olds.'

'Ah!'

'Yeah, they can behave badly. Get up to all sorts of things...'

'Like what?'

'Oh, lots of things. It can be quite tiring!'

'Like...' I prompted in a teasing voice.

'Just... their constant backchat,' he said, the laughter dying on his lips. 'They obviously think I've never heard the F-word before...'

Andrew wasn't laughing any more. He had turned an impressive shade of pink.

My mushroom risotto wobbled precariously on my fork. 'Oh.'

'It can get a little tedious. Quite grating, really, constantly having to lecture them – don't throw that, stop standing by the window, sit down, where's your book, why did you leave it at home.' He caught sight of my expression and tailed off. 'Oh, sorry, Nicola.'

'It's fine,' I said, waving my hand. 'It's clearly a bit stressful.' I shrugged it off, not wanting to embarrass him any more. I sipped my wine. I took a spoonful of risotto. 'Hmm...' I said, pointing with my fork. '*Great* risotto.'

Andrew looked at me vacantly.

I repeated my observation. 'Yummy,' I said, showing him my fork.

He blinked and mumbled something so quietly that I had to lean forward to catch it. 'Last week they brought in fart spray and the classroom still smells.'

'Sorry?' I said, straining to hear him.

'Last week they brought in... fart spray,' he whispered.

I leant back. 'Oh.'

'And one boy graffitied the desk, saying *Mr Moore likes to wank*, which is both offensive, and untrue,' he spluttered.

I began to feel a little uneasy.

Andrew became increasingly impassioned. 'I have seen the Deputy Head about some of the things they're saying, because though they are only children, Nicola, it can be very hurtful stuff. I mean, how would you like it if you read on a toilet wall that someone thought you were a "tosser"?' He spat out the word and accompanied it with the appropriate hand gesture.

I choked on my mouthful. 'Um. Well, I would... er...'

'Indeed, Nicola. One time they left some deodorant on my desk. It can be very damaging to your self-confidence.'

My heart went out to this harmless man.

'They are always saying, "Do you live near a sewage works? Were you a bin man before you were a teacher, sir?" It can make any person worry. And the trouble is that the parents just spoil them rotten. When you tell them what you think of their little darlings they accuse YOU of being a bad teacher!' He dabbed at his brow with the napkin. 'It's one of the reasons my doctor has put me on the pills. And it doesn't *matter* if they are children, Nicola. Abuse is abuse. It can be very wearing. Sometimes I wonder how I'm still doing the job. I mean, I'm thirty-four and I'm losing my hair.' He clutched his temple and pulled back his hairline to show me.

I nodded sympathetically. What had I begun?

'*Mr Moore you're such a bore* is their favourite little chant,' he spat bitterly. 'They know that it winds me up. But we're powerless to stop them. Bring back corporal punishment, I say.' He banged the table with his fork so that my plate jumped. 'These kids have to learn.'

'Er, quite. Well, what about the good eggs in the class?' I asked, desperate to try and find the silver lining. 'You know, the kids that are just caught up in the wrong crowd?'

He looked at me blankly. 'The *good* ones?' he repeated, as if it was a wholly original thought.

'Er, yes. Surely there are a few you like?' I gave him an encouraging smile.

Andrew was now deep in thought, tapping the fork on his mouth so that little specks of cheese sauce stuck to his upper lip.

'I don't mind Milly,' he said finally.

'Oh good,' I replied, relieved. Well done, Milly.

'Yes, she can be a joy when she isn't calling the rest of her classmates "little fuckers".'

'Oh.' My eyes watered. 'More wine?' I asked, pouring the majority of the bottle into my own glass and taking a large gulp.

'And Josh has actually begun to work, but only because his parents are going to buy him an air rifle if he passes the year.'

'It's a start,' I said, horribly enthusiastically.

'I suppose,' he relented. His face softened a fraction. 'Then there's Adam. He's a nice guy.'

'Really?' I encouraged, swallowing the last mouthful of my risotto.

'Yes, he reminds me of me when I was that age,' he said wistfully.

I didn't dare ask what Andrew had been like in his youth. I certainly didn't expect 'popular, confident, go-getting' to make it into the description.

'Yes, Adam isn't appreciated by the other students, but one day they'll realize Adam has a lot to offer the world.'

'Absolutely, I'm sure *Adam* will.' I smiled, almost with a wink. These positive thoughts of Adam had, I think, managed to bring Andrew back from the Dark Side, and he returned to the pleasant version of himself I'd met at the start of the date. I straightened in my chair, pleased to have been some help to Andrew. It felt good.

The coffee passed without further mishap. Andrew seemed... all right. But my stomach was hardly flipping at the thought of seeing him again any time soon. In fact, at ten o'clock, I was keen to get home to my book and a hot-water bottle. The fact that Andrew seemed less of an appealing option than a hot-water bottle solidified the notion that he probably wasn't *The One*. It was with these thoughts whirling through my mind that I found myself outside the door to my apartment block with Andrew looking a little nervous by my side. I gave him a slightly awkward smile and indicated my door.

'So! This is me.'

'I've had a lovely evening.' He smiled.

'Yes. Thank you for dinner. It was delicious.'

'It was,' he said. 'And it was excellent to meet you, Nicola. You are a very special lady.'

'Well, thank you.' I offered my hand for him to shake. It instantly felt wrong. He took it and we did an odd sort of limp shake. Damn. I should have given him a kiss on the cheek. But would that have given him the wrong idea? I was so out of practice.

'We'll have to do it again some time,' Andrew said cheerily.

'Yes, yes. I *am* quite busy with work at the moment.' His face fell. I felt bad. 'But, um, well, a film might be... um...' I shrugged awkwardly.

'There's a new Coen Brothers film coming out next week if you're interested? Maybe we could go to that?'

'That might be possible,' I said, searching my handbag for the door key.

'That would be *wonderful*,' he gushed.

'Possibly. Right, well.' I indicated my door again. 'Long day tomorrow and all that.'

Andrew moved determinedly towards me. I backed away, jabbering. 'Lots to do, sleep. I need some sleep! Okay, so I best...'

Andrew was leaning in so closely that my entire field of vision was taken up by his head. The flecks of cheese remained on his top lip.

'Goodnight,' I yelped, whipping round like a ninja, plunging my key into the lock and throwing myself over the threshold. I shut the door firmly behind me, catching a last glance of Andrew standing in the dark of the street. Another date? I didn't think so. I'd have to think of a nice, encouraging, non-self-esteem-destroying way to dissuade him. I sighed and headed upstairs to my flat. I plonked down into the sofa. That hadn't been an *enormous* disaster, but it hadn't got me any closer to finding true love with a capital T, capital L either. Obviously, I hadn't expected to strike gold and be whisked off my feet on the first date with a total stranger, but it would have made this whole thing way easier if Andrew had been *The One*.

I turned on the lights in the flat, kicked off my heels and flung my feet over the side of the chair. Picking up yesterday's newspaper, I idly flicked through the articles. A headline caught my attention. 'Puppy Love', it announced in bold capitals. The piece was accompanied by a soft-focus picture of a woman and her dog. It was one of those tiny poodle-type dogs, all fluffy tight curls and spindly legs. She was holding it up to one cheek. I read on.

'I'd given up on finding love but then love found me,' the woman was quoted as saying. Below, was another photo – a passport-sized picture of a reasonably normal-looking, smiley-faced man.

'I met Peter out walking our dogs and we just clicked. Our love of our pets brought us closer together...'

Maybe that was it, I mused. Andrew and I lacked a shared passion to bring us together. Perhaps I'd meet someone more suited to me if I searched for a man who enjoyed the same things I did. I *sort* of enjoyed dogs. Perhaps I could meet someone while out dog-walking? That might work. I yawned, hand over my mouth, noting as I did so that I didn't actually have a dog.

But I could work around that.

CHAPTER ELEVEN

Single girl WLTM nice
man with a good smile
and no deeply disturbing
emotional problems.

Contact: Box No. 1583

CAROLINE JUMPED on me the moment I arrived at the office the next day. I couldn't resist a smile.

'You are incorrigible,' I said, as she wandered over under the guise of watering the solitary plant on my desk.

'What? I'm not doing anything!' she insisted, her face the picture of innocence. 'Sooooo... Fun night?'

'Yes, thank you, Caroline.'

'Enjoy dinner?'

'Yes, thank you, Caroline,' I said again, trying to concentrate on my email inbox. I'd had about eight from that wretched dating website Caroline had signed me up to. Apparently someone called Geoff had winked at me. Delete.

'So, how is Andrew?' she asked, changing tack.

Ah, clever. I couldn't avoid this one.

'He's very well. Busy teaching, obviously, but well.'

'Teaching?' Caroline repeated, wrinkling her nose. 'I didn't know he was a teacher.'

'He said he's been a teacher for a long time. Caroline, how well do you know Andrew?' I frowned.

'Oh, he's an old friend,' she said airily. 'He seems awfully sensitive to be a teacher, though. He's the only man I know who cried when we watched *Titanic*.'

'Oh, great,' I muttered. 'Something you could have mentioned before.'

'What? Why? Men can cry,' she argued, crossing her arms over her bosom. 'Ben cries all the time!'

'Caroline, Ben is six years old,' I pointed out.

James popped his head out of his office. 'Nicola, can you bring me the info on that Channel 5 docu-drama?'

'Men can cry, can't they, James?' cooed Caroline.

'Sorry?' James said from the doorway.

'You don't think less of a man if he cries, do you, James?' she repeated.

'Er, where are they crying?' he asked.

'Oh, you know, around, just in general. Do you think less of a man if he cries?'

'I don't mind men crying when someone dies,' he said thoughtfully. 'So I suppose, no, I don't mind men crying.'

'Thought so,' Caroline sing-songed.

'Glad to have cleared that up,' he said, returning to his office with a puzzled look on his face.

Caroline turned back to me with a wistful expression. 'Yes, Andrew was always a tiny bit on the sensitive side.'

James re-emerged. 'I bloody hate it when people cry when they lose the football, though, so it *does* depend on the circumstances.'

'Hmmm, you have a point.' Caroline nodded in agreement.

I watched this exchange in amazement.

'What do you think, Nicola? Men crying or not crying?' asked James.

'Oh, um.' I blushed at being put on the spot. 'Not crying, I think.'

'Yes,' he said decisively, 'men should be men.'

And with that he slammed his office door so hard the glass almost smashed. It was very *manly*.

'Andrew is definitely the crying type.' Caroline nodded.

'Yes, I think the kids at school make him cry.'

'Oh, how awful,' she said, a very brief look of concern flitting across her face. 'So, any other dates lined up? You've got to see who else is *out there*, Nicola.'

James popped his head back through his door. 'Um, Nicola, have you got the Channel 5 stuff?'

'Of course, of course, sorry,' I spluttered and, throwing a look at Caroline for distracting me, raced to his door.

Wandering aimlessly down town at lunchtime, I enjoyed the bright winter sun and tried hard not to brood. Valentine's Day was not that far away. The red circle on the calendar was a permanent reminder that I had a task to do. Without realizing which direction I'd been walking in, I ground to a halt outside the entrance to a small dusty-looking shop with a green facade.

I'd never noticed the pet shop before. The newspaper article about the dog walkers destined for love immediately sprang to mind, and before I could really think about what I was doing, I pushed open the door.

The smell of sawdust and animal hit me instantly. A wall of cages held scurrying rodents. Brightly coloured fish gaped at me from large tanks. A parrot in a cage called out to me. I was surrounded by hay and feed and cat toys and fake bones. I turned to leave. But before I could, an enthusiastic-looking, round-faced pet-shop assistant dressed in a lilac aertex T-shirt appeared by my side. I glanced at his name badge. Roger.

'Can I help you?'

Flustered, I stuttered a quick, 'Oh no. I'm just looking.'

'Are you sure?' Roger asked, with a kind smile on his round face.

'Well, I suppose a dog,' I mumbled, almost to myself.

Roger frowned. 'Something for your dog?' he asked.

'No, um. I was just wondering if you lend dogs? I'd like to borrow a dog.'

'Borrow?' Roger frowned.

'Yes. I mean, well, I might be in the market for one,' I explained. 'But, you know, what if a dog isn't... for me?' I wasn't quite sure where I was going with this, but I carried on. 'Maybe I could, you know, borrow one. Like a test drive?'

'A test drive?' Roger said, his eyebrows meeting in the middle.

'Well, ha ha, you know. Just so I could take it for a spin. To see if it suits me.'

'A *spin*?' Roger frowned for a moment before shrugging. 'Okay... Any particular breed catch your fancy?'

'Well, I...'

'Follow me and let's go and meet some, shall we?' He swept me confidently through the shop. Wow. Was dog borrowing a *thing*?

Twenty minutes later Roger had shown me many pictures of dog types and provided me with a list of local breeders' numbers. Then, before I could stop him, he'd picked up the phone and started dialling. 'Hold on, I'll just try Garry. He might be able to help.'

I tried to interject but Roger put up a hand and smiled encouragingly. He spoke to Garry.

'Lady says she's interested in your Cockapoo or something similar, Gar.'

He put his hand over the receiver and turned to me. 'You definitely just want to *borrow* him?' he checked.

I nodded.

'Borrow like rent him?' Roger confirmed.

'Yes, just for maybe an hour or two to see, you know, if we get on.'

He spoke into the receiver, his eyes never leaving my face, 'Doesn't look mad... Women, mate, isn't it...' Eventually he put down the phone and looked at me. 'Garry said he knows someone who'll lend you their dog,' he said, disbelief etched on his face.

'Oh super,' I stammered.

'If you leave your mobile number with me, we'll put you in touch with the lady who provides this service.'

'Right, okay,' I said, scribbling my number down as quickly as possible, thanking him profusely and practically running out of the door. I scurried out into the street, wondering what I had just done.

Roger called me that evening and I arranged to meet Sandra outside the pet shop that Friday, when I would be 'set up' with a dog for an hour's walk. Yes – I had a date with a dog! Maybe I'd be like that woman in the paper – I'd stumble across Mr Right in the park. Then I would get my own dog and we would walk them together. I smiled as I poured myself a glass of Chablis, rootling in the back of the cupboard where I knew I kept a slab of dark chocolate for cooking purposes. I snapped a couple of squares off and popped them in my mouth just as I heard the doorbell ring.

CHAPTER TWELVE

THAT EVENING Mark decided to stop by with a 'cool surprise' for me. I had come to hate surprises because of the unpredictable nature of them; I liked knowing what was in store for me. Plus, I was doubtful that any surprise organized by Mark was going to fill me with delight. I just had my fingers crossed it wasn't any kind of bat in a box.

It wasn't a bat, thankfully. It was, in fact, a brand-new helmet he'd bought himself. It had neon go-faster stripes up the side. I had to pretend to examine every inch of its surface and polish the visor for twenty whole minutes before I was allowed to get up and make some coffee.

'So, I was mentioning you to a friend of mine who also owns a motorcycle, right,' Mark called as I put the kettle on.

'Mark, it's a moped.'

'No, it's a *motorbike*, and anyway you don't really understand because you're a girl,' he reminded me kindly. 'Anyway this friend of mine, Steven, is keen to go on a date with you, and I thought—'

'Okay, go back, go back. What do you mean you "mentioned me"?' I asked suspiciously, as I emerged from the kitchen with two mugs of coffee.

'I just mentioned that you are, you know, single and dating. That's all.' I handed him his mug with a stony expression. 'Don't worry, sis! I didn't make out you were a desperado or anything.'

'Oh, *thank you*,' I said, voice loaded with sarcasm. 'You are too kind.'

I sat down at the table and sipped at my coffee.

'Yeah, well, he is keen and said he'd take you out.' Mark joined me at the table. I rolled my eyes.

'Mark, you make me sound like a charity case. I'm not an outreach programme you need to get your friends interested in!'

'No, no, that's not what this is. He's a really nice guy and he is up for it.' He gave me a thumbs up.

I shook my head. 'No. No date with your friends, thanks, Mark. I'm not that desperate... at least not yet.'

'Fine, fine, fine,' Mark said, throwing up his hands. 'Do you know what you need to do though, sis?'

'Watch a film and go to bed?' I said, smiling sweetly at him.

He waved his hand dismissively. 'You need to get *online*, start socializing again. Get on Twitter, actually, get on Facebook. Then you can meet people on your terms and see who turns up.'

'Hmmm.' I shrugged hesitantly. 'Haven't I missed the boat a bit for Facebook?'

'No! Everyone's on Facebook. You have to be nowadays. How else do you stay connected with the rest of the world?

Look, sis, it'll be good for you. You can get back in touch with some of your old friends.'

'I don't know,' I said, not meeting his eye.

I'd been avoiding social networking websites for a few years now. Surely everyone who wanted to be in touch with me, was in touch with me? I didn't get the whole thing. Why bother? Then Caroline's face swam before my eyes and I thought of the dare. Of the promise I'd made to myself and the feeling that it was time to face up to the past.

'Come on. Let me get you started.' Mark grabbed my laptop from the floor and opened it up onto the table.

I gave him a reluctant nod and Mark went about setting me up on the websites.

'Right, I've transferred all your email contacts onto Facebook. Now just wait, sis, everyone will be messaging you...'

I took a breath and sat down, reading what he'd already written under my profile.

'You all good?' Mark said, shrugging on his coat. 'I'll be off then. See you soon and I'll tell Steven he can call you about this weekend.'

'Hmmm?' I muttered distractedly, wondering what my 'Hobbies' were.

'Steven, my friend,' he prompted.

'What?' I looked up, and then remembered, 'Oh no, Mark. Don't worry, I'm fine, really.'

'Oh go on, sis, you'll like him. He's a good guy.'

'Well, I... What's he like?' I relented.

'He is good-looking apparently, say the girls, and he likes

sports. He has a good job in the centre of town and he's a, well, you know, he's a…'

'Good guy?' I hazarded.

'Yeah! So he's up for it. I've already given him your number so expect his call, okay?'

'You've GIVEN him my number already? Oh gee thanks, Mark. Give me some element of choice, why don't you?'

'What's that, sis? I can't hear you,' Mark yelled, diving out of the flat and closing the door behind him.

Grrr.

Steven called me pretty much the moment my brother left and I found myself agreeing to meet him, 'wearing something warm', on Saturday morning. I returned to roaming around the internet and promptly forgot all about it.

Twenty-four hours later and I was still online. Okay, so I did go to work and eat breakfast, but the entire next evening had been spent in front of the laptop screen. It was midnight on a Thursday and I was firmly in cyberspace. I was looking at a friend of a friend of a friend on Facebook. I didn't know this girl. She was a perfect stranger. I didn't even know this girl's friend, who was a friend of my friend. So why was I here staring at her face? Why did I feel the urge to trawl through her cover photos? Why had I noted the groups she'd joined? Why was my stomach twisting at the sight of this sleek individual with her toothy smile and horribly shiny blonde bob? Why did I care? She was just a friend of a friend of someone I used to know.

The trouble was the someone I used to know. He was on Facebook. Brazenly, right here. His profile photo was an image of him on a skateboard, which, on anyone else, would look daft, but on him was cool in an ironic sort of way. I looked at his friends list and didn't recognize any of them. To be fair, it had been more than seven years since we saw each other, but still. Stumbling across him had come as an enormous, uncomfortable shock. I wondered what he was like now?

I knew I shouldn't have let Mark set me up on here.

CHAPTER THIRTEEN

THE NEXT day, feeling both apprehensive and slightly ridiculous, I approached the pet shop on my lunch break. I was wearing a wax Barbour jacket I'd unearthed from a trunk in my bedroom and had pulled on some filthy Adidas trainers to complete my 'dog-walking' look. A woman was waiting outside the pet shop, a small-to-medium-sized ball of fluff sitting on hind legs by her side.

'Sandra?' I asked.

'You must be Nicola,' she replied. Then she turned to the dog and said in a baby-voice, 'You said this pretty lady was her, didn't you?' She then scooped the dog up into her arms and made me shake its paw.

I glanced up to see Roger in the window, eyeing us both.

'Great. I'll just take him for a spi... a walk and then we'll meet you back here in an hour.'

'Do you have the money?' she asked, as if we were involved in some kind of drugs drop.

'Oh, I do, sorry.' I rummaged in my bag for the cash.

'I want to go to Primark while you're gone, you see.'

'Right. Okay.' I handed over a tenner, wondering how

many items she could get with the note. Loads, probably.

'Well, I'll say goodbye then,' she said, lifting the dog up so that they were face-level. 'He likes his walks, yes he does, yes he does,' she said in the baby voice, shaking him a little and then rubbing her nose against his. Ew. She handed the lead to me. 'I'll meet you back here in an hour. You kids have fun!'

We walked off up the high street and I swear he started dragging his back two legs, already missing the affections of his owner.

'Come on, dog, come on, doggy,' I said, copying Sandra's sing-songy voice in the hope I could fool it into trotting after me.

Pulling on his lead, I headed round the corner of Park Street and up towards Brandon Hill – Bristol's premiere dog-walking spot.

I was quite enjoying myself. The dog and I were entertained by numerous games of chase-the-stick and I loved the feeling of being out in the fresh air, doing something a little different from my normal everyday routine. I realized I had barely noticed if there were many men around to talk to and, as I stopped to catch my breath after a particularly brutal over-arm throw, I reminded myself that the whole point of this exercise was to find a like-minded soul. If I didn't find someone soon, Caroline would set me up with another eligible young bachelor from her list. I shuddered.

'Aw, what's its name?' came a voice from nearby.

I looked about myself and spotted a middle-aged woman with a black Labrador attached to a lead beside her. I was about to engage in my first dog-walker talk! Only, I realized, I had forgotten to ask what the dog was called.

The woman approached and patted the borrowed dog enthusiastically, as her Labrador sniffed at my shoes, its tail wagging. She looked at me, expecting an answer.

'Oh, um, it's called. It's called... It.'

'It?' said the woman, with a frown.

'Er, yes, short for... um... short for... Kermit... It.' I nodded slowly, feeling like an absolute fool.

'Kermit...' The woman looked at me, then back at the dog and then back up at me, a worried expression on her face. 'How... nice. Kermit. Like the frog.'

'Yes, ha... ha.'

'Funny name for a dog, isn't it?' She laughed.

'Yes. I suppose it is. Anyway, I best get on,' I said with false gusto. 'Come on, It! Come on, you,' I said, tugging at his lead and wandering away.

He or, rather, *It*, grumpily waddled after me, sad to be leaving the lady and her Labrador.

I scanned the fields in search of any eligible-looking men to strike up conversation with, but there were none, unless you counted the very old man over there, walking a Dachshund attached to a piece of string. I suspected he wasn't *The One*. I sighed. This was no good. And It didn't seem to like me very much at all. 'Oh come on,' I said to It. 'Let's get you back.'

As we were walking back down Park Street I decided to drop into the office and show him to Caroline. There was still a bit of time before I was supposed to meet Sandra, and

Caroline just loved dogs. I pushed the door open a fraction and indicated to Caroline with a finger to my lips that she should keep the noise down. But, of course, the moment she saw the little dog she started clapping her hands and squealing like I'd just announced it was an unexpectedly early Christmas...

'Oooh, he's lovely,' she said, scooting out from her desk to come and pet him. 'I didn't know you had a dog, Nic?'

'Oh, I don't he's a... friend's.'

'What's going on out there?' James' voice sounded out from his office.

Caroline giggled.

'We should go,' I whispered, backing away from Caroline and towards the door. 'Back soon.'

It, having clearly taken to Caroline, chose that moment to let out a round of noisy barks.

James appeared in the doorway. I was sure I was about to get into trouble, when James surprised us both. His face lit up and he practically fell over the corner of my desk in his haste to join us. He scooped the dog up into his arms. 'He's brilliant.' He put him back down onto the floor and ruffled his ears. 'Good boy,' he said, in a voice strikingly similar to the one he used when speaking to our trickier clients. He picked up a packet of Jaffa Cakes from Caroline's desk and removed one. 'Have a biscuit, doggy, have a—'

Caroline reached over, plucked the Jaffa Cake out of his hand and put it straight into her mouth.

James looked aghast.

'What?' she mumbled through munching. 'A waste of

perfectly good chocolate. Don't you dare. And, anyway,' she said, sponge spraying out of her mouth, 'Jaffa Cakes are *not* biscuits. Everyone knows that. It has something to do with Marie Antoinette, or tax, or something.'

James took the dog gently by the ears and shook his head. 'Who's a mean lady? Who's a mean lady? Yes, boy, you bark at the mean lady.'

I laughed.

James looked at me. 'I never thought of you as a dog person, Nicola.'

The smile died on my lips. What was that supposed to mean? What was a 'dog person' anyway? What, just because I didn't parade around the office in a T-shirt advertising 'Pedigree Chum,' or make annual trips to Crufts, didn't mean I didn't like dogs.

'I always pictured you with a cat,' he said, smiling up at me, his grey eyes crinkling at the corners.

A CAT person! Does he think I sit alone in a bedsit, drinking wine from the bottle and crocheting, with nothing but the TV guide and a fat tabby for company? I mean, fine, I do live in a small flat and yes, some do say that knitting is the poor man's crochet, but still...

'He's lovely,' James said.

'Hmmm. We have to get back,' I announced, nose in the air.

As I walked back down the stairs I heard James ask. 'What's up with her?'

I was still quietly seething that evening as I sat on a bench overlooking the Suspension Bridge. The sun had long since set, but the lights looping along the bridge always looked magical and there was no traffic, so it was reasonably quiet. The gorge yawned open, the River Avon making slow, silent progress below. Did others see me in the same way as James did? Was I the sad, mad lady with hundreds of cats, a woman with only feline company to look forward to of an evening? Pah. I would show James. I would show myself. I was *not* some desperate case to be pitied. Standing up, I hurried home. I needed my beauty sleep because tomorrow was Date Number Two.

CHAPTER FOURTEEN

T HE START of the weekend and I was standing on the pavement on the corner of Park Street. The Wills Memorial Building, with its sandblasted walls, soared above me. Students walked by in chatty clusters and cars inched past me on the road. Smoothing down my top, I waited.

Following the advice I'd read in one of Caroline's magazines, I was wearing the most minimal of make-up in an attempt to look like I was wearing none at all. It had taken me an hour to perfect this. I was dressed 'warmly' in a big cream polo neck, which was tickling my chin, and some jeans and wool-lined winter boots. I was feeling pretty nervous, but my curiosity had won over and I was feeling excited for the date.

I wondered what Steven had planned. Would we leave the city and spend the day in front of a warm country pub fire? Would we get out into the forest and wander around under the bare trees? Would we... my heart suddenly leapt as I spotted a gorgeous light-silver Aston Martin convertible working its way up Park Street. My tummy jumped. Hadn't Mark mentioned that Steven had a good job? Good job normally equalled good car and I was already imagining what the cool leather interior was going to smell like, my back eased into a cushioned passenger seat, some Brahms playing quietly through the sound centre, the air-conditioning heater warming us as we motored along in style.

I craned my neck to try and make out the driver's face but he was still too far away and his progress was currently being hampered by some idiot student in a shabby Peugeot 306, which was pottering up the hill with what looked like an enormous canoe balanced precariously on its roof. Aston Martin Man was now travelling at approximately 2 mph in a nervy stop–start way as if waiting for the canoe to break free of its flimsy straps and slide right down to the bottom of the hill, taking any unfortunates in its path with it.

Fortunately, the lights turned green and the cars were on the move again. My face broke into a welcoming smile in case Aston Martin Man was looking for me on the side of the road. Yes. The car was slowing down and my smile widened. I went to lift my hand into a wave and then startled as he leant on his horn. I peered down to look into the car, but there was no man inside. Just a frustrated blonde woman, all pearls and cashmere, yelling expletives in the direction of the Peugeot. The canoe-topped car had stopped and was now blocking the road and, inside it, a rugged-looking scruff was making apologetic gestures at the driver of the Aston Martin. What the hell was going on? The scruff in the canoe car started gesturing at me. Wait... What did I have to do with... Oh God, he was beckoning for me to come over. I looked behind me quickly, in the hope that he was trying to catch the attention of someone else, but—

'Nicola,' he shouted.

Great.

I gave him a weak smile and slunk over.

'Quick!' he said, flinging the passenger door open.

I manoeuvred in, cringing as I heard the rustle of a discarded crisp packet beneath my bottom. The exact moment I shut the door, we squealed off, car bumping back onto the road so furiously that when I went to grab the seat belt I was almost catapulted through the windscreen.

'Sorry about that!' Steven said, indicating the convertible behind us and its furious blonde driver.

I jammed my seat belt into the clasp, pulled the crisp packet from under me and dropped it into the footwell.

'That's okay.' I breathed quickly, turning to look at him.

Blue eyes, blonde hair, enormous shoulders. He gave me a wide smile and I began to relax. He had an open face, a little rumpled, but I imagined that was from lugging the gigantic canoe about the place. He looked friendly. Aside from the crisp packet, the car was relatively clean. There *was* a slightly strange smell, like coconut, but otherwise it was bearable.

I had just about got over my Aston Martin disappointment when Steven asked, 'So where's your flat? I completely forgot to tell you to grab a bikini.'

I looked at him, aghast. 'My *bikini*?'

It *was* November, wasn't it? It wasn't just my imagination? It was only thirty-six days till Christmas, wasn't it? He couldn't possibly mean my bikini, my actual, I-wear-it-in-the-summer-in-the-SUN bikini?

'Yep.'

'Oh.'

'It's St Georges Street, isn't it? Mark mentioned you live there,' Steven said with a smile, oblivious to my rising panic.

'Are we going swimming?'

'No,' he grinned. 'It's a surprise.'

'Right. Er. My... St George, yes, my flat, is on St George's. Up here on the left.' I indicated. Ooh, unless we were going to spend the day at a country spa? My hopes lifted momentarily and then plummeted when the massive tip of the enormous canoe blocked out the passing sun. Instinct told me no, no spa.

'Just here,' I pointed, feeling like I was about to cry. Why was I even doing this? Should I just go up to my flat and never come back out? I jumped out of the car and fumbled for my keys. Cursing myself, I rang the doorbell.

'Mees Nicola,' Julio said, opening the door with a flourish.

'Sorry, Julio, I can't find my keys.' I raced off up the stairs before he could reply.

I let myself into my flat and stood with my back to the door, breathing heavily. The flat had never looked so welcoming. The sofa had never looked so inviting. The television seemed to wink at me, light bouncing off its glossy surface. 'Come and watch box sets on me, Nicola, come,' it seemed to say. 'We could finish season eight of *House* today if we really focused on it.' Gahhh.

I considered staying put, closing the blinds, never going back outside. My country-pub-fire hopes were a distant memory, my frosty forest walk was crushed. Outside, Steven pipped his car horn. Damn. I couldn't back out. We'd made plans and I hated to let people down. I sighed, sloped through to my bedroom, grabbed my bikini from the summer section of my wardrobe and ran back down the stairs.

Julio was waiting poised at the door to see me out, occasionally glancing suspiciously in the direction of Steven.

'Have good day, Mees Nicola.' He waved.

'I will,' I yelled back at him, in case Steven's window was open and he was listening. I got back into the car. 'Got it,' I said, patting my handbag where one of the bikini straps could be seen poking out of the top.

'Okay then, let's go!' He veered wildly off the pavement once more and this time I was thrust backwards into my seat as he simultaneously drove and switched on *The Beach Boys: Greatest Hits*. Christ. 'Round, round get around I get around...'

At around Weston-Super-Mare I had psyched myself up enough to get chatting.

'So, go on, what are we doing today then?' I asked in what I hoped was a casual way. My knuckles turned white as I gripped my legs. I was a *little* tense about what lay in store. Steven's manic driving didn't exactly help matters.

'Oh well, of course we're taking this baby out, aren't we?' He nodded his head in the direction of the roof.

I was under no illusions as to what *this baby* was. Oh dear. I gave him a strained smile and he added, 'Don't worry, I've got all the kit you'll need. You won't even be aware it's winter.'

That made me feel marginally better. Up to that point I'd thought he might be under the illusion it was in fact summer. I mean he was wearing shorts, we were listening to the Beach Boys, and we were headed to the West Country. It was basically Bank Holiday. I settled back into my seat and decided to make more effort on the small talk. The CD had moved on to 'In my Room', which made for a slightly calmer atmosphere, at least.

'So, are you quite into The Great Outdoors?' I asked, gesturing to the patches of passing fields as we whizzed along.

'I guess you could say that,' he said with a vague chuckle. The chuckle made me edgy again. I looked back out of the window.

Focus on the horizon, Nicola, we can do this.

'What about you, Nicola, what kind of hobbies are you into?' He gave me a quick sideways glance.

'Oh, I like...' Hmm. This was a tricky question. All my 'hobbies' seemed so dull. Reading, watching films, having a glass of wine, cleaning the house, making photograph collages... 'Photography,' I announced suddenly.

'Interesting.' He nodded. 'Did you get to see the Matthew Brady exhibit when it was on at the City Museum?'

Bugger.

'Oh, er, no. I was... away.'

'Abroad?'

'Yep,' I said quickly, pleased to have avoided the photography faux pas.

'Where?'

'Hmm...' I turned to him. He'd taken his eyes off the road and was looking at me expectantly.

'Where did you go?' he repeated.

Oh bollocks.

'Madrid!' I said suddenly, my eyes wide. The lies were flowing freely now. The truth was that I hadn't left the country in five years. And even that had just been Brittany, which really didn't count as it cost a pound to get there on the ferry and we'd only stayed a few hours before my brother managed to hospitalize himself by clambering onto a statue of Arthur III, losing his grip on his sword and plunging to the ground with a broken ankle.

'It's a great city, Madrid,' Steven said enthusiastically. 'I spent a year out there with work.'

Curses.

'That's great,' I shouted, hoping to match his enthusiasm. 'Oh look...' I pointed out of the window as we sailed past a sign on the M5. 'Taunton.'

'Er, indeed,' Steven said. 'So, where did you stay in Madrid?' he asked.

I cringed. 'Um, just near the centre,' I said, waving my hand dismissively.

'Centro or more towards the Arganzuela district?'

Bloody hell, what was up with this guy? Did he write for *Lonely Planet* or something?

'Um, more Centro,' I said, trying to mimic his pronunciation. He'd done something funny with an 'O'. I spat on his dashboard.

'It's very lively, isn't it?' He grinned, not seeming to notice my spittle. 'I went out there with the football team I played with. We spent the most awesome night in Bar Salamanca, which is ridiculous because it's not even in that district.' He roared with laughter.

I laughed along, a split-second too late, and then trailed off.

'Did you go?' he asked.

'Go?' I said, lost now.

'Bar Salamanca, in the centre,' he repeated.

'Oh no, we didn't,' I said, trying to sound gutted. 'We, er... walked past it, though.'

'It's an amazing place. They serve you beers and shisha pipes on low cushions on the floor. I'm off drink, obviously, but the atmosphere is just fantastic.'

'Off drink?' I prompted, trying to steer him away from the original topic and risk exposing my theatre of lies.

'Well, it gets in the way of training, so I tend to avoid it.'

'Training for what?' I asked.

He shrugged. 'Whatever I happen to be doing at the time. When I was in Madrid I was in training for the football season, but I was also running the Barcelona Marathon that year.'

'Oh wow. You sound very sporty!' I said, amazed that someone could have so much stamina. 'Are you training for anything now?'

'A competition in four months, actually,' he replied, manoeuvring the car round a lone caravan, the canoe rattling a little as the speedometer edged up to 80 mph.

I hastily looked away and tried not to think too much

about potential canoe-related car crashes. 'Competing in what exactly?'

'A mixture of stuff. It's a triathlon, you see.' He swerved back into the outside lane.

My triathlon knowledge was about as detailed as my canoe knowledge, but I nodded appreciatively and said, 'Gosh.'

'Yeah, it's the second time I've done it. It's called The Iron Man competition. It's pretty mad actually.' He gave a low laugh and indicated off the motorway.

'In Bristol?' I asked him.

'America, actually.'

'America, really?' I raised my eyebrows. 'Ooh.'

'Yep.'

'So, um, what do you do for it exactly?'

'Well, you start with an ocean swim, then cycle, then run a marathon to finish,' he explained.

'Right... Gosh,' I said again. That didn't quite seem to convey enough enthusiasm, so I added a 'golly' for good measure. 'Gosh... Golly.'

'Hmm.'

'You'll probably want to kick back for the rest of the year after all that, I imagine?' I said in a slightly strangled tone.

'God, no.' He laughed. 'I've got to raise money because my friend Tom and I are doing the Himalayan 100 Mile Stage Race in October next year.' He registered my blank face. 'It's a run.'

Had he said 100 miles? A run that is 100 miles long. Isn't

that the distance from Bristol to London? Isn't that a car journey that requires a sweetie stop?

'Yeah, it's quite intense,' Steven explained, spotting my astonished expression. 'It's like running a marathon a day for five days, in the Himalayas. The high altitude can make it a little harder to breathe, so it can be quite challenging.'

This silenced me. *Quite* challenging. Surely there could be nothing on this earth more challenging than five marathons in five days up a mountain range where people die walking with picks and ropes? This was a man who liked to test himself. This was a man who was focused on winning, endurance and pushing his body well beyond its capabilities. This was a man I was about to get into a canoe with. My stomach plummeted. I wanted to go home. But it was too late. We pulled into an empty car park.

'We're here,' Steven said, beaming at me. 'Looks like a light sea breeze!' The glee in his voice was palpable.

'Super!' I swallowed, watching him climb out of the car and almost instantly getting knocked off his feet by the 'light' sea breeze.

I took a breath and opened the car door. This was it. My hair whipped around my face. I looked over at Steven. He was inhaling deeply and rolling his shoulders.

'Let's get the kayak down!' he said, clapping his hands together. He had the LOUDEST CLAP IN THE WORLD. I flinched.

'Oh, kayak,' I said, nodding quickly like a mad person. 'I thought it was a canoe.'

'Hahahaha.' He laughed heartily at me. 'A canoe! That's a good one.'

'Er, right. Haha. So how do you do it?' I asked, attempting to match his enthusiasm and failing. I copied his deep inhalations and shoulder rolls in an effort to look like I was trying.

Following much strap pulling and heaving, the kayak was on the ground beside the car. If possible, it now looked even bigger. Steven was fixing some complicated seat pad things to it with various straps and attachments. I stood looking around myself, hugging my arms to my chest, already freezing.

'In the bag in the back there's everything you need. I've brought you my sister's wetsuit, it should be fine, and then there's boots and things like that. You'll feel like a princess.' He laughed, clearly very excited to be preparing for our adventure.

A princess.

I tried to get into the spirit and practically skipped to the boot of the car to get the bag. 'Okey dokey!' I wondered if it was the wisest choice to use that phrase now for the first time.

'There's a public toilet over there you can change in,' Steven said, pointing to a distant block of cement. I looked at it with narrowed eyes. I knew there was little point in complaining. This was a man who planned to spend a week defecating in a pot in the Himalayas, so I didn't think moaning about these facilities would meet with a huge amount of sympathy.

I pushed the door open and instantly gagged from the damp, musty smell. The loo seat was up and the toilet was streaked with yellow. The flush had lost the bit on the end of the chain and the sink was not an adequate size for even a five-year-old child. There was no loo paper and no hook for my clothes. There was no real manoeuvrable space, so I was in for a really fun five minutes.

I tried to breathe through my mouth. As fast as I could, I whipped my jumper off and flung my jeans in the bag. My flesh was already breaking out into goosebumps and I gritted my teeth as I plunged into my bikini. Grabbing the wetsuit, I struggled for another few minutes, stretching the material over my limbs. It was a little on the small side. I put on the boots, leaving a thin strip of skin around my ankle laid bare to the elements. Also in the bag was some kind of hat made in the same material as the wetsuit. It looked as if it hooked under the chin. I inspected it in disbelief. Surely not. I would look like a skittle. Stuffing it back in the bag, I collected up the rest of my things and ventured out into the elements, feeling highly self-conscious.

'Great!' Steven said as he jigged enthusiastically about by the kayak. He was wearing the hat. He did indeed look like a skittle. Oh God. 'Do you want me to do your hat up for you?' he offered.

I nodded silently. I slowly tied my hair back in a ponytail and let him tug the hat over my head for me. My left eyebrow was stretched uncomfortably taut and a piece of hair on the other side of my face was tickling me where it had escaped The Hat's clutches.

'Okay.' Steven clapped his hands for a second time. The sound was only slightly dampened by the hat covering my ears. 'Let's hit the sea! You take that end and I'll lead the way.' He pointed to a toggle at one end and I lifted it, instantly dropping it again as I realized how heavy it was.

'You'll probably need to use both hands,' Steven called behind him.

I was tempted to poke my tongue out at his back. Mentally preparing myself, I took a deep breath and grabbed the toggle with both hands. I lifted, lurching forward as Steven set the pace. I half-walked, half-hopped along behind him, trying to keep hold of the kayak, block out the wind hitting my face and ignore the pain as I realized the small wetsuit was rubbing my legs and crushing my boobs down. Then we rounded the corner and I saw the sea. All other thoughts emptied as I watched the waves roll in, crashing dramatically onto the shore and throwing up white surf. The grey expanse of dark clouds overhead reflected the foreboding I felt. Up ahead, a man, wearing at least eighteen layers of clothing, was walking his dog. There was no one else in the water.

'You'll be in the front,' Steven gestured to the first seat. 'And I'll be in the back doing the steering and providing the brute strength.' He grinned warmly at me. I realized he was making a big effort and I managed to smile back at him.

'Hop in, Nicola.'

I gasped as the water hit the bare patch of ankle and, with a slight wobble, I managed to settle myself into the kayak. A few seconds later a wave washed past us, spraying a little water over me. I shivered. Feeling a great surge of weight behind me, I realized Steven was in. He handed me a paddle and shouted instructions.

'Right! We're going to head out and try and make it round the coast, depending on conditions,' he yelled. 'If you paddle, I'll copy you and you'll be fine.' Then he roared with excited delight and his laughter carried on the air like a maniac's.

I started to paddle straight at the waves. I squealed as a second wave headed towards us. My squeal soon died on my lips as it crashed over the kayak, smacking me full in the face. I was so shocked by the icy cold that I simply stopped paddling and opened and closed my mouth in wordless surprise.

Steven was yelling, 'Just keep paddling, Nicola, this is the hardest part.' But all I could make out was, 'Blank, blank, Nicola, blank, something, Mardi Gras.'

Gritting my teeth, I paddled on. Another wave hurtled over us, unbalancing me and blasting water down the gap between my hat and the wetsuit. My spine tingled and my body jerked. I was going to die today. In the sea, in November, canoeing with a stranger. Oh sorry, KAYAKING with a stranger.

'Nearly there, Nicola, we're nearly beyond them!' (Blank, blank, Nicola, something blank bee, blank them!).

I could feel Steven powerfully manoeuvring us over the waves and, after another two had passed us/smashed me in the face, we were out beyond what I now knew, thanks to Steven, was the break line.

'Sorry, Nicola. That's always the worst bit, but at least you're used to the temperature now, eh?' He laughed, absolutely loving this, which was unfathomable to me. I tried to nod my head so he could see I was coping, but I wasn't, so my head just wobbled a bit as I tried to bite back the tears. I really didn't need any more saltwater on my face.

'Okay, we're heading to the left so start paddling,' he called on the wind.

I put a paddle in and tried to work into a slow rhythm, not sure if I was going too fast or too slow. Not really sure of anything, to be honest, except the slight ringing in my ears as the cold seeped in and the pain around the bare strip of my ankle, where I imagined they were going to have to amputate.

The trouble was that every time a rogue wave threatened to blast me in the face, I stopped rowing and our paddles clashed together, putting us out of sync. Steven kept calling out helpful instructions like: 'If you could just keep a steady rhythm, Nicola,' and 'You see our paddles hit if you change the pattern of your paddling!' So that really helped me to focus. After what seemed like an hour in the water, we appeared to have travelled around one hundred yards.

I tried to stay positive in the face of near death. I tried to focus on sticking the paddle in the left and then again in the right. I tried turning my head to one side so the water didn't hit me full in the face and instead just got my cheeks. I tried to think of warm places (a beach in the Caribbean, a sauna, the fires of hell, etc.), but instead, I imagined I was being forced to paddle for my life. That if I stopped I would die (which I suspect was, in fact, the truth). I started to pray to many, many gods for this ordeal to be over. I lost track of the time as I moved in as steady a rhythm as I could manage.

Steven and I were just two skittles paddling the high seas together.

At long last, thank you, Jesus, there came the blessed call. 'Let's head back!' Steven yelled.

Heading back! Yes, yes, yes, yes, let's DEFINITELY do that.

'It should be a little easier as we are moving *with* the current now,' he called.

We started to turn and my whole body jumped happily with the notion that we could soon be warm again. I paddled with all my might, throwing up seawater and heading for the sand. Steven was right. It was easier. I was only hit once in the face and the rest just got my lower body parts. And I hadn't been able to feel those for the past half an hour anyway. Before I knew it, I was wobbling out onto dry land, watching Steven drag the kayak higher up the sand and away from the water.

Thank God.

'Right, let's get warmed up,' Steven yelled over at me, throwing me a towel. I grabbed at it gratefully but my arms, numb with cold, failed to react in time. The towel slapped me on the chest and fell onto the soggy sand. I watched it fall in slow motion, my mouth rounded into a silent 'Nooooo'. I scooped it up without a word and put it over my head like a tent. Get me off this beach.

'Let's get this back to the car. I brought tea in a flask,' he sang, grinning at me. I thought he was going to add a *TA-DA*, he was so damn perky.

I tried to lift the kayak and watched as the toggle slipped from my frozen grasp. My fingers had turned a pale whitish-blue colour. I looked up at Steven the Skittle. 'I can't,' I whispered.

Steven examined my face briefly and then made a decision. Handing me the paddles, he pointed to the car park. 'See you back there,' he said, and, just like when Superman lifts that van in the film, Steven hoisted the kayak onto his back and headed up the path towards his car. I slowly traipsed behind the kayak with dead legs, dragging the paddles, reckoning that if I were twenty degrees warmer, I would find this image funny.

I entered my flat, Steven's jaunty goodbye still ringing in my ears ('Well, Nicola, hope I haven't put you off the ocean for life, HA HA HA!' MASSIVE CLAP OF HANDS), and straight into a Disney movie, as I found Basia cleaning the bathroom taps and singing: 'The hills are alive weeth sound of musica'. On seeing my expression, beneath the streaked mascara smears, she muttered something like, 'I see kitchen now' and scampered out.

Five minutes later, and exactly three hours after I'd entered the ocean, my body was cocooned in my massive towelling dressing gown, and yet I was still cold. I rubbed my arms, trying to get rid of the goosebumps that still covered my skin, and pulled a blanket over my legs. I felt cold to my core. I felt cold in my organs. I felt like I would never be warm again. Ever. I dialled Mark's number. This was his fault.

'Ahhh, Prick Face,' I said slowly, when he answered. Prick Face had been my name for him when I was twelve. It seemed a wholly appropriate time to resurrect it.

'Ahhh, hey, sis. How was the date? How's Steven? Did you say I said *Hi*?'

'You said he liked sport,' I said in a low, dangerous voice.

'Huh?'

'You. Said. He. Liked. Sport,' I spelt out slowly.

'Er, he does...' came the confused reply.

'Yes,' I said, gritting my teeth, 'I *know* he likes sport, Mark.'

'Good,' he answered, not gauging my tone. 'So how was it?'

'He doesn't just *like* sport, though, does he, Mark? He *loves* it.'

'Yeah, I suppose he is quite into it. So anyway, what did you guys do tod—'

'Quite into it?' I repeated. '*Quite* into it? Mark, Steven LOVES sport,' I exploded. 'He loves sport to the point of obsession. He lives, breathes, dies for sport.' My breathing turned heavy. 'He loves sport like I love cleanliness and you love bats, Mark. He LOVES IT. If sport were a woman, he would have asked it to marry him years ago. Steven wants to get sport *pregnant*.'

'I do like bats,' said Mark, chuckling in a way that only annoyed me more.

'I have never in my life met anyone so into a hobby. He can't get enough sport in his life, Mark.'

'Sorry, sis, I don't get what your point is?' Mark seemed perplexed by my angry rant. 'I mean, everyone has to have interests. So did you say I said Hi?'

'No, brother,' I hissed. 'In between the whole being

116

slammed by tons of freezing seawater thing and trying to ensure my body temperature remained capable of sustaining life, I forgot to send him your love and kisses.'

'No need to be like that, Nic,' Mark lectured, beginning to sense the date he'd set me up on hadn't been the triumph he'd anticipated.

'I'm not being like anything, Mark. I am cold. I have spent the day in a kayak—'

'A kayak,' he interrupted, 'cool, yeah, his last girlfriend was into water sports.' He chuckled.

I hung up.

Reaching for the remote, I tried to map out the rest of my day. I brought up the TV listings and scanned the channels, searching for anything mindless and comforting. Basia poked her head out of the kitchen.

'All done,' she chirruped. I'd completely forgotten she was here.

'Great.' I smiled weakly at her. 'Thank you, see you next week, have a nice evening!'

'Okay, I am leave to go on the tiles,' she said, miming a pretty indecent dance move for my benefit.

'Er, great!'

'See you on the next week, yes?' she called, shrugging on her coat in the hall. 'You good week hoping I. Byeeee!'

I sighed and snuggled deeper into my sofa, daydreaming of roaring fires, boiling water and steam rooms.

CHAPTER FIFTEEN

```
Single girl WLTM man who
enjoys darts, board games,
crosswords, watching TV and
cosy nights in.
```
Contact: Box No. 5811

'**YOU LOOK** exhausted,' Caroline said when I arrived at the office the next day.

'Thanks,' I scoffed, swinging my bag down by my desk. 'I appreciate your lovely compliment.'

Caroline noted my grumpy expression and giggled. 'Oh, you look pretty too, Nicky Wicky, just a teeny bit tired... Up all night, were you?'

I threw the nearest thing to hand, a pink highlighter, at her but she just ducked out of the way.

With mock horror, she said, 'Nicola Brown, are you CLUTTERING our office space?'

I poked my tongue out at her just as James walked through the door.

'Very mature, Nicola. I'm sure she deserved it.' He smiled,

as I felt my cheeks get hot.

'Good morning, James,' I mumbled.

Caroline was openly laughing at me.

When James was firmly settled into his office next door, I told Caroline about my sea kayak experience of the day before, relishing retelling the gory details, remembering just how cold the sea had been, and loving the varied expressions of shock on Caroline's face.

'He made you get in the water?' she gasped. 'In *November*? He's as mad as a box of toads.'

I was pleased that someone else thought this was particularly abnormal and reminded Caroline that during this entire nightmare I'd been dressed top-to-toe in figure-hugging neoprene. Hat and all.

'Honestly, I looked like a skittle.' I shook my head as Caroline rocked in her chair, laughing at the image.

James re-emerged from his office, 'All I can hear is you two laughing. What is so funny?' he asked with a raise of an eyebrow.

'Nicola has taken up kayaking,' Caroline said, exploding into another bout of giggles.

'*Nicola*?' he enquired, turning to me.

I mumbled a potted version of the story I'd just told Caroline, excluding the fact that it had been a blind date, and looked up in confusion as James started chuckling as well. I couldn't remember ever making him laugh before. Well, except for the time I'd been cleaning under my desk and fallen off my seat, head first, into the bin. But on that occasion he'd been laughing *at* me and not with me. This was new. It felt good. For the first time in twenty-four hours I was genuinely glad to have been out with Steven yesterday. It wasn't that I was reconsidering making winter trips to the ocean, but I realized I had a good story to tell. I'd done something outrageous this weekend and retelling that tale was part of the fun. I gave myself a small, and imaginary, pat on the back.

So when I received a text from Mark later that morning that read: 'Sorry about Steven, have got another lined up... interested?' I didn't instantly recoil from the idea. Fine, so me and Steven were never going to be future life partners, but he hadn't been a horrible person. Aside from his fanatical desire to push his body to its physical limit, Steven had been a perfectly decent human being. He hadn't been rude, hadn't been unpleasant, hadn't been dull. He hadn't taken recreational drugs on our date, he hadn't had *deep* psychological problems, he hadn't appeared violent, abusive or needy. It could have been worse. In the warmth of the office, retelling the tale, it sounded comical, adventurous, exciting. Not enough to repeat the experience, obviously, but enough to see who else was out there. Buoyed up by these thoughts, I texted Mark back. 'Okay, I'll do it. Get him to give me a call.'

Clearly surprised by my positive response, Mark immediately rang my mobile.

'That's the attitude, sis! Try, try, try again. I'll get Lewis to call you. You'll like Lewis; he's like the opposite of Steven. He's not outdoorsy at all. But he's not fat,' he tacked on, just in case I assumed that if you weren't running a few marathons a year you were bound to be obese.

'And what does Lewis do?' I asked.

'Lots of things. He's a bit of a handyman, but, you know, educated.'

'Age?' I enquired.

'My age. Oh, hold on, Carol is calling me over. I better go!' he gushed.

'Have a good day, run off to Carol.' I laughed.

The phone went dead and I was left staring at the handset.

Excitingly, James had decided that we could all do with a nice team-bonding lunch out, so Caroline and I pretended to work, while really clock-watching, until James emerged from his office and announced time.

He'd booked a table in one of the restaurants on the river in the centre of town. It was a magical winter's day. My breath hung in icy clouds and frost sparkled in the sunlight. Everyone was bundled into big duffel coats, holding gloved hands, their noses pink.

I'd splurged on a cherry-red woollen dress and a faux-fur hat that made me look, in Mark's words, 'very Anna Karenina/ like a silver-haired bat.' My black leather knee-boots were keeping my feet toasty warm as the three of us walked down Park Street amidst the buzz of the shoppers.

James was wearing a thick grey topcoat over a russet cashmere jumper that made him look like he'd stepped out of an advert from the Ralph Lauren's men's catalogue. His mobile started to ring. His wide shoulders hunched as he spoke into the mobile and he curved his body away from us. I shivered and tucked my hands around me protectively.

'I'm going to have to throw it in the river so he can't work over lunch,' Caroline sighed, eyeing James' mobile.

Almost as if he had heard her, James hung up and ambled back to rejoin us. Our eyes met for a brief second and a hint of something in his expression made me look away quickly, eyes darting anywhere but his face. We walked along the quayside until we got to the restaurant, a converted canal boat moored next to a low stone bridge. Ducking inside, we were immediately greeted by a baby-faced waiter and shown to a small round table tucked in a corner, ivy strewn along wooden shelves behind us, candles flickering as we sat down. James pulled out my chair.

'That colour really suits you,' he said, indicating the dress.

I mumbled back at him, barely acknowledging the compliment, racing through possible replies. 'You too,' just sounded odd. 'Thank you,' dismissive. My mouth half-opened, and then my shoulders sank in relief when I was interrupted by the waiter. James immediately ordered a jug of mulled winter cider, which we drank while we chose what to eat. I scanned the lunchtime specials, freezing in panic when my foot brushed up against a leg. The table leg? Caroline's leg? James' leg? I sneaked a look at them both for a response. *Table leg,* I reassured myself. What had come over me? I fanned myself with the menu, impossibly hot in my woollen dress.

'I'm having the full roast dinner,' announced Caroline, smacking her lips already and tucking her napkin into her purple shirt, which made us both laugh.

'A good call,' James agreed. 'Nicola?'

'I'm...' I stopped fanning myself and scanned the menu

again. The words blurred into tiny black smudges. I couldn't think straight. I wasn't sure why I was so flustered. I quickly added, 'The same.'

The waiter bustled over and we ordered main courses and more cider, hands round our mugs blowing on the surface of the drink and feeling the alcohol warming us from the inside. I looked out of the window onto the river and smiled as a double kayak went by. An elderly couple appeared at the table next to us and James turned round, chatting amicably to them as they settled themselves. I grinned as the old lady roared with laughter at something James said, and realized I'd missed something Caroline was telling me.

'I didn't catch the last bit,' I apologized.

'I noticed,' she said, one eyebrow raised.

I felt a blush creep into my cheeks as James turned back to the table.

'Caroline, Nicola,' James inclined his head at us both and then raised his glass. 'For keeping my show on the road, I thank you!'

'Cheers.' We all clinked glasses.

Moments later, the waiter appeared with three plates, pushing cutlery out of the way to make room. Just as we were settled, forks poised, a mobile went off. James swallowed a hasty mouthful and fished in his coat pocket, pulling it out and silencing it with a tap.

'So, will you be going away for a Christmas break?' I asked him.

He shook his head, 'No, very much England-bound, relative-boun—'

He was cut off by his mobile again. 'Sorry,' he smiled, reaching to switch it off.

A text message beeped and he clicked on the phone and read it, before wordlessly shoving the phone back into his pocket.

'You?' he asked.

Another text message beep. He looked heavenwards, seeming to lose an internal battle with himself, and scooped the phone back out.

'I think this will keep going if I don't get it. I'll be back in a moment.' He scraped his chair back and ducked outside, stamping his feet to keep warm as he held the phone to his face.

Caroline frowned. 'That's odd,' she commented.

I chewed a forkful of beef and potato, barely tasting it as I saw James mouthing into the phone, rubbing a hand across his forehead. He looked like he'd aged twenty years in less than a minute. His forehead was pulled into a frown and his kind grey eyes had lost their usual sparkle. Whoever he was talking to, it was clearly not a pleasant conversation.

He hurried back inside and stood over our table. 'I'm sorry, ladies. This is terrible timing, but I'm afraid I have to be somewhere.' He picked up his scarf from the back of his chair and swept it quickly around his neck. 'Please order what you like, *do* get dessert,' he stressed, and tried to raise a smile. One side of his mouth lifted, but his eyes looked so horribly dead I panicked that something really terrible had happened.

'Is everything okay?' I asked, automatically standing up and reaching out to place a hand on his arm. He looked down at it and I snatched it back, feeling suddenly embarrassed.

'Yes, I'm being summoned.' He attempted a hollow laugh. 'Long story,' he said, not quite meeting my eye.

I nodded slowly, feeling something shift. Swallowing, I opened my mouth to say something, wanting to help. Caroline stood up too. 'Off you go then, get it sorted. We'll eat your lunch for you.'

There were false laughs all round and James left, answering his mobile again as he ducked out of the restaurant.

CHAPTER SIXTEEN

DAYS PASSED and the weather worsened so much that heading into work usually meant the death of at least one umbrella between us. On the first reasonably mild day in an age, I hit the shops in my lunchbreak. I had decided to make an effort to dress up for my next date. I felt glamorous and excited as I whisked round the stores trying on dresses in colours I didn't usually plump for. I settled on a green floral tea dress that was smart enough for the office but girly too (fine, this is exactly how the shop assistant described it, but I agreed). I'd bought a deep red lipstick to wear with it and some cute vintage T-Bar heels. Lewis had called me at home the night before and we'd agreed to meet for a drink in a bar in the centre of town the next evening.

I arrived promptly at the agreed time of 7.30 p.m. The bar had a Mexican theme; lots of garish yellows and bright reds clashed in dramatic fashion. On the walls, pictures of men looking swarthy, moustachioed and muscular hung alongside mini guitar ornaments. Low, squashy sofas lined the back of the room, all currently occupied, so I perched on a stool at a small round table by the window and sipped on a glass of wine.

Lewis was late, and after half an hour of waiting, I shuffled over to the bar to buy another white wine from a miserable-looking waiter in a sombrero. I tried to look anywhere but at his hat, which was tricky – it was so big that it cast a shadow down the entire length of the bar. The waiter grunted and handed me my change. I scuttled back to my stool, perched on high once more. I didn't really hold out huge hopes for this date, especially considering how late he was, but I felt a nice hint of intrigue about meeting someone completely new, about the possibilities of the evening. Until, of course, it occurred to me that Lewis might have stood me up.

I suddenly panicked. What if he had simply decided *not* to come? Was I about to spend my evening sitting in a Mexican bar, rain streaming down the windows outside, ploughing my way through a bottle of wine and a few tequilas, attempting to raise a smile from the grumpy waiter? What if Lewis had called Mark to cancel and Mark hadn't passed on the message? This wasn't impossible. Mark's mobile was about as old as Mark himself – a 'Pay-as-You-Go' with some kind of hologram sticker on the back.

How long should I wait? I'd already been here for over thirty minutes. Should I leave now? Should I pretend to answer my phone and have a fake conversation with a fake friend and then leave? That would perhaps be less sad. But what if the phone rang while I was having the fake conversation? That would be worse. I rolled my eyes. This was a nightmare. This was rubbish. This was... a man, coming into the bar and glancing in my direction. This was Lewis, thank God.

Lewis bounded over to the table, apologizing for his lateness. Then, exactly like an overkeen Labrador puppy, he took off his coat, shaking the rain from it, splashing our table, and me, with droplets. I was relieved that he hadn't stood me up, however, so I smiled indulgently at him, dabbing discreetly at the droplets. Things could only get better, I reasoned.

'Nicky.' He beamed, grabbing my hand and nearly knocking over my wine with the effort. *It's Nicola*, I thought. *Nic-o-la*. I was about to correct Lewis out loud, when he turned his back on me to yell at the miserable waiter. 'All right, mate!' The waiter seethed at him.

After slinging his wet coat over the back of a chair, Lewis proceeded to blow his nose with one of the paper napkins close to hand. Then, noticing I was already halfway through my wine, he went off to the bar and bought himself a drink, not bothering to ask me whether I might care for a top-up. He left the paper napkin screwed up on the surface of the table and I spent an uncomfortable couple of minutes trying to distract myself from thoughts of what lay inside its folds.

He finally joined me, downed most of his beer in one go and, leaning back in his chair, took a good long hard look at me, as if I were a horse at an auction. I took the opportunity to get a better look at him. He was tall, with dark brown hair. All of his features were in the right place (although his nose had been broken at some point), and he didn't appear to have a dire dress sense. I was marginally concerned that it wasn't just the rain that was making his hair glisten under the lights, but, relatively speaking, he was passable.

We swapped small talk about our lives, our houses, the city, our jobs. From what I could gather, Lewis worked in a call centre. Dressing up his title as 'Sales Executive' really didn't make it any more glamorous, but I didn't want to be snobby about it.

'So, what are your hobbies?' I asked, taking a quick sip of my drink and hoping to find something we might have in common. 'What do you like to do?'

'Oh, this and that, Nicky, this and that,' he replied helpfully.

My shoulders dropped.

'Among other things, I MC at gigs,' he continued.

'MC?' I queried, trying to work out the acronym in my head. Mexican Cookery? Model Cardigans? Make Cakes?

'*MC*. You know, DJ, MC, like rap.'

'Rap! What, you're a rapper?' I exclaimed, astonishment clearly apparent on my face.

'No, it's a bit different, Nicky. Rappers plan the words they're going to rap. I freestyle on the spot. I make it up *literally* ON THE SPOT,' he stressed.

'So, you don't learn it beforehand?' I asked, but only to piss him off as I'd already worked out that he made it up ON THE SPOT.

'The words just come straight out of my mouth when the DJ plays the music,' he pointed at his mouth as he said this, which made me like him less.

'What do you MC about?' I asked.

'Oh, everything. The world around me, Nicky.' He opened

his arms out wide to demonstrate the world around him.

'Like what? The room, where you are, or the world outside?' I asked.

'I can do it about anything.' He shrugged, trying to look modest, and failing.

'Cool.' I nodded. My shoulders slumped and, twiddling with my straw, I awkwardly looked around the room.

Then Lewis piped up. 'I'm just going to the bar to get a drink and then we'll have a think.' He stood up and clicked his fingers at me.

'Sorry, what?' I replied.

'Yeah, yeah, Nicky. I'm, like, going over there, but feel free to fix your hair, yeah.'

Oh my God. Was Lewis MCing for me?

'I'm MCing for you, Nicky, I'm not taking the mickey,' he said, sauntering to the bar, a renewed swagger in his gait.

I was left mouthing silent questions. Questions like: 'Oh my God, why are you doing that?' and 'What have I done to deserve this?'

I didn't have the guts to leave. I just sat there patting my hair at the back, nervously, and thinking of the *Doc Martin* repeat I could be watching right now. And I was not even an avid fan of *Doc Martin*. Frankly, an entire series of *Splash* seemed a more attractive prospect than this.

Lewis strutted back over and I spotted the triumphant look in his eye from twelve paces. 'Here you go, I've got a voucher so this one is free. Yeah, Nicky, that's right, that drink's on me. Word.'

My mouth fell open.

'Er, thanks. That's kind,' I said, pulling myself together just enough to take the drink from his hand. He had a voucher for this bar. And he was still rhyming. And we both had full drinks, so this wasn't ending any time soon. I felt an overwhelming urge to cry.

'Thanks,' I whispered again, huddled over the tall table.

He nodded. Was he disappointed? Should I have rhymed? Oh God, he was beginning to squirm in his chair. I took a breath and straightened up. 'Um, that's really kind. You've a nice, er, mind?' I finished uncertainly, feeling fucking stupid.

Lewis looked delightedly at me. I'd clearly given him the green light. 'So, like, I'm going to sit with you and chat and we'll get on like that.' He clicked his hand as he said 'that'.

'Good,' I said as enthusiastically as I could muster to a man who seemed to think we were in some kind of Eminem film.

'So, you got me here, to drink a beer, so let me ask you about your...' Then he stopped. His eyes widened and he panicked. Deer, fear, mere, peer, tier, queer, I could see him rushing frantically through the alphabet, knowing he had lost his rhythm. A vein throbbed in his neck. I suddenly felt a surge of sympathy for him.

'Career?' I offered.

'Yeah, career, yeah. No fear,' he rapped, the relief palpable as the tension eased from his neck.

'Um... well...' I muttered, desperate to not prompt any more. 'I, um, I work in town for an agency. We represent actors, models, promotional staff, that sort of thing,' I explained.

'Musicians?' Lewis queried, suddenly looking even keener.

'Er, no. No musicians,' I replied.

His shoulders sagged, but then he brought his hand to his face and started making a sort of 'Boom, boom, wicka, wicka' noise repeatedly. I looked around me. Other couples were engrossed in their own conversations; a hen party was concentrating on consuming as much tequila as was humanly possible in a few short minutes. No one appeared to notice as Lewis continued to 'Boom, boom, wicka, wicka', his hands moving at his lips as he started up once more. 'Because, Nicky, rapping is an art form, rapping is a skill. It's music to your ears, right, so call it what you will.' Then he finished with another 'Boom, boom, wicka, wicka'.

I couldn't pretend any more. I just looked at him aghast.

'I, I, um... I have to be somewhere,' I gabbled, downing my drink and looking around for my jacket.

'But, Nicky, we're just getting started. Don't leave, baby, you'll regret it if you...' Then his eyes widened once more. I couldn't bear it. I didn't even suggest 'departed'. I just looked at him, pity in my eyes. He was still struggling to finish the sentence, and then his head drooped forward and he reached for his coat.

'Let's call it a night,' I said gently. 'All right?'

He nodded once, eyes cast down.

We both left the bar and, without a backwards glance, I hailed a passing taxi.

'It was good to meet you, Lewis,' I said, as I clambered into the back of the cab. I didn't bother to make up another lie about where I had to be, why I had to leave so soon. He knew.

*

'Never again, Mark,' I said, the moment he answered his phone.

'But—' he began.

'No, no, no, no, no,' I chanted, refusing to be interrupted. 'No more setting me up. I'm doing this on my own, if I'm doing it at all. Frankly, after the disaster of a date I've just had, I am seriously questioning ever agreeing to meet anyone of the opposite sex ever again.'

'Nic, you're being a bit extreme,' Mark protested.

'Never,' I said indignantly, and then, suddenly, completely out of nowhere, I started laughing hysterically.

Mark was stuck in a baffled silence on the other end as I continued to laugh, then hiccough and then giggle again.

'Er, Nic,' he said, between hiccoughs, 'Nic, are you okay?'

I collapsed onto my sofa, gave one last little snort and then sighed. 'Actually, I think I am,' I said, dropping my head back onto the cushions. 'Just no more disastrous dates this week, please, brother dear.'

'Fine. I promise. By the way, when are you going home for Christmas?'

'Oh, lordy, is it that time of year again?' I said, stretching out my legs and wiggling my toes in front of me.

'Be nice, Nicola,' Mark warned.

'She provokes me,' I protested.

'I know, but you're younger and prettier, so it's your duty to be nice to her.'

'No, she's older and wiser,' I corrected him. 'And my *mother*.'

'I'll be there to get you through the dark times,' he said teasingly.

'I know you will. What do you want for Christmas?'

'Really?'

'Yes, really. Apparently it's traditional to exchange gifts at Christmas.'

'Well, now that you mention it, I have been thinking about getting a chinchilla or my own domestic fruit bat.'

I groaned at this announcement. 'Can't I just get you a book, or a DVD?'

'Fine, sis, fine.' He sounded disappointed and I felt guilty. Maybe I could stretch to a rodent for his home. I made a mental note to research this possibility. I could call Roger at the pet shop.

'So, I'll see you at home then,' I said, about to hang up.

'Can you come over tomorrow night?'

'Tomorrow?' I shrugged. 'I suppose I could after work.'

'Awesome. I have something to show you,' he said, excitement creeping into his voice.

'It's not another moped helmet, is it?'

'*Motorbike*. And no.'

'All right, I'll be there. Oh, and Mark,' I said. 'At Christmas – please don't bring any random friends home with you. I can assure you now that they are NOT my type.'

CHAPTER SEVENTEEN

'**D**ATING IS officially dreadful,' I announced as I arrived at work the next day. We were now into the last week before Christmas, but even that thought hadn't been able to cheer me.

'Oh dear, not another dud?' Caroline asked, bringing me a tea and perching on my desk with a look of concern. She held a chocolate Hobnob aloft, on the off-chance I was tempted to stray from the routine. Where was the harm? I ate the biscuit.

'Tight, tedious and into rapping,' I stated, rattling off the characteristics on each finger.

'Into napping?' she asked, brow wrinkling.

'Rapp— Oh never mind. It was dreadful,' I wailed.

'That bad?' She grabbed the full packet of Hobnobs (it was an emergency after all). I noticed Caroline staring at me as I scarfed down two in quick succession.

'*That* bad,' I confirmed, one hand over my mouth so as not to spray crumbs around. I swallowed. 'Honestly, never again. It was just awful,' I said, reaching for a third biscuit. 'Totally embarrassing.'

'Oh dear.'

'No more dates for me. No more, no more,' I repeated. 'I just can't face it.'

'But you must, Nic,' insisted Caroline. 'Look, this is a setback, but the right person *is* out there.' She said it with such confidence that even I believed her, for a split second.

Then I shook my head again. 'Nope. The dare is off. I can't do it. I don't want toooo.'

'You *can* do it,' Caroline urged. 'Maybe you've been trying too hard. Maybe that isn't the way forward. Maybe you need to relinquish control,' she mused thoughtfully. 'Let fate lead you to the right path.'

'Fate?' I repeated sceptically. 'What path might that be, Caroline? The path that leads to where the *decent* men hang out?'

'Exactly!' she said triumphantly.

I groaned, putting my head in my hands. 'No, I need to give up,' I said. 'It's horrible, humiliating and simply not getting me anywhere.'

'Rubbish,' Caroline grumped. 'We just need a new approach. Honestly, Nicola. I know you've had a couple of, er, less-than-wonderful dates...'

I scoffed at this massive understatement.

'... But you do need to keep going. You need to see what life has in store for you. And at least you're *living* life now, not hiding away in that cold flat of yours—'

'*Cold*?' I interrupted, looking up with a frown.

'Oh well, no, it's lovely, of course,' Caroline immediately gushed. 'All those fresh, clean lines and that, er, white decor.

All I meant was that it's quite sterile. Well, not *sterile* but...'

I broke into a smile and held up my hand. 'It's fine, Caroline, I'm not offended,' I promised.

She seemed visibly relieved. Before she could put her other foot in it, James appeared in the doorway, startling us both. 'Nicola, help,' he started, waving his right hand at me, while his left waved a bunch of papers.

I raised an eyebrow at Caroline and turned to James. 'Er, sure.'

He had already run back into his office. I got up to investigate the source of his dilemma.

I found him rummaging in the filing cabinet, a concerned look etched on his face, hair mussed up in crazed spikes.

'How can I help?' I asked in a gentle voice.

'Nicola, where do we keep the contracts that have expired?' he asked over his shoulder, still rifling through a drawer that I knew contained CVs and headshots only.

'Not there,' I stated firmly, joining him at the filing cabinet.

He stopped mid-rummage, blinking like a frightened rabbit in the headlights.

'What exactly do you want? I asked, trying to avoid noticing how close to me he was standing.

'A contract for that Channel 5 series Chris did,' he explained.

'Chris as in...' I asked, knowing the answer already.

'Chris Sheldon-Wade,' he confirmed.

'Right, that's fine.' I sank to my knees and opened up a drawer near James' feet.

'Apparently they're repeating it, and Chris wants to know if he's entitled to repeat fees,' James said from above my head.

'Ah, okay,' I replied, flicking quickly to the 'S' section.

'And I can't remember whether we wrote it into the contract. I mean, I'm sure we would have, wouldn't we? Otherwise it's just money we'll never see, but I just can't seem to remem—'

'Er, James.' I craned my neck up. 'Don't panic.' I gave him a calming smile and, getting up from my feet, felt heat flood my cheeks as I bumped into him slightly. 'Um... here you go,' I said, handing the contract over.

'Great.' He took it and quickly scanned its contents. His shoulders relaxed. 'He does, we do, thank God.' He looked at me with a relieved expression and leant against the cabinet. 'Thanks, Nicola. Right, I have to go out for the rest of the afternoon, around,' he checked his watch, 'ten minutes ago, actually.' He laughed nervously. 'So if Chris phones, give him my mobile number. No, actually, tell him I'll call him back. Actually, no, maybe just tell him—' He'd started to jabber again.

'Shall I deal with it?' I suggested quietly, holding out my hand for the contract.

'Brilliant, brilliant. Yes, do that. He likes you and we have to keep that man happy!' He slapped me on the back so that I lurched forward. 'Oh, sorry, er, right, must go.' Grabbing his jacket, he headed for the door. 'Bye, Nicola.'

I waved the contract at his back. 'See you tomorrow.'

'Bye, Caroline,' I heard him call from our office.

'Oh, don't forget lunch, James! You'll pass out!' she cried out, as he raced down the stairs and out onto the street.

I hurried to the window and watched him walk briskly down the road, one hand fiddling with the collar of his jacket, the other reaching for his mobile to make a call. He seemed so distracted lately, the bags under his eyes back with a vengeance. I hoped he was all right.

I didn't have to wait long to hear from Chris. The landline trilled and I answered the phone in James' office with my usual brisk: 'The Sullivan Agency, Nicola speaking.'

'Ah, I hoped it would be you, Nic-o-laaaaaaa,' sang a male baritone. I held the phone away from my ear as he finished the note.

'Chris,' I said, trying desperately to sound efficient and formal.

It seemed to work, as Chris stopped singing and replied, 'Nicola,' in a vaguely sensible voice. Progress.

'I assume you're calling back about the repeat fees for Channel 5,' I continued in the same uber-professional tone.

'Well, then you assume wrong,' he retorted.

'So why are you ringing?' I asked, beginning to worry that I *did* need James here after all.

'I'm ringing specifically to hear your dulcet tones, Nicola,' he smarmed.

I groaned inwardly, 'Right, Chris. Look, if by some chance you do also want to know about your repeat fees, I can confirm that you will be receiving them once the show has been aired. And if you don't, then of course let us know and we can chase them up for you with the company.'

'That is *super* kind of you, Nic-o-la.' He laughed.

I gave him a curt, 'Not at all,' in reply.

'So, Nic-o-la, I actually also need to send in my contract with the agency, as it's coming up for renewal.'

Yes, this was important, I thought, hand tightening on the receiver. Chris was one of our most successful, and therefore profitable, clients. We had to keep him on our books.

'But, you see, I don't feel like signing it unless you guys do something for me...'

'Chris, I'm sorry but you'll really need to talk to James, I mean Mr Sullivan, about that because I don't have the power to alter your contract with us, and any queries regarding percentages and—'

'Nicola, Nicola, Nicola,' he interrupted.

I stopped.

'You *can* help with this.'

'Honestly, Chris, this really isn't my area of experti—'

'Nicola,' he repeated lightly, 'I won't sign the contract at all if you continue to make excuses.'

I stopped talking instantly.

'Now,' he purred down the line. 'I will only sign the new contract if, and this is where you come in, you agree to come to dinner and then to my New Year's party as my,' he lingered over the last word, 'date.'

'What?' I exclaimed.

'You heard me. So will you, Ni-co-la?' he asked.

'No! That's, don't be silly. I can't, well, it's just tha—'

'Plans already?' he asked.

'Well, no, but...'

'It's settled then,' he said decisively. 'I'll sign the contracts, you'll come to my party,' he confirmed, as if it were all so simple.

'It's very kind of you to ask, but—'

'The theme is celebrities, so dress up glam, Nicola. Not that you'll need to try very hard,' he crooned. 'I'll call you about further details; I have your mobile number.' He laughed once more, a loud bark that reverberated down the line. 'It's a date, then.'

And with that, he hung up. I was left staring at the receiver, a fairly usual pose for the end of a phone conversation with Chris Sheldon-Wade. I replaced the handset, mind working overtime. How on earth could I keep him on side but *not* endure an entire evening as his date? My shoulders slumped as I realized that I didn't have much choice. I'd have to go. His business was far too important to the agency, and I could make this small sacrifice. I pictured James' wild hair, the new lines round his eyes, and found my resolve firming up. I was going to help him.

I left James' office and walked slowly back into the main office, shaking my head at the thought of Chris Sheldon-Wade.

Caroline gave me a sideways look. 'Are you going out for lunch, Nicola?' she asked.

'Yes, you know I am,' I said, perplexed by her question. Earlier that morning, I'd spent a good five minutes describing, in detail, the baguette I'd set my heart on (a few bits of bread weren't going to hurt me, I'd argued, and

Caroline had been quick to agree). A new deli round the corner sold the most mouth-watering sandwiches, and a melted goat's cheese Panini had been dancing through my mind all morning.

'Good. See you when you get back,' she said, nudging me out of my baguette-based daydream and getting up from her desk. Then, without warning, she threw my handbag at me and bustled me out of the office.

'Caroline, quit it! I'm going, I'm going! I just need my coat,' I protested.

Before I'd even finished this sentence, however, she had found said item and was holding it out for me to take.

'Bye then,' she breezed, and promptly closed the door on me.

I stood, bewildered, at the top of the stairs. What a day! I needed that baguette. I set off down the street with my eye on the goal. Melted cheese and peppers...

After gorging myself, I went to do a little shopping. A bit of retail therapy really helped lift my mood and wiped away the manic morning I'd had. I bought the usual Pledge, Vanish, a new carpet cleaner they'd been advertising on TV that week, dusters, a light yellow jumper, and presents for various family members. Christmas was coming around fast. I got back to the office with four bags in each hand, pushed open the door with my bottom and shuffled backwards into the room. Our usual strip lighting didn't seem to be on and the office was cast in an eerie orange glow, unusual for this time of day. I poked at the light switch on the wall with my nose, finally managing to turn it on by the fourth go. The room was flooded with light and, as I turned, I heard a tiny squeal, felt something rush past me, and then everything darkened again.

'What is going on?' I asked, completely disorientated. The blinds were down, and a scarf draped over the lamp in the corner gave the room a strange sepia effect. 'Caroline, what are you up to?'

In the half-light I could see Caroline standing in the centre of the room and a strange figure sitting at my desk. 'Caroline, what is going on?' I asked again.

'Shh, Nicola, come in, come in.' Caroline beckoned, taking my bags from me. 'This is Clara,' she said, gesturing towards my desk. Using the same slightly husky tone, she added, 'Clara, this is Nicola.'

'Nicola,' repeated the figure at my desk, bowing her head a little in my direction. My eyes began to adjust to the gloom and I could make out the figure in the shadows: a woman. She seemed to be wearing the most unusual clothes: a silvery triangle of shawl edged with sequins covered her shoulders and chest, a large piece of cloth acted as a bulky headband, and enormous jewelled earrings glinted at me in the semi-darkness. I assumed she was one of Caroline's more quirky friends, someone she'd met at a pottery class, perhaps – a hippie woman who listened to whale music, carved Aboriginal jewellery in the evenings and danced naked over fires on festival days. I'd met one such woman at one of Caroline's infamous guacamole and fajita parties. She'd spent the evening teaching me the words to a rare Buddhist chant and had shown me how to shape a napkin into the image of a rose.

Realizing Clara was waiting for my response, I whispered an, 'Er, hello,' and then decided to bow back at her.

What was going on?

'James is out all afternoon, so I invited Clara over to assist us,' said Caroline in a hushed voice. 'I wanted to get everything set up before you returned.'

'Er, assist us with what?' I whispered back at her.

'Our project,' she said, motioning for me to sit in the empty seat by Clara.

Something winked in the half-light.

'Is that a *crystal ball*?' I squeaked, completely abandoning my hushed tone.

'It is,' drawled Clara, giving me an enigmatic smile.

'What is "our project" exactly?' I asked, turning to Caroline.

'Er, you.' She gave me a none-too-gentle shove towards the ball and the woman in the shawl.

I sat down sharply in the seat and squinted at Clara.

'I just figured you haven't had the best luck so far,' explained Caroline, shrugging her shoulders. 'So I thought we should call on the cosmos for a little guidance.'

'The cosmos,' I muttered, unable to meet Clara's eye, which wouldn't have mattered as I realized her eyes were shut and she seemed focused on emitting a low humming noise, head tilted towards the ceiling, hands on the orb. I shot Caroline a look. But Caroline was now back at her desk mimicking the movements of Clara, her eyes shut, her hands resting on her desk.

'Nicola,' Clara said, suddenly reaching out her hand for mine.

I looked at it uncertainly.

She searched my face with her piercing blue eyes. I didn't want to hold this woman's hand. I was already jumpy. What if she put a spell on me? Her eyes wandered over my face. I tried to avert my gaze, lest she hexed me and I was sucked into her dark magic.

As if she could read my thoughts, she said, 'Calm, Nicola,' in a slow, controlled voice.

It frightened the crap out of me.

'You are searching for something,' she stated, continuing to stare at me with those startling blue eyes.

'Er...' My voice was a whisper. 'Yes,' I confirmed.

This wasn't an enormously impressive start. I assumed Caroline had given her some background. Still, those eyes...

'The journey will be hard,' she started, then stopped and took my hands, turning them over so the palms were facing up. 'You will be faced with choices, difficult choices. Some paths might be blocked and others beckoning to you.'

I nervously looked about me. She actually spoke like I'd imagined fortune-tellers to speak. All weird half sentences and obscure metaphors.

'You must learn how to recognize the path you should travel. But sometimes you can do this only by taking the road you should not.'

'Um, so what you're saying is, I should try to um...' I petered off. I was still going over 'the path I should travel, some I shouldn't' speech in my mind.

She went on. 'You must be wary of being blind to the right path,' she warned.

'Okay,' I said, but only to fill the gap.

'The new project is good, but you must ensure you do not deviate. It will be hard but you will learn things about yourself. By doing this, your goal will be realized and you will be fulfilled.'

'Well, that is good to hear.'

'Follow the path.'

'I will,' I said, confusion edging into my voice once more.

'Soon, you will meet someone who seems perfectly suited to what you are searching for,' Clara added.

Caroline looked over and gave me a thumbs up.

'That's good,' I acknowledged. It sounded promising. 'So, er, when will that be?' I asked, hoping she'd offer up a specific calendar date.

'Soon,' she repeated, obviously keeping her (metaphoric) cards close to her chest. 'Although sometimes we think we know what we want, and we do not,' she said cryptically.

Caroline's thumbs up wavered uncertainly and she returned to closing her eyes.

'I sense that recently times have been hard. We must always use our trials to make ourselves stronger,' she said: very Oprah.

'And round the corner there's trouble with your mother,' she warned.

'There's always trouble with my mother,' I sighed, beginning to think Clara might have lost her thread.

'You will be headed for one destination on the plane.'

I was getting lost again. A plane? An aeroplane? The astral plane? It was very hard to tell.

'Repeat after me,' she said and began to chant.

At this point, Caroline opened one of her eyes. My mouth was gaping.

After a couple of minutes of embarrassed attempts to copy her chanting, I gave up. 'I'm sorry, Clara, I'm not really a chanting sort of person,' I said apologetically.

'That is part of your problem,' she scolded (I think she was quite miffed, but I imagine Caroline was paying her, so she soldiered on).

'Can we go back to what you were saying earlier,' I suggested. 'The meeting someone thing you were talking about.'

'Yes, as I said, you will meet someone...'

'Right, um... What does he look like?'

'He will be what you're hoping for,' she said in her mysterious *I-own-sixteen-different-types-of-incense* voice.

This wasn't quite the detailed description I'd been hoping for. I'd been thinking more along the lines of brown hair, 6ft 2, will be wearing cream chinos and a blue jumper when you meet him.

'But you can't rely on someone else for your own contentment. You need to find peace within yourself,' Clara continued.

'Sorry, Clara,' I interrupted. 'So going back to, er, what he looks like again... It's just, how will I know exactly...?'

She gave a resigned sigh. 'He will be tall, well-built and he will...'

This was more like it.

'... have thick hair and excellent dress sen—'

Just at that moment there was a coughing sound from the doorway. I jumped up, swaying slightly as I realized James was standing in the doorway with a baffled expression on his face and a beautiful girl on his arm: Thalia, the fashion-designer girlfriend. I flung myself across the room and hit the light switch in the hope that this might help. It didn't. Our bizarre scene was now fully illuminated for James and his stunning girlfriend to see. They looked highly confused. Caroline blinked like a newborn animal emerging from its cave into the sunshine and Clara was, well, seated calmly at my desk looking like she'd been well aware we were to be interrupted. I suppose she'd known, what with being able to see into the future. I wondered if she could see how much trouble I was going to get into? Could she see what other jobs were available in the Clifton area?

'Ladies, what, um... what is going on?' James laughed a little nervously.

'James, I'll be in your office,' Thalia said, staring at us with narrowed eyes. She closed the door to James' office behind her. I looked up at James. He looked concerned, eyes wide, hand loosening his tie. I suppose he was right to be worried, we all had the air of 'Mad Extremist Cult' about us. It didn't help that Caroline had attempted to draw a complicated henna tattoo on the back of her hand in thick blue biro and Clara's outfit looked like Joseph and his Technicolor Dreamcoat had thrown up on her.

No one spoke. I couldn't think of any kind of reason as to why we'd all been sitting in the half-light, curtains closed, a strange woman with ball telling me I was about to meet a tall, dark stranger. Caroline, it seemed, had also lost the ability to speak, or indeed function at all, besides opening and closing her mouth like a goldfish. Clara stepped in.

'You have a very impressive quality,' she announced, moving towards James, one arm extended. 'You are a successful and determined man,' she added.

James' mouth turned up, his eyes creased. This was brilliant stuff. Clara's a frigging genius. Why hadn't I thought of that? It was just good old-fashioned sucking up.

'You also have terrible taste and are veering away from the course that is right for you.'

I cringed as James' face fell. *Back up, lady, back up, back up.*

'And someone with a name beginning with T spells T for trouble.' She looked like she was enjoying herself. Caroline gazed at her in unabashed awe.

Oh God. Thalia. I glanced at the door to his office. Clara, shhh. She wasn't finished though, oh no, she was clearly getting into the swing of things as she turned a shaky finger on James and said, 'And don't think you will be able to avoid a difficult situation by ignoring it.'

Oh God, it was getting worse. I looked frantically at Caroline for help, but Caroline was still staring at Clara with a look that bordered on the religious. Oh, who was I kidding? Bordering on? If Clara started recruiting disciples, Caroline would be the first to don a toga, learn a chant and follow her round with a candle.

Clara had apparently finished her brief synopsis of the various people and situations that were going to bring disaster raining down on my boss's head. There was a strange silence.

'Well!' I clapped my hands. 'Very authentic, particularly that improvisation at the end. Thank you for popping down to see us. We will let you know,' I said.

Caroline eyed me, brow furrowed, and then, catching on, started nodding her head in agreement. 'Oh, yes. Well thank you, Clara. You've been excellent and we'll let you know.' She geared up to bundle her out of the office.

James, shaking his head in disbelief, made to move towards his office. I ran over to open his door. He looked at me in a very peculiar way, before walking through.

Within minutes, Caroline and I had managed to hustle Clara, and her ball, back out into the street, and not a moment too soon as James' door burst open and Thalia stalked out, giving both Caroline and me a barely concealed sneer as she marched past our desks. As she descended the stairs I let out a breath and, putting my head in my hands, sank into my chair.

'Oh God,' I whimpered.

'I'll explain to James,' Caroline said, edging towards his office.

Somehow this just made me feel worse and I stopped her. 'No, no. I'll go, I'll think of something,' I said, smiling weakly at her.

'Are you sure? It *was* my idea...'

'It's fine. I'll explain it to him.'

Caroline smiled gratefully. 'Thanks, Nic.'

I got up from my chair. Right, okay, fine. James wouldn't

be that cross, would he? I mean, we were wasting valuable office time doing something that, to his eyes, might have resembled a seance, but I couldn't be fired over that. I mean, he might yell, but he'd been very pleased with my contract finding earlier. He was a nice man and a good boss. *Save it, Nicola*, I warned myself; don't waste the good compliments in your head. Right. Breathe out, good. I was ready.

'Okay, so it must have looked a little strange, that, er, episode,' I said, bursting into his office before I lost my nerve. 'But, you see, she was, she was...' James just stood there, face full of expectation. 'She was someone we were thinking about taking onto our books,' I finished triumphantly. 'Yes, yes, you see, we're trying to look for some middle-aged women for some um... jobs going on this ITV drama. And they are, um, they're seeking women of, um... Well, anyway, it doesn't matter. She was a little strange, wasn't she?' I rattled on before he could answer. 'So, basically, it's a No for the er... the ITV people. I mean, her range is quite limited. How many times are they going to need to cast a mystical middle-aged woman? We just don't get auditions like that, really. We need people who are more mainstream...' I trailed off as I realized James was looking at me sceptically.

'Hold on. That woman was an *actress*,' he said with a frown.

'Yes, yes. Just someone who sent in her CV to see if we are interested. Caroline invited her in for a meeting and, um... we went along with her for a bit and then, well, you showed up,' I explained.

Know when to stop, Nicola. Know when to stop.

'An actress,' he repeated, still sounding bemused.

'Yup, so we'll keep looking for that casting then,' I said in a very gung-ho voice.

'Why did Caroline pay her?' James asked.

'Hmm...' I mumbled. 'Oh that, Caroline is... Caroline is... Caroline is...'

I gave up.

James started laughing at me. Roaring, in fact.

'Honestly, Nicola. I thought I'd walked into a coven. Any moment I was expecting her to cast some spell on my goolies and disappear in a puff of green smoke. I assume you have your reasons for inviting in that er... guest and I wouldn't want to delve further into the deep, dark secrets of this office. It is very illuminating to know what goes on when I leave for one afternoon.'

'I'm so sorry. We really didn't...' I went to protest but James put his hand up to hush me and I fell silent.

'It cheered me up,' he said, then started chuckling again. 'Don't worry about it, Nicola. Honestly, it's fine. You should get out of here anyway, it's holiday season after all. No one should work this hard around Christmas.' He called through to the next office, 'You too, Caroline. I know you can hear me.'

'The cheek!' a voice said.

I skulked out, wondering how I was going to look James in the eye tomorrow. What MUST he have thought?

'Oh, Nicola,' he said innocently, making me turn round in the doorway. 'I trust that you got the answers you desired.' He said the last bit in a spooky voice while moving his hands up and down in a spell-casting kind of way.

I felt my whole face burning. 'Yes, thank you,' I squeaked and scuttled back to clear up my desk and go home.

CHAPTER EIGHTEEN

Single girl seeks man by
normal means. No love
potions, no spell casting,
no black cats or crystal
balls.

Contact: Box No. 06660

AFTER THE day I'd had, I just wanted to get home, stick the kettle on and start getting ready for Christmas. The last thing I wanted to do was find out what ridiculous surprise my brother wanted to show me. A new biking jacket? A DVD on the nocturnal habits of the Peruvian Short-Haired bat? Jumping in a cab, I reasoned that I could be there and back on my sofa within an hour.

'Why have you dragged me here, Mark, at the end of a long day? Some of us have real jobs in which we have to work and get tired. *And* I need to wrap presents.' I piled into his house and recoiled at the sight that greeted me.

Mark lived in a shared house just off Gloucester Road, on a street so cool the graffiti had been photographed for a council art project. The house itself had seen better days (last decorated circa 1970) and Mark's living room was a cross between David Attenborough's workspace and Hell. Photographs of exotic species of mammals lined the walls, a big poster of an enormous-eyed, winged creature stared back over his sofa, and the round table was littered with discarded beer cans and Opal Fruit wrappers (or 'breakfast' as Mark called it).

'And, by the by, do you know you are disgusting?' I said, still standing, due to a lack of clean sitting areas.

Mark flapped his hand and put down the black marker pen he was holding.

'I needed you here because I have a cunning and brilliant plan and wanted you to witness it,' he explained, marching over to a cupboard and pulling out a large flipchart from inside.

'What IS that?' I asked, curiosity piqued.

'This,' Mark huffed as he propped it up in the middle of the room, 'is "The Carol Plan".'

I groaned as he went on. 'Oh, Mark, no. Let her go,' I said.

'No, sis, impossible. You see, all your searching for love got me thinking. I *have* to have this girl.' He turned over the first sheet to reveal a blown-up photograph of Carol's face, surrounded by lots of drawn-on arrows pointing at her head. It looked like a serial killer's target. I sat down on the arm of his sofa.

'Er... Mark...'

'Shh, sis. Your search got me thinking. I don't want to continue to court these random people any more. I have always known who I should be with and I need to make this a reality. So, I have come up with this plan.' He turned the next sheet over to reveal two stick people standing next to each other lifting something between them.

'What are they doing?' I asked, squinting at the picture.

'Holding up a poster as they are hosting the planetarium's children's event in the New Year, of course.'

'Of course,' I nodded.

'That good-looking cad is me,' Mark pointed to one of the stick people, who had four strands of hair. 'And this gorgeous beast,' he paused to circle the other one, 'is Carol. Obviously.'

'*Obviously*.'

'So, we come together to host the planetarium's children's Christmas event and we spend time arranging the event, making plans, maybe even meet up in the evening to discuss things over a pint.'

He stressed the word *evening*, extending the 'eve' into a long noise so it sounded super sinister. 'And we gradually become closer.' He turned the next sheet to reveal two stick people embracing each other.

'Riiighhhhhttt.'

'Then, after hosting the planetarium's children's event over the Christmas holidays we are closer than ever.'

He flipped over the last sheet to reveal two stickmen lying on the floor together, one on top of the other and one...

I moved closer to the picture, eyes narrowed.

'Mark, what is that...? Eugh, Mark!' I backed away.

'That is my penis,' Mark confirmed.

'I need to get back to my flat,' I said.

'But, sis, what do you think of the plan?'

'Very thorough.'

He seemed pleased.

'I did think of everything,' he nodded.

'Quite.'

Before I left, he turned over to the very last sheet and there were two stick people surrounded by loads and loads of little stick people. And some birds in the sky that were obviously...

'Ah, bats,' I said, gathering my stuff to leave. 'You're nuts, brother dear.' I shook my head.

'You just wait, Nicola Brown. Just watch and learn...'

So Mark had his plan, and I needed to get back on track with mine. As I meandered slowly through town, watching people spilling out of the theatre, chatting outside the pubs, I smiled to myself. I couldn't believe my disastrous search had motivated him. He was about to launch himself into his own project because of my attempts to get a love life. Music pumped out of a nearby bar and I watched as a young couple greeted each other outside with a kiss. The guy threw an arm round the girl's shoulder and showed her in. As I watched, I realized that apart from Chris, who didn't count as it was for work, I had no further dates planned. The thought made my stomach sink slightly and I realized I didn't really want to abandon the dare. This notion caught me off-guard and I came to a halt in the street, forcing an old man behind me to swear under his breath.

'I'm sorry,' I murmured, moving on again.

What had I gained? I thought back over the last few weeks. They'd been fun, they'd been busy, they'd had a... *purpose*. Maybe I didn't need to arrange blind dates to keep the dare going. There were plenty of other ways, easier ways, surely, to meet men. The safest place, it seemed, was the internet. At least I could screen the people who lurked there. I couldn't let the dare take on its own life and drag me on any more useless nights out with people I had nothing in common with. Maybe if I could communicate with my potential date in some capacity *before* being thrust together, it would work better when we eventually met face-to-face.

I'd been dipping in and out of the dating website Caroline had set me up on and I'd been winked and nudged and generally prodded by a host of strangers. None of them appealed. They were just that: strangers. I'd received emails from old friends, had been sent photos from my school days and it had felt good to hear from people I'd assumed had forgotten me long ago. As for the men I had heard from, Jon-who-had-sent-me-a-Christmas-card-Allen, was now known as Married-Jon-who-had-sent-me-a-Christmas-card-Allen, while Alan-who-had-asked-me-to-join-him-for-coffee-once-Pope, was now Gay-Alan-who-had-asked-me-to-join-him-for-coffee-once-Pope. I hadn't heard from Him, Man-Who-Broke-My-Heart-Seven-Years-Ago, but recently, to my surprise, my pulse hadn't quickened when I logged on. I didn't feel the same curiosity about what he was up to and who his friends were – not even the girl with the impossibly shiny hair. All the hurt I'd been carrying around for so many years was becoming blurrier around the edges, as new, happier thoughts jostled to be heard, and memories of the old, fun me began to nudge me into action. It was time to get the old Nicola back. It was time to get a life.

One person to emerge from my new cyber world was a guy I'd known at university, Dan Mitchell. He'd written 'Hey' on my wall and following that we'd swapped a few private messages, mostly inane sort of comments similar to the type you'd make at a drinks party. After seven of these messages, he had suggested we meet casually at the cinema to see a film together and I'd agreed. We'd then swapped another three messages in order to handle such complicated questions as *what film?* and *which cinema?* before it had been settled.

My university memories of him were sparse but not all unpromising: he'd been on the tennis team, had a large head of blonde hair, was good-looking in a clean-cut way (Ralph Lauren jumpers knotted over the shoulders, boating shoes when not on a boat, etc.), he'd snogged my friend Teresa in a Tesco Express petrol station, and had been on my English course. Also, once a group of us had gone to Weston-super-Mare pier on a day trip and Dan and I had managed to win big on the 10p machines and shared a bag of sugared doughnuts together, so, as I mentioned, not all unpromising. By the time I had reached the door to my flat I felt fired up once more. Perhaps my cinema trip with Dan qualified as a real date? It would surely be more of a success than meeting a stranger. After all, we'd sat in the same lecture theatre for three years together, he had attended my 'American poetry: from Bates to Whitman' seminars. That was a fairly firm grounding, and at least we could fall back on university-related conversation. What did you do with your degree? Do you still enjoy American poetry? Do you see anyone else from the course? Do you... Okay, so three questions is more than adequate. LOTS in common.

CHAPTER NINETEEN

I WAS RUNNING, fine, tottering, to make the fair on time. The Annual Bristol Christmas Fayre, held in The Mansion House in Clifton in aid of whichever charity my mother and her friends had decided upon this year, appeared on my calendar every twelve months and was an absolute three-line whip. There was one time, in 2009, when I'd been ill with suspected appendicitis, that my brother had actually appeared at my flat, an apologetic look on his face and an ominous warning that he was to 'fireman's lift me out of there' if I refused to go.

Today, I'd abandoned my Christmas present-wrapping halfway through and hotfooted it out of the flat, making the brisk walk through Clifton. Sweeping across the gravel path, staring up at the mullioned windows and deep red bricks of the elegant Victorian house, I checked my watch. I pushed open the door and, following signs to the Drawing Room, appeared in the doorway only two feet from where my mother was standing, hair set in a sweeping chignon, large jewels flashing on her ears.

'Darling, good, I thought you'd forgotten.'

My mother looked at her watch and raised one perfectly drawn-on eyebrow. I glanced at the clock on the opposite wall. I wasn't great with Roman numerals but even I could quickly deduce I was only one minute late. She cut me off before I could protest.

'You're here *now* and that's the important thing.' She turned and waved to a woman wearing a terrifyingly large, lilac hat. 'Penelope, I've found her, thank God, we haven't been let down.'

'Mum,' I hissed.

'Right, darling. We've got you an outfit this year. We all thought the event could do with "jazzing up" a little.'

'Hmm...' I said, my heart sinking.

She thrust a carrier bag at me and shooed me to the corner of the room, where a heavy oak door announced in faded gold scroll that 'Madames' could enter.

'What do you mean, outfit?' I spluttered, peering into the top of the bag and making out some green cloth. 'I thought I was selling cakes!'

'Penelope's daughter, *who arrived early*, is already on the cake table and doing a fine job. Anyway, I said you'd be delighted. Do be quick, it's for the children, darling, don't forget.'

'Mum, we're raising money for Kidson Keyboards not the starving of Africa,' I stated.

She checked her hand. 'Oh damn, I think I've chipped a nail.'

Ten minutes later I was standing in the cubicle, absolutely refusing to emerge.

My mother's voice swept over me. 'Nicola, we're all waiting. The children want to see you.'

'Oh God,' I muttered, looking down at myself in hopeless resignation.

I sighed, rearranged the green felt hat and stepped out of the cubicle. Staring into the gilt mirror opposite, I didn't recognize myself. My bobbed hair was all but hidden under the hat that was slightly too large, my entire body was encased in the colour of freshly mown grass, and over my shoes I wore large pointed elf feet that curled up at the ends. Thrusting the rest of my clothes in my bag, I reminded myself that we were raising money for charity and I had made my mother a promise. I gave myself a crooked smile, splashed my cheeks with water, wiped under my eyes and headed reluctantly out into the fray.

After doling out sweets and posing for photos, I was now being forced over to the corner of the room to talk to three children swinging their legs as they sat on ornate padded chairs. As I walked towards them, pulling up my elf belt as I went, I felt a flash go off on my right. I turned to see Caroline standing there grinning at me, her two children in tow.

'Don't you look a treat,' she laughed, clutching her stomach in mirth. 'I wouldn't have recognized you.' She leaned down to her offspring. 'Ben, Alice, do you remember Nicola from the office? In her spare time, my loves, she is one of Santa's helpers.'

Ben's eyes grew so wide I could make out all the whites around his irises. 'You help Santa?' he whispered, awe written all over his cherubic face.

I knelt down to his level. 'I do,' I said solemnly. 'And he has a message for you.'

Ben looked up at his mum and grinned. 'Whoa.'

I leant forward. 'It's a secret message, though, so I have to whisper it. Is that okay?'

Ben nodded twice, brushing his fringe out of his eyes. Caroline smiled, giving me a thumbs up. I cupped a hand around my mouth and bent to whisper in Ben's ear. He stepped back a moment later and nodded solemnly at me.

'No one,' I said again.

'I promise,' he whispered.

I stood up, feeling a warm glow as Ben hopped from foot to foot in excitement. Giggling, I turned to Caroline. 'One very good boy guaranteed till Christmas.' I laughed.

'I'll hold you to that.'

'Right, I think I've done my bit for the kids,' I said, going to take off my hat.

'Nic, you've been here all of ten minutes! You look cute!'

'Cute? There are other words I could use,' I said, catching sight of my feet.

'Oh, by the way, you did get that contract in the post for Chris yesterday, didn't you?' she asked.

I looked at her blankly. Oh no. I put a hand to my mouth. 'Er...'

'I put it on your desk for a signature?' she prompted.

'I got it, I just, Oh God, Caroline. I never... I forgot...'

Moving quickly to scoop up my bag, I looked at the clock. I had twenty-five minutes until the Post Office closed and the last post would be sent off. If I hurried, I could just about make it.

'Oh God, Nic, you don't need to do it now! I shouldn't have said anything.'

'No, I should I have done it. I have no idea how I forgot. He'll need it. The job starts this Wednesday.'

'Well I can pop back and—'

'Mum,' I called, to where she was chatting to Penelope by a tombola stand. 'Emergency,' I mimed, not giving her enough time to manoeuvre herself round from behind Penelope's hat as I raced to the door.

I wished I hadn't forgotten my coat that morning as I scampered up Park Street, a streak of green felt, earning myself plenty of looks from passers-by and a jeer from a small circle of men clutching pints in a fenced-off area outside the pub. The jingling from the bell in the hat reminded me of my horror but I was too cold to remove it. Anyway, I was nearly at the office. I could change there.

Taking the stairs two at a time, I pictured the contract where I had left it on my desk. It should take me all of ten seconds to find it and send it out. I took out my key and as I put it in, realized the door was already unlocked. I heard voices coming from inside. Opening the door, I stumbled in to see two figures standing in the middle of the room, metres apart, raising their voices at each other.

They turned towards the noise and I realized it was James and Thalia. She was panting slightly, her cheeks two pink spots. He looked grey, two-day-old stubble on his jaw, bloodshot eyes. His mouth was frozen in an 'O' as I stepped inside the room, remembering far too late that I was dressed in top-to-toe green felt and I jingled when I walked.

'I'm sorry,' I mumbled, feeling the heat in my face. 'I didn't think anyone would... I'll just be two... I just came to get...'

'Oh no, please.' Thalia put up a manicured hand, stopping me straight in my tracks. 'We're finished,' she said, staring across at James and then sweeping up her handbag from the floor. 'James,' she said in a low voice.

'Thalia,' he sighed heavily.

'Shall we go home?' She lingered over the word 'home'.

I rushed across to my desk and tugged at the piece of paper I needed and shoved it into my bag. I threw James an apologetic glance. 'I just knew you needed it sent out now,' I babbled. 'Please don't mind me.' I backed away towards the door, stumbling over my pointy feet.

'Well, aren't you just the most wonderfully helpful elf,' Thalia said, hands on hips.

'Nic...' came James' voice.

I didn't get a chance to hear what he said as I spun round and slammed the door, pausing only briefly to close my eyes and run through the entire scene in my humiliated head. Beautiful, sleek Thalia and her designer handbag, me dressed in a violent shade of green looking like the Christmas hobbit. I breathed out, hearing her voice start up again from the other side of the door, and made it towards the stairs and home, blessed home. But first a rather long walk and a wait in the Post Office. I pushed back onto the high street and waited for more catcalls and choruses of 'Jingle Bells'.

CHAPTER TWENTY

Single girl seeks man
quite quickly as she has
a deadline to meet and no
one does anything over
Christmas.

Contact: Box No. 2500

I WAS IN my bedroom at the family home in Gloucestershire, perched on the edge of an open sunbed. Across the room, past the dressing table on which was balanced the entire Clinique collection, underneath the pink dumb-bells, massive inflatable ball and strange wire contraption that promised 'Fab Abs', was my sad single bed, complete with sad stuffed teddy bear that peered at me accusingly out of its sad solitary eye. I sighed and lay down on the sunbed. I didn't close the top but rested my head back onto the little leather cushion and allowed myself to drift away in the peace and quiet.

I'd been home for all of three hours and my mother had already made me want to take the teaspoon I'd been using to stir my tea and use it to scoop out my own eye.

'Nicola, that top, it's very ageing,' she had announced on opening the door to me, airily giving me a double kiss on the cheeks in an effort to sweeten her harsh words.

'Thanks, Mother,' I replied, knowing she loathed anyone reminding her she was the mother of two children. Especially two *adult* children.

She looked suitably put out as I manoeuvred myself out of her clutches.

Her latest husband, Guy, had been outside on the patio, barking down a sleek and sophisticated-looking mobile phone and had managed to raise a hand in greeting. I had raised one back and suspected that might constitute the extent of our seasonal bonding session.

'Nicola, must you really keep wearing your hair in such a severe style?' Mum had asked, sighing as she looked me up and down. 'Penelope was saying to me, seconds before you abandoned us the other day, that she thought you'd suit a longer style...'

Fortunately, she had then realized her Hatha yoga session was starting any moment and had rushed out to do the 'Reverse Warrior' pose with a bunch of manicured local ladies for the next hour.

I took my suitcase upstairs and arranged my belongings in an orderly fashion. Placing a hand on the banister, I turned to look at my reflection in the hall mirror. I dropped the suitcase and walked forward, smoothed my hair down and ran the ends through my fingers. Maybe I would let it grow a little longer. This bobbed haircut showed off my long neck and large grey eyes but, perhaps, it could be a little softer. Maybe I could even pop some highlights in it. I blinked and looked away, feeling silly at my sudden intense scrutiny.

Padding through the upstairs hallway, I stopped next to a pile of boxes ominously labelled 'Nicola'. A flash of silver caught my eye and I moved across to a box in the corner, under a large canvas of my mother and Guy kissing by a turquoise sea, to see a photo in a frame lying on the top of a pile of dog-eared books, pens and other paraphernalia. I had the brief feeling of being at the top of a roller coaster about to plummet down as I bent, now in automatic, to retrieve the picture. I hadn't seen this photo in years. It used to stand tall on my bedside table. I'd often gaze at it before reaching to turn off the bedside lamp. I picked it up and felt the hurt wash through me. Seeing us together, so confident, happy, made my heart lurch. It wasn't like seeing him on Facebook, disconnected from me in his new, separate life. This was a stark reminder of how we used to be. How I used to be. I felt the old pain resurface.

He had one arm on my hip, I had one arm round his waist, a hand in his back pocket. I was looking up at him, grinning at something he had said. He was wearing the blue jumper I'd given him for his birthday, my body pressed up against the soft wool. I was wearing my favourite short cream dress, vintage lace around the neck, capped sleeves, brown knee-high boots that he'd loved so I'd worn them long after the scuffs and scrapes should have consigned them to a bin. We'd been at a friend's party. It had been two weeks before the day it had all ended. I'd thought we'd spend the rest of our lives together. I'd really thought I had landed on my feet, used to smugly cock my head to one side as friends told me their tales of terrible dates, overbearing men, selfish boyfriends. I'd feel relief that I had found the one good man. The exception to all the disasters I listened to. I placed the picture back on the pile face down so that he was no longer smiling at me from seven years ago, my happiness, my world, in his hands.

My eyes had been closed for what felt like all of two minutes, when I heard the sound of Mark's moped turning into the driveway outside. It was faint because I'd had to close the top of the sunbed to block out the sound of Guy screaming at someone called Marie about some stocks she should have sold at least an hour ago. Mark would be quick to help Mum relax and distract us all with some story from work, some documentary idea, or some grizzly animal DVD. I opened the sunbed and waited to hear his familiar resigned sigh as he took in the latest carpet colour (currently a tasteful stone-grey wool) my mother had had fitted. I got up to greet him at the front door. I heard giggling, followed by girlish squealing. Frowning, I went to investigate. As I peered over the landing banister, I watched in amazement as Mark tumbled through the front door with an attractive woman in his wake. I was yet more amazed to hear him call her 'Carol'. I instantly liked her when I heard her insisting, 'Mark, it's a MOPED.'

I started down the stairs with a smile on my face.

That night we were herded into Guy's Land Rover, which looked so clean I was convinced he'd hired it for the occasion, and taken to a Christmas drinks party in an enormous house just outside the village where my mum lived. Amazingly, Mark had shaved and was wearing a new dark blue suit and tie. His arm was draped proudly round Carol, whose green-silk wrap dress contrasted with her red hair perfectly. I felt a bit drab in my steel-grey pencil dress. My mum had been quick to agree.

The drive was lined with lanterns hanging from the trees and the honey-coloured manor house was bathed in a beautiful golden glow from the fairy lights hung along every available surface. The hostess greeted us in a waft of lavender and Je Reviens. Her husband, a foot shorter and a few inches wider, rushed forward to bury his head in my mother's breasts, which seemed to be sparkling with a powdery sheen. As he emerged, I stifled a laugh at the fine layer of glitter now covering the tip of his nose. Guy, oblivious to the greeting, having been on his mobile since slamming the door of his Land Rover, shook the host's hand vigorously, an automatic smile clamped on his face, his eyes already roving to the scene beyond. Duly introduced, we trailed into the large hallway where, beneath a huge Christmas tree decorated in silver and red that still managed to fill the room with the smell of pine needles and Christmas, waitresses greeted us with overloaded trays of canapés and champagne. Other guests clustered in small groups around the room, sipping from crystal flutes, and surreptitiously eyed up each other's outfits. Lofty ancestors peered down from the enormous oil paintings that lined the walls and I tried not to feel intimidated as we chatted and drank.

Carol and I found ourselves parked beneath a portrait of a heroic-looking soldier with a stump for a leg.

'Oh dear,' Carol commented, pointing at the missing appendage.

'Oh dear indeed.'

'Let's hope we don't get absolutely legless tonight,' she went on, nudging me conspiratorially.

'That is dreadful,' I choked, a little bit of champagne dribbling down my chin. 'The poor man.'

Carol looked suitably chastised.

'It can't have been an easy life,' I continued. 'He was probably hoping to have a good knees-up on his return.'

Carol snorted. 'He might not have been able to foot the bill,' she chuckled.

'I take it you are both busy cackling over some poor unfortunate,' Mark said, appearing at our sides and giving me a friendly squeeze of the waist. 'Hey, Nic, have you seen who's here,' he said, jerking his head towards a huge bunch of flowers that were sadly not quite enormous enough to block out the person he'd indicated.

'Oh God,' I muttered. 'Kill me now.'

'But it's Stannnnley.' Mark laughed, turning to Carol to fill her in on the details. 'Total, massive, stonking crush on Nic here ever since she sat on him at some dinner do... long story, she'll protest...'

I was mouthing angrily.

'Mother thinks he's completely divine,' Mark continued, refusing to be interrupted. 'Because he's utterly filthy rich.' He turned to me. 'Nicola, you must go and say hellooooo, you must, you just must, dahling,' he pleaded in a frighteningly accurate impression of our mother.

'Shut it, Mark,' I said, alarmed that Stanley would sense all the attention and turn round.

'He doesn't look dreadful,' Carol commented, sizing him up.

'Hmm...' I muttered, taking a peek at Stanley who, even in a dinner jacket, still managed to look ridiculous. His hair was matted and worn in a straggly ponytail, fastened with a crushed velvet bow for the occasion. His suit seemed two sizes too big because he was a man who had been waiting most of his adult life to 'grow into things'. His thin face was covered in tufts of unshaven beard that he thought made him look sexy and relaxed but really made most people want to take a blade to his face. It wasn't so much his physical appearance that had really turned me off Stanley, however. It had been his high-pitched voice and his snobbish, uppity manner.

When we'd first been introduced, he'd said to me: 'Your mother tells me you are a PA, how lovely, I've always rally, rally wanted one of them myself.' It wasn't absolutely clear what Stanley's occupation was, but, from what I'd gathered, it seemed Stanley spent much of his time on his parents' estate, making sure the 'damn gardener' was doing the right things, whilst he played his mother at backgammon. He was a real mummy's boy through and through, still living at home in his early thirties. In fact, I noted with an audible groan, Mummy was here tonight. Red in the face and bursting out of a hot-pink taffeta dress that would make it possible to balance a collection of canapés on her ample bosom, she was squawking at someone standing to the right of Stanley; something about the polo season and that 'gorgeous gel Zara'. As she swung round to introduce some frightened-looking blonde to her son, she almost smacked him in the face with her breasts. I hurriedly looked away before it was too late.

Mark noticed the movement. 'Aaahhh, see, Carol, she's smitten. She has the look of love in her eye, check it out. She is practically drooling over him.'

'I am not!'

'She is not!' Carol and I chorused.

'Hey, Nic. Maybe Stanley could be part of your new project,' Mark suggested, popping a prawn vol-au-vent into his smug mouth.

'I warn you, Mark, this sausage comes on a skewer and I will use it on you,' I said, waving it threateningly at him.

'Ouch, Nic. Come on, he's perfect, and you need a new participant in *The Project*,' he insisted, miming a quotation mark with his one available hand.

'Shh, Mark, stop it,' I giggled. 'And anyway it is not a project.' I paused. 'It's a hopelessly futile attempt to get a love life.'

Carol stared at us both. 'What are you two blathering about?' she asked, stealing the last of the canapés from Mark's hand.

'Oh dear, please don't judge me too harshly,' I said, as Mark launched into a long tale that charted all the various humiliations of the last month of my life. Carol fortunately laughed at the appropriate moments, gasped at the appropriate moments, and slapped Mark at the appropriate moments ('Sea kayaking, in November... how could he?').

'Sounds interesting,' she commented when Mark had finished. 'You know, I've actually got a cousin who—'

'Stop right there,' I said, holding up my hand to her. 'No more setting me up. Truly,' I insisted as they opened their mouths to argue. 'I'm going about things in a new and different way.'

'Like what?'

'The minute details of my cunning plan are yet to fully materialize...'

'Huh?'

'She means she hasn't thought of them yet,' translated Carol.

'Thank you, Carol.' I nodded at her. 'But rest assured, I am going to come up with something. It just won't involve any more blind dates with total strangers.'

'But I...'

'But we...'

'I have to pee,' I declared loudly, and then I turned round slap bang into Stanley. 'Oh, I...'

'Doesn't one always have to at the most inopportune moments?' he leered and I raced away.

'Where are the blinking, blinding toilets?' I muttered five minutes later, still searching the long, dimly lit corridors for a lavatory. My feet ached in my new heels as I tottered past paintings of serene rural scenes; cottages, mills, farmers in big hats doing things in the fields, which I assumed to be hoeing or raking or some such. I heard the burble of voices getting further away as I continued, past sculptures and large suits of armour glinting dangerously in the shadows, before entering a wing of the house I was sure I'd already ventured down. Rounding another bend, I pushed open a heavy oak door. The room was lit by the rosy glow of candlelight, and a fire roared beneath an ornate mantelpiece, over which hung a large gilt-framed mirror. The room was too big to be a toilet, and the rows of bookshelves climbing to the ceiling seemed quite over the top for some light bathroom reading; I must have stumbled across the library. I turned to retreat, but a voice called out from the depths of the room.

'Come in, dear,' it said.

Hoping the voice was not a figment of my imagination or the Ghost of Christmas Past, I followed the sound to a vast leather armchair placed next to the fire. As my eyes adjusted to the dim lighting, I made out the slight figure of an elderly woman.

'I'm so sorry, I've got the wrong room,' I said quickly.

'Not at all, come in, sit down,' she said, indicating another armchair placed opposite her.

The fire crackled, sprigs of holly hung from the mantelpiece, Christmas cards stood to attention, and the whole scene seemed enormously comforting.

'Wine?' she offered, producing a glass from a tray beside her.

'That would be lovely,' I said, going over and taking the glass. 'Thank you.'

I sat down. 'I'm Nicola, by the way,' I said, pointing slightly unnecessarily to my chest, as if she wouldn't be aware who I meant.

'Esther,' she said, sipping at her wine.

She must have been at least eighty, I guessed. She leaned forward, pouring the wine with two hands to steady the bottle. Dressed in a simple navy dress with a neat string of pearls round her neck, she looked elegant and well at home in this enormous house. Her hair was short and showed off little pearl-drop earrings which sparkled when she moved. Her eyes glinted in the firelight as she spoke.

'So, why have you squirrelled yourself away here then?'

'I'm looking for the loo is my excuse.' I blushed. 'You?'

'Oh, just a bit of quiet. My ex-husband is out there. Both of them in fact.' She cackled.

'I see.'

'Yes, one's brought his new wife to show off. She looks like the Christmas turkey, trussed up in layers of what looks to me to be turquoise tin foil.'

I wrinkled my nose at the thought.

'Never did marry well,' she said, swilling the wine round in the glass.

'Why?' I found myself blurting out.

She didn't look annoyed; her brow wrinkled as she sat and thought for a while.

'Nothing in common,' she concluded, sipping again at her wine.

'Like?' I ventured.

'Like fine wine.' She cackled again, pouring another glass. 'And music, and dancing, and a sense of humour and books. They didn't read a book between them,' she went on. 'Just sport – fishing, shooting and bloody horses. I can't stand bloody horses, or rather bloody polo. If I had to watch another polo chukka, I'd end it all right out there in the hall.'

'Wow, you *really* don't like polo,' I commented.

'How about you, Nicola, are you married?'

'No.'

'Courting?'

I laughed. 'Not courting, not seeing anyone in fact, I am...' I paused.

'Shopping around?'

'Exactly.' We both laughed.

'Well, you keep shopping, Nicola. You need to find someone you can share your life with, someone you have something in common with... although a handsome face always helps... and good legs. They're vital.'

'Absolutely. Thank you for the wine.' I lurched over and gave her a hug. Then straightened up, feeling embarrassed. 'Sorry,' I laughed.

She just smiled. 'You're a gem,' she said simply.

'Thank you.'

'Nicola,' she called as I reached the door.

'Yes,' I said, turning, anticipating a wise word, a piece of advice or some thought-provoking proverb.

'The loo's on the left, dear.'

Tottering out of the loos and realizing I might have had one mulled wine too many, I couldn't avoid the looming figure of Stanley, who was standing next to an alarming sculpture of a naked man with long, flowing hair, one arm pointing towards the sky, the other resting on his hip as if frozen in a dance move from *Saturday Night Fever*. This thought made me giggle. Stanley lit up and walked purposefully over to me so that I was pinned back against the wall.

'You're looking rally, rally, lovely this evening,' he said, smoothing his ponytail down with a hand and licking his bottom lip.

'Thank you,' I squeaked, a hand flying self-consciously to my chest.

He leaned closer. 'Just been having a rather enlightening tête-à-tête with Mark,' he said.

'Have you?' I said, playing dumb.

Note to self: kill Mark.

'And I'm planning to act on it,' he said in a whisper.

'Gosh, really, well, that's nice. Oh, look! They've hung tinsel from the beams, how gorgeous.'

'Nic,' came a shout. Carol waved at me from the end of the carpeted corridor. I exhaled loudly.

'Coming.' I waved back, scooting under Stanley's arm before he could stop me. 'Lovely to see you, Stanley,' I threw over my shoulder. 'Happy Christmas.'

Carol linked arms with me as I appeared.

'Bloody Mark,' I said in a low, dangerous voice.

*

Many mulled wines later, we piled back into the Land Rover, Guy talking into the hands-free as he drove us home. Mother sat silently next to him, her right eye wandering as it always did after too many glasses of wine. I told Carol and Mark about meeting Esther on my trip to the loo.

'Esther isch right. Isch about interests. We *have* to have the shared intereschts.'

Carol turned to Mark with a hiccup. 'What are you intereschrested in?'

Marks eyes were crossed. 'You 'n bats.'

'Yesch, but you're a bit weird.'

'Yeah, but we did schpend a lot of time in the same places when we met.'

'Yesch, but you just followed me to them, which is called stalking, so waschn't a coincidence.'

'Thish is true,' Mark said. 'But *sometimes* we met by accident in the same place because we do have similar intereschts.'

'True,' Carol said, leaning across to peck him on the nose. She turned to me. 'Men juscht love cars, tools and football so you should do something with that.'

'Amazshing idea. I will,' I announced, lurching forward as Guy parked the Land Rover in the driveway.

We tumbled out and crunched up the gravel path to the house, laughing stupidly as Mum missed the keyhole three times.

Sniffing about us behaving childishly, she seemed surprised when I gave her a warm hug. 'Night, Ma,' I said, pecking her on the cheek.

'Goodnight,' she said back, one hand on the banister.

Guy didn't look up from his BlackBerry as he called a 'Goodnight' from the staircase.

I joined Carol and Mark in the kitchen.

'Let'sch get on the internet and sign you up for stuff, Nic,' Carol said, clapping her hands.

'Good thinking!'

We pulled up short, seeing a pan half full of mulled wine on the oven.

'Another glass to *mull* over the situation?' Carol asked, which cracked Mark up for a good ten minutes.

Mugs of mulled wine in hand, we proceeded to spend a drunken hour signing me up for carpentry classes at the local university.

'That's where they'll all be,' said Carol, gesturing at the screen, her pretty green dress now sporting a trail of red wine down the front.

'By Valentine's Day, sis, you'll have met a man, AND you'll be able to make me a wooden tray using a lathe,' Mark read from the advertising blurb on the website. He pointed at a man standing by a machine. 'You could meet him,' he whispered.

'Excellentsch work,' Carol and I chorused, before collapsing onto Mum's white leather sofa.

CHAPTER TWENTY-ONE

HUNG-OVER AND head thumping, I practically crawled into the kitchen the next day to pour myself a coffee and forage for breakfast. Mark and Carol were still not up and Guy had left a note on the kettle that said, 'Meeting'. Mum had left a second note saying, 'Back soon'. I felt like writing a third note that simply said, 'Dying', but didn't have the energy required to find a pen.

The kettle bubbled. I reached for a mug and shook coffee granules into the bottom, already anticipating that first caffeine hit, and feeling it was a win–win, when I discovered a year's supply of paracetamol in the cutlery drawer.

Reaching into the fridge for milk, I frowned as the doorbell rang.

I poked my head round the kitchen door, making out a shadow of a man in the frosted glass. Could I ignore him? As if in answer to my question, the doorbell went again. Postman? Lone carol singer? I opened the door.

Standing outside was a man in a full three-piece tweed suit, complete with flat cap on top of his straggly long hair. Stanley.

My mouth fell open and I automatically drew my tatty towelling dressing gown protectively around me.

'Nicola,' he said, taking off his flat cap with a flourish and leaning forward to kiss both my cheeks. 'How wonderful to see you! Rally, rally wonderful.'

'Stanley, I—'

'Golly,' he drawled, taking in the dressing gown over faded pyjamas and flip flops. 'You look frightfully like one of those women on that television programme, *Eastenders*. Ma in?' he asked, looking round as he stepped inside, *uninvited*.

'No, no, Ma's, I mean Mum's out. Back soon,' I said, parroting the note.

'Shame. Is that the kettle just boiled?'

With a defeated sigh, I realized I had a house guest. 'Yes. Tea? Coffee?' I offered.

'Earl Grey if you have it, old gal, lovely, lovely.'

I fetched a mug and noticed Mark's head appear round the door, wide-eyed, and then hastily withdraw. I followed him into the hallway but he'd already escaped up the stairs.

'Mark,' I hissed.

He mouthed things at me from the top landing, out of sight of Stanley, and made a hanging mime of a dead man on a rope, tongue lolling out, rocking sideways. I was too groggy to laugh and shuffled back into the kitchen, realizing, sadly, that there was no hope of backup.

Stanley flicked his long hair behind his shoulder as he marched around the kitchen taking the lids off things to peer into them for no reason.

'Well, Nicola,' he said as I handed him an Earl Grey with

a slice of lemon, just how he liked it. 'You must be rally surprised to see me here?' He eyed me over his mug, before taking a sip, pinkie out.

'I guess so!' I confirmed.

'Just thought I should pop by and tell you I am in the neighbourhood.' He leaned forward.

'Right.'

'Didn't feel we really caught up properly last night.'

'I suppose not.'

'I'm around the corner,' he said, nodding slowly.

'Sorry?'

'*A-round the corner*,' he emphasized each word.

'Um...'

'Available at a moment's notice if you wanted a... play date.' He winked.

'A *play da—*'

'A rally *fun* play date.' He winked again.

'Oh! Okey dokey,' I said, draining the last of my coffee and wrapping my robe even more tightly around myself.

'We could rally have some fun, you and I. I thought of you last night in that gorgeous dress of yours, and do you know what I thought?'

'Er, what did you think, Stanley?'

'I thought...' He paused, gaze travelling slowly up my body, before meeting my eyes. 'I rally have to make that girl realize I am keen if she is.'

'Ah. Well, that is kind,' I said, my toes rubbing the back of my heel in awkwardness.

'Quite. We're having our annual Christmas backgammon

tournament this afternoon,' he guffawed. 'So I best get back to Mummy, but, Nicola... Just remember... Around the corner, there is a friend. A friend who could be more than a friend.'

'I'll remember that, Stanley,' I croaked, nodding dumbly. 'Thank you for er... thinking of me.'

'I'll leave my mobile number here,' he said, sliding a card across with one finger. 'And you can ring it day or night. Day... or night, Nicola.'

'Thank you,' I squeaked, suddenly overwhelmed by the awful urge to laugh.

'Well,' he said, adjusting his flat cap. 'I'll be orf.'

And, striding out into the hallway, he was gone. I was left blinking in the kitchen.

When the front door closed I heard an explosion of laughter from the landing above, as Mark and Carol chorused: 'Day or Night, Nicola. Day or NIGHT.'

'Was that Stanley Holloway I just saw leaving?' my mother asked, sweeping into the kitchen moments later, her head still craned towards the front door.

I groaned inwardly. 'It was,' I said, refusing to divulge more. 'Tea?'

'Green.' She nodded. 'You know, Nicola, you could do a lot worse than Stanley Holloway. Believe me.' She perched herself primly on the edge of the white sofa. 'You wouldn't have to work for a start,' she said, noticing a speck of something on her skirt and brushing it off immediately.

'I *want* to work,' I said.

'I know, darling – you've always been eccentric – but you wouldn't *have* to,' she stressed.

I rolled my eyes and waited for the kettle to boil.

My mother waved a hand. 'Well, I'm glad you want to move on but you can't be so fussy, Nicola.'

'God forbid,' I muttered.

'Mark tells me you are getting back *out there*...'

Did Mark? I glanced at the stairs with a scowl.

'... And maybe that will put an end to this constant work and no fun. You used to be quite fun,' she mused.

'Thanks, Ma,' I said, handing her a mug.

'Good luck with it.' She raised the mug in a toast. A flicker of warmth passed between us and I smiled at her.

'Thanks, Mum.'

She sipped at her tea. 'Too strong,' she sighed and poured it down the sink.

CHAPTER TWENTY-TWO

AFTER THREE whole days and three whole nights in the family pad in leafy Gloucestershire, I was ready to return to Bristol for my casual cinema trip with Dan and the chance to catch my breath. I was glad to be back.

Flinging my suitcase into the doorway of my flat, I ventured straight back out to buy a newspaper and a coffee. Heading for the nearest place that sold caffeine by the double shot, a newspaper folded neatly under one arm, I already felt in better spirits. The barista gave me a smile and a 'Happy Christmas' as I picked up my mug from the counter. Settling myself in a window seat, I had a leisurely read of the articles, finishing up with a peek at my Virgo horoscope.

'A new year, a new you! Be bold!'

It continued to tell me that there was a moon in Uranus and something about this being a significant moment, whatever that meant. I heard my phone beep and took it out of my bag. Oh! I'd missed a call from a number I didn't recognize. I rang my answerphone.

'Ni-co-la. Happy Christmas. Seeing you in a few short days. You *promised* you'd come for dinner and then on to a party. It'll be rocking. Call me. Don't break my heart.'

I stared at the mobile. I stared at my horoscope. I realized that, although I was only going out with Chris to help James keep him as a client, I *was* actually looking forward to it. New Year, New Me! On the way home, I decided it wouldn't hurt to pop into the office. I could check any emails and tidy up the post so that there wouldn't be a huge pile to wade through when we returned after the Christmas holidays.

Unlocking the door to the agency, I headed straight upstairs to our floor. Pushing open the door, I was surprised to see we had no mail. Not even an advert for double glazing, or a festive card from a desperate actor keen to send us Christmas salutations and his new show reel. I jumped as I heard movement in James' office beyond. Before I could seize a weapon, the man himself emerged, an umbrella held aloft.

'We have no cash on the premises,' he called out. 'No cash on the premises.'

He stopped, took one look at my frozen face, bag halfway to the floor, feet planted in panic, and burst out with a relieved laugh. 'Nicola! Thank God. You scared me!' He dropped the umbrella to a less threatening height.

'*I* scared *you*,' I managed, almost dropping my bag in relief.

'Hmm. Good point,' he said, noting my pale face.

A second passed and then we both began to speak at once.

'I just thought I'd pop in and check on—'

'I can't believe you are back in the office on your holi—'

Immediately, we fell into a self-conscious silence and I ambled awkwardly across to my desk.

'Right, let's start again,' he said. 'How was your holiday and why aren't you still on it?'

'Holiday was lovely, thank you, and I only popped in to pick up the post. You know, and just make sure everything was okay,' I explained.

'Well, it is okay. I don't expect you to come back here at Christmas, Nicola,' he said. 'Go home, have fun, be merry, etc, etc...'

'Okay, fine.' I laughed, putting up my hands in mock surrender. 'I won't be long.'

'Time for a coffee?' he asked, slinging his coat over his arm.

'Um, no thanks. I'm fine. I just, um... drank.'

I reached for my bag and bashed the corner of my head on my desk.

'Ow!' I flinched.

James hurried over. 'Are you all right?'

'Yeah,' I said, rubbing my head where it had knocked the corner. 'Ow,' I repeated, tears stinging the back of my eyes. Oh, brilliant. Was I going to cry like a baby in front of my boss? Wonderful. The humiliating notion thankfully made the tears retreat. I smiled weakly at him.

'Best get on then,' I said heartily.

James grinned. 'Right... I suppose I'll be off then.' He paused in the doorway. '*Unless...*'

'Yes?'

'Well, if you really are set on making yourself useful, you *could* help me with a task I've been putting off for weeks.'

'What's that?'

'I'll show you,' he said mysteriously, bolting through to his office. 'Wait there.'

I heard him scuffle about, dragging something heavy across the carpet. Then there was a thud, followed swiftly by a 'Bollocks'.

'Er, are you all right in there?' I called.

'Yeeesss fiiine,' he grunted. 'Hold on.'

'Okay,' I mouthed, tapping the top of my desk.

There was a load more rustling and what sounded like Sellotape being removed, and then finally James called out in a triumphant voice: 'All right, come in!'

I edged open the door curiously and found James proudly patting the top of a large rectangular cardboard box, with a makeshift bow made of sellotape perched on the top.

'Ta-da!' James announced. 'Happy Christmas! Don't say I never give you things.'

Perplexed, but delighted, I rushed forward. 'Oh, wow, you shouldn't have...' Then I spotted the writing on the side of the box – *Office 4-door Filing Cabinet* – and stopped short. 'Ah... you really shouldn't have!' I exclaimed, slapping James on the arm.

It was an odd moment in my life. Physically assaulting one's boss was not something I'd tried before. James looked as surprised as I felt, and then, rubbing his arm in an over-the-top panto gesture, he started roaring with laughter.

I gestured with my hand. 'I'm so sorry, James, I...' but the movement of my hand was too much for him. He shielded his face.

'Stop, Nicola. Please don't!' And then, grinning at me,

he lowered his arms. 'I can't take another beating,' he whispered shakily.

I pouted, hands on my hips.

'Fine,' he huffed. 'I suppose I might have deserved the slap.' He handed me a pair of scissors. 'Now cut the Sellotape, Nicola. Don't get me with those, I don't want to spend the New Year in A & E.'

I cut the tape and, together, we ripped open the cardboard until its remnants were scattered all about the floor. It looked like we were building an extension onto the office, not a filing cabinet. There were slats of wood, packets of bolts and screws and random metal objects littered everywhere.

'Ah, flat-packed furniture,' James sighed. 'My favourite type of furniture.'

I picked up one of the many clear packets. 'I've never seen so many nuts.'

'Quite,' James agreed.

I looked up sharply, convinced he was mocking me, but he smiled innocently back.

After ten minutes of pointlessly clanging various pieces of metal against various pieces of wood in the vain hope they would suddenly all make a filing cabinet, James had run to get coffee while I was left scooping the instruction manual out of the bin, where it had been flung in the first five minutes by a frustrated James. By the time he returned with two cappuccinos, I'd successfully attached Part A to Part B with Screw J. I was pretty smug about it too.

'Brilliant! We have clearly earned a rest,' James said,

sitting on the carpet and leaning back against his desk to sip at his coffee.

'We?' I queried with a raised eyebrow.

'Fine, Miss Winner of the Flat-Pack Furniture Assembly of the Year Award, *you* have earned it.' He handed me my cup.

'So,' James said, 'how come you've run back here so soon? Bad Christmas?'

'No, not really. Just exhausting Christmas, the usual kind, I imagine.' I smiled.

I told James about my family. My opinionated, yoga-loving mother, and Guy, constantly glued to his mobile. I told him about my bat-obsessed brother and his delight over the present I'd given him – an enormous framed picture of a Cyttarops alecto (Short-Eared Bat from Brazil). James reciprocated with tales of his mad aunt who'd spent the entire Christmas dinner asleep in her mashed potato.

'Oh dear.' I laughed, noting that in amongst all the goings on James hadn't spent Christmas with Thalia, Queen of Fashion. Not that I cared, either way.

'I didn't realize you had a niece and nephew,' I said, imagining James at home, not James the boss of the office.

'I haven't been a very hands-on uncle,' he admitted. 'I'm always a slight loose end with children. It's been ages since I was one and I'm never quite sure what they like doing. I mean, I liked building train sets and playing Scalextric but kids today...' He shook his head as if he were an old-age pensioner. 'It's hard to tell what they're into, isn't it? My nephew was given a Wii for his Christmas present and started talking about its WAP capabilities and its something dual function. I was completely lost.'

'I'm pretty sure most of them love to do anything that involves running around and getting dirty.'

'Sounds about right... So, Nicola Brown.' He rubbed his hands together and frowned at the many metal and wooden pieces lying on the floor between us. 'I suppose we'd better try and build this thing.'

By 4.36 p.m. the filing cabinet resembled a giant wooden jigsaw puzzle and a pile of scrap metal. It could probably pass for some kind of abstract modern art sculpture. As for holding files? No way.

'Hand me the thingy,' James said, waving his hands at me.

'What thingy?'

'The thingy that goes on the wood thingy.'

'You'll have to be more precise, I'm afraid,' I said, quite enjoying his frustration.

'*Fine*, you know, the thingy that screws onto the corner bit of the wood thingy,' he said in an exasperated tone.

'What, a cross dowel?' I peered at the instruction manual. 'Part L.'

'Is Part L the metal bit shaped like an "N"?'

'Yes.'

'Then yes,' he said, sounding relieved. 'That's the one.'

'I haven't got it, you must have it.'

'No, I don't.'

'Maybe it's by one of the Part H's over there.'

'It's not, I've looked.'

'Well, I don't have it.'

'It must be here somewhere,' James grumbled, manoeuvring himself onto his knees to scan the carpet.

'You're sitting on it,' I observed, scooping it away in time.

'How embarrassing.' He coughed. 'One doesn't normally like to sit on one's cross dowel.'

'Indeed not,' I agreed.

After what seemed like an eternity, the last bloomin' dowel had been put in the cabinet and we had performed the Opening Doors Test, which essentially involved exactly that. They all opened and therefore we deemed the test an enormous success.

We sat back and observed our handiwork for a few minutes. I hopped up and patted it on the top. 'You know, every time I put a file in it I will feel—'

'Nervous it's going to fall to pieces in your hands?' James interjected.

'*No.*' I laughed. 'Proud is the word I was going for.'

'What's the time?' James asked. It had grown dark outside.

'Um...' I checked my watch. 'Ten to six.'

'Christ. It would have been quicker to build one from scratch!'

'Hmm, maybe I'll learn,' I mused, thinking about the New Year carpentry class Mark and Carol had drunkenly persuaded me to sign up for.

'Learn what?'

'Oh.' I blushed. 'I'm heading to a carpentry class next week to, er, learn how to... carpenter... things.'

'Carpenter things, I see.' He nodded.

'You know, make stuff out of wood.'

'Yes, Nicola. I got that.'

'Of course. Thought so. Just checking.' I giggled.

'Right,' said James, grabbing his coat from the back of his chair. 'Can I drop you off anywhere?'

'No thanks, I live just up the road,' I said, my face feeling flushed by the central heating.

'Sure?'

I nodded.

He reached for the door, opened it and then paused, spinning back round to face me. 'Time for a drink?'

'Oh, I can't. I have a da... a thing,' I said, suddenly regretting my planned catch-up with Dan.

'A thing,' he repeated. His face dropped slightly and I wished again that I was free.

Noticing his jumper, I wondered if it had been a Christmas present from Thalia. It looked so appealing and soft and I felt the sudden urge to reach out for it. It made his eyes look almost navy. Heat surged through my cheeks.

James cleared his throat. 'Well, thank you for today. I would have hacked it to pieces hours ago without you here to help to, er... build it. I didn't know my nubbin from my oojamaflip. See you in January, Nicola,' he said in slightly too loud a voice.

'See you!' I said, matching his hearty tone, waving an Allen key at him for good measure.

Before he left he turned round. 'And make sure you stay away from the office until then.' He grinned warmly.

'I will.'

'Happy New Year.'

'Happy New Year,' I said, waving the damn key again.

From the window, I watched as he walked up the street, his head down against the cold. A small smile crept over my face. I felt a sudden surge of love for Christmas. I ran across the room clutching the Allen key and kissed the filing cabinet.

CHAPTER TWENTY-THREE

MY GOOD mood didn't fade and I was humming as I got ready for the casual date with Dan that evening. I pulled into the cinema car park and found a parking space. In the Ford KA next to me two teenagers were snogging and I tried not to catch their eyes as I checked my make-up in my rear-view mirror. They can't have been more than seventeen, and the very sight of them made me feel ancient. They would have thought me old, of a different generation, maybe even past it. I mean, I was turning thirty for goodness' sake. What could I possibly have in common with them? They were born at the end of the nineties, when I was reading Evelyn Waugh, experimenting with liquid eyeliner and listening to Enya.

Fortunately, the boy was far too concerned with attacking his girlfriend's bra strap to give me a moment's thought. I made a concerted effort to close my door quietly and sneak away before they could accuse me of dogging.

I pushed open the heavy revolving doors of the cinema and instantly the sickly sweet smell of popcorn hit my nostrils. The sound of children racing from arcade to sweet shop and back to arcade, their harassed parents calling out to them, and the hubbub of a hundred people milling around, surrounded me, assaulted my ears. The whole world seemed to have descended on this one cinema complex for the evening and I carefully navigated my way past one family's hot-dog-related argument and a group of pre-pubescent boys debating whether 12A really meant they had to have an adult with them. As I joined the mammoth queue for tickets, my mobile rang. I pulled it out from my handbag.

'Hello,' I answered, leaning over and cupping my hand to my ear, barely able to register any answer due to the sound of crowds around me.

It was Dan. I could just make out his voice above the noise. 'I'm here already. I was a little early so I got on with it! I'll wait for you in the foyer by the toilets.' He hung up.

Oh phew, I thought, manoeuvring my way out of the queue. No need for me to line up for another fifteen minutes, crushed uncomfortably against perfect strangers. I looked around for Dan's location by the toilets and spotted him, with a slightly nervous expression on his face, holding a bucket of popcorn and a bag of sweets. He hadn't really changed since university. He was good-looking in an American sitcom sort-of-way, lots of teeth and smooth, tanned skin. Like he had just come off the slopes. I took a deep breath, put on a smile and approached him.

'Dan!' I waved.

He looked up and waggled three fingers at me from underneath all the foodstuffs he'd purchased. 'Nicola, hi.' We wandered over to Screen Two, where a burly man waited to collect our tickets.

'Tickets, please,' he said, stretching out his hand.

I turned to Dan with an expectant smile.

'Tickets,' I repeated. 'Do you want me to take some of that stuff?' I offered.

'Oh, um, I got myself a ticket but, um, I didn't, well, I didn't think… I thought you would get, um…' Dan stuttered.

I looked at him in exasperation. The ticket man let out a loud sigh. Quite, I thought.

I headed back to the heaving queue of people and called over my shoulder to Dan, 'Give me five minutes.'

Dan looked sheepish when I returned. 'Great. Sorry, Nicola, so thoughtless of me,' he muttered, leaning in to give me a belated kiss of greeting. I hadn't anticipated this manoeuvre and the kiss landed in between my chin and lower lip.

The ticket man didn't even try to disguise his mirth. He was still chuckling when he handed me back my ticket and waved us both through to the screen.

When we were settled in our seats, Dan clearly decided to try and make up for the ticket debacle by leaning over and listing his thoughts on many of the recent releases to have hit the cinema. It was like being in the presence of Jonathan Ross on speed. I could barely keep up as he rattled through all the latest movies he'd seen, why American blockbusters were obsessed with the Middle East, why animated films had such weak scripts but such brilliant effects, why he liked the IMAX experience but it wasn't appropriate for this type of film. The trailers began, and still Dan continued in a steady stream of patter. He had run out of films to comment on and had now moved on to critiquing all the adverts to appear. He knew all the words to the latest Orange one. He clearly went to the cinema a lot.

'Hmm, yes, I've heard this film has had excellent reviews,' I replied to his latest barrage of commentary.

My reply seemed to relax him and he settled himself into his seat without another word. I squidged down in my seat and exhaled slowly, feeling better. I felt my stomach rumble and realized I hadn't eaten anything since lunchtime. I looked over at Dan's items neatly placed on the armrest and reached for the popcorn. Yummy. I lifted a handful of delicious sweet popcorn to my mouth, inhaling the smell. It was wrong, but so, so right. Caroline would have applauded at my indulgence. Ooh, look! He had pick 'n' mix. I loved pick 'n' mix. I still got a cheap thrill on entering the supermarket and filling a little bag with fizzy cola bottles, pieces of fudge and pink shrimps. I always walked out without purchasing them, of course, but just choosing them was often enough of a buzz. I peered in to ascertain his sweet selection. Brilliant. Dan had excellent pick 'n' mix taste. I reached for a sweet in the shape of a smiley face. Suddenly Dan's hand appeared from the semi-darkness and batted mine away.

'Sorry, Nicola, but there isn't really enough,' he explained.

'What?' I whispered back, too amazed to register what he was saying.

He leaned in towards me. 'I just didn't get very much so...' he trailed off and I was left looking startled, my hand still hovering over the bag.

Was he denying me sweets?

He moved the bag away. He was!

I stood up so suddenly that the couple sitting behind us started muttering grumpily. Dan gave me a curious look.

'What are you doing?' he asked.

I didn't have the nerve to whisper anything truly cutting. Instead, I hissed, 'I need food.'

Dan nodded and reached for his bag of pick 'n' mix.

The ticket man gave me a quizzical stare as I pushed past him into the foyer. Grabbing the shovel, I heaped mountains of sugared sweets into the bag.

'That's six pounds forty please,' said the man behind the counter.

Good, I thought as I handed over a crisp tenner. *Should be enough*. Deciding I was thirsty too, I added a bucket of lemonade to my collection and stalked back into Screen Two, laden down with MY treats.

I arrived just as the opening credits started. I sat down, determinedly staring at the screen so I couldn't catch Dan's eye, and placed my drink and bag of sweets in between us to create a food wall.

It was a good film. Lots of explosions and action involving attractive, if often sweaty, men who you'd choose to sleep with only after you'd given them a good wash. I shovelled sweets into my mouth to keep up with the quick-fire special effects and the pace of the dialogue. Parched, I reached for my drink. It wasn't in the cup holder. Confused, I glanced down by my feet, but it wasn't on the floor. I turned round slowly. I couldn't believe it. Yes, this was *outrageous*. My lemonade was being SUCKED ON BY DAN.

I stared at him as he slurped on MY lemonade. Fortunately for the cinema audience, at that moment a car exploded on screen, or they'd all have heard me saying, 'I don't bloody believe it!' Even Dan missed my outburst, but then he was utterly focused on the sucking of MY straw.

I didn't even take in the last ten minutes of the film. I just got progressively angrier, running through all the put-downs I could muster in my mind so that, when the movie had finished, Dan would feel my wrath. I was really psyching myself up; I was going to do this. I was going to tell him that his behaviour was unacceptable, that he was ungenerous and that he couldn't just willy-nilly go sucking on other people's straws. Although I might not phrase it like that. Good, the end credits were rolling. Dan was already on his feet and heading for the exit, barely registering if I was behind him or not. I walked briskly, knowing the sooner we were out, the sooner I could let rip.

We pushed open the heavy doors and I turned to him, opened my mouth and heard myself saying, 'Well!' But in a hugely cross sort of way.

'Drink?' Dan offered.

'Well, I...' I'd started to flounder. *Come on, Nicola, have it out with him. Tell him what you think of him.* 'I... um... Yes, that would be nice.'

I'd bottled it.

We walked across the foyer, out into the street and over to a nearby restaurant. A waitress showed us to a cosy table near the back of the room. *Clean slate, clean slate*, I thought as I removed my coat and sat down. I ordered a mineral water because I had so much sugar running round my system I really didn't think my body could take much more.

Dan settled himself opposite me and raked his hand through his hair. I nodded and smiled. I suppose at the very least, it'd be nice to reminisce about old times.

'Didn't you have long hair at university?' Dan asked, indicating my bobbed haircut.

I patted the ends self-consciously. 'I did.'

'Yeah,' he nodded. 'I think you should grow it long again.'

'Oh.'

A further silence descended. I waited for our drinks, drumming my fingers on the tabletop and looking around the room. He hates my hair and he steals my food. I really didn't think things could get any worse but after ten minutes of limping down various conversational cul-de-sacs involving people we'd both known at university, the conversation ran dry.

Halfway through telling him a sorry anecdote about the time I jammed the photocopier (not one of my top ten tales), I became aware that Dan was glancing at my breasts. I moved the story on to the part where I'd had to ring the photocopier manufacturers to enquire about the paper feed, but even this scintillating turn of events failed to distract him. He was definitely still looking at my breasts. The trouble was that, interspersed with the tit staring, he was also occasionally glancing up at my face, so it was difficult to accuse him of ogling my boobs for a concentrated period of time. I continued to talk, becoming more and more uncomfortable. My story ended (happily I should add – we could still use the photocopier) and I crossed my arms in an attempt to distract Dan from my cleavage. It didn't work.

'Out of interest, Nicola, what bra size do you wear?'

'I'm sorry?' I gasped, flummoxed by his cheek.

'What bra size? Because I think it might be wrong.' He gestured at my chest.

'I... I can't remember,' I gabbled.

'There's no need to be embarrassed,' he said breezily. 'You see, I worked at Marks and Spencer's in the underwear department, and you need one that hoists them up a bit, if you don't mind me saying.' He held his hands up in a gesture of innocence. 'Many women get it wrong, it's very common.' He nodded, in a very knowledgeable sort of way.

This was surely my moment to silence him, surely my moment to tell this man what I thought of him? But I couldn't. I just couldn't do it. Dan seemed to think my lack of reaction was an invitation to continue talking to me on the subject of bras in general. He added: 'Did you know that ninety per cent of women in this country wear the wrong bra size and many develop problems with their backs because of this? Not forgetting the increased risk that their breasts will lose their elasticity in the future.'

As Dan talked and I sat in shocked silence, my mind raced. How did I manage to meet these people? I was a good person. I was trying to 'get *out there*', but if this was what was *out there,* did I want to be *out there* with them? Was I not better inside, behind closed doors, with the television for company? *I should get up and leave. I really should. I should go now. I could. I could just make my excuses and leave.*

'Dan, I...'

'Another drink?' he asked enthusiastically, waving the waitress over. 'Same again, please,' he said, even though I had barely touched my mineral water.

Fine. Another drink, another few minutes, I thought, slumping back into the seat. At least Dan had moved on from the previous conversation and was now bemoaning the plethora of fat people he had witnessed on his lunchbreak from work.

'It's their fault,' he ranted, in an irritatingly know-all voice, a sort of nasally whine – how had I never noticed this at university? 'Some say it's genes, but that's rubbish. It is because they eat too much. You know, I think they should charge them more on planes.'

'Hmm,' I replied weakly.

'I imagine many people out there would agree with us,' he continued. 'Yet it won't change things. Political correctness, see, that's the damn problem. If I was a politician I'd ban—'

Before he got progressively worse, I found myself standing up. Turned out I did have a limit.

'I need to go home,' I announced, gathering my bag.

Dan looked slightly put out. 'I'll get the bill then,' he said, beckoning to the waitress. She appeared as I reached for my coat.

'Right. Well, thank you, Dan, it's been... er...'

Dan frowned up at me, clearly surprised I was leaving, and held up his hand. 'Hold on,' he said. He took the bill from the waitress, read it, looked at me and said: 'Your drinks were four pounds forty.'

I rummaged in my bag, threw a fiver down on the table and spat, 'Keep the change.' I knew he would.

CHAPTER TWENTY-FOUR

SPEEDING BACK from the cinema, I felt my breathing slow. Bristol looked wintery and magical as I drove back to the flat. Frost had formed so that stone houses and cars seemed to sparkle under the lamplight. Couples weaved back from the pubs, bobble hats bent in conversation. A group of girls wearing Santa hats wobbled in heels as I raced past.

Stepping out of my car, I glanced up at the flat. There was a newly manicured lawn area outside of our apartment block. Julio had obviously been attacking it with shears. He'd clipped the low hedge along the front into a straight line and had bought a couple of pots to brighten up the place. Moving closer, I realized the pots were full of small clumps of lavender. The scent made me stop in my tracks, key wavering. I was drawn to a memory, blinking as I was swept back seven years.

I'd been rushing back to our flat with a pot of lavender. I'd had the idea of making window boxes for our bedroom — we had wide sills that would be perfect. I pictured waking up in the morning, limbs entwined, watching the sun come up, an open window allowing a gentle breeze into the room and the smell of lavender nudging us into consciousness.

I noticed the light on from the street and realized he was home from lectures early. Smiling, I started planning an ambush in my mind, excited already to think of his amber eyes crinkling in delight, his mouth breaking into laughter.

Creeping into the flat, trying not to giggle, I'd put the lavender down on a side-table, padded softly over to the kitchen and peered my head round the doorway. No one there. I frowned and wandered to the living room, removing my top so that I'd appear in my red bra, make him laugh at my brazen behaviour. Throwing the door open, I noticed his clothes already on the sofa. I chuckled to myself. The cheeky thing – he was beating me at my own game!

Laughing, I walked across the corridor to our bedroom – a box room so tiny there was only enough room for a bed and our whispered nothings. I turned the doorknob and prepared to dive-bomb him.

As I walked in, the 'TA-DA' died on my lips. I took in the scene before me. Flesh, naked flesh, long blonde hair, clothes scattered and my boyfriend, the man I had moved in with only a month ago, the man I had planned my future with, made promises of a life together with, was wrapped around my very best friend. Her flushed cheeks and sparkling eyes open in surprise at the intrusion.

I had stood there dumbly as they scooped up clothes, apologized, muttered things. I couldn't get my head around

209

what I was witnessing. My whole world had shrunk in the space of a few seconds.

His ever-confident gaze met mine. His face was practically a smirk as he'd said: 'Well, this wasn't quite how I planned to tell you.' My stomach lurched.

Charlotte clutched her jumper to her chest in a pathetic attempt to cover herself up. She couldn't even meet my eye. Our friendship shattered in that moment. All the hours we had spent pouring out our woes over a glass of wine, giggling over a tin of Roses, cramming before exams, the things I had told her about him, the times I'd taken her home to sleep on my floor when she'd got drunk and needed somewhere to crash. I'd believed in our friendship, assumed she would be a bridesmaid of mine, a loyal side-kick as we grew up.

I only just made it to the bathroom in time, before throwing up. Then I stumbled out of the apartment, straight into the street below, not knowing where to go, but knowing I would never, ever go back.

CHAPTER TWENTY-FIVE

Single girl WLTM someone to
kiss at midnight.

Contact: Box No. 08366

IT WAS New Year's Eve and the evening of my dinner with Chris Sheldon-Wade. We'd be following dinner with a New Year's party he was co-hosting with someone who I swear he'd called 'Nobby' – a good friend of his from public school.

I'd taken forever to decide what to wear, knowing that people would be looking at the girl on Chris's arm, and I'd splurged on a short electric-blue dress and a pair of ridiculously high strappy silver heels. For a moment, I'd felt like I used to feel, the old excitement as I'd dressed. I spent time putting my make-up on, a brilliant slick of red lipstick coupled with smoky grey eyes, using the eye shadow Carol had given me for Christmas. I completed the look by pinning up my hair at the back.

I waited in my flat, perched on the edge of my sofa, feeling nervous. When I'd looked in the mirror earlier I'd been pleasantly surprised by my makeover. But now the dress seemed too short, the lipstick seemed overdone and the shoes an absurdity. I tugged at the hem of my dress. I couldn't stand Chris. He was petulant and self-absorbed, but he was a man the agency needed to keep sweet, a man whose fees paid my rent, and I knew being nice to him was important, especially for James.

The intercom buzzed and I answered it, hearing, 'Niiicolllaaa, the taxi's on a meter,' before hanging up. I practically pulled a muscle racing down the stairs of the apartment.

Chris was looking effortlessly gorgeous in a black suit with a thin deep-blue tie, and I became tongue-tied as I gripped the inside of the cab and tried to find something to talk about that wasn't work. Fortunately, it took us less than five minutes to reach our destination and I managed to cover: the weather (unpleasant but normal for December) and his tie (Hugo Boss).

The restaurant was full to bursting; couples were waiting in a reception area, clustered round low tables, clutching their half-empty drinks and looking expectantly at any passing waiter. We were swept straight through by the maître d'. I felt a small, guilty glow and tried not to catch any of the narrowed eyes as I passed.

It took us about forty-five minutes to reach our table. Chris knew practically every other diner so we had to stop for a good deal of air-kissing. We finally sat down in a corner next to a fish tank filled with bright, exotic-looking fish. Chris shifted his seat slightly, to be 'out of the way of the draught', but coincidentally managed to settle himself right in front of a large square of mirror positioned behind me.

We then spent a few tense minutes trying to catch the eye of a waiter. Every time I tried to start a conversation, Chris craned his neck round to continue the waiter hunt, thus silencing my efforts. Finally, a waitress with a cute blonde pixie-cut and a mini-skirt showing off long legs casually sauntered over. She barely bothered to look in my direction but instead drawled the day's specials so quietly to Chris that I was forced to lean across the table to hear. Not totally effective, as all I heard was 'salmon, herb, asparagus' repeated intermittently, so anything special from the kitchen was going to have to pass me by.

Chris ordered for both of us, salmon en croute with dill sauce. I'd have plumped for something different but kept quiet. After all, he did know the restaurant better, and the day's specials had just been whispered in his ear.

When the waitress exited, with one final giggle and wiggle at Chris, we sat looking at each other. He fiddled nervously with the napkin in his lap, which was actually quite endearing. I hadn't really thought about it from his point of view, but here he was taking out a colleague, of sorts, and trying to come up with some conversation. Maybe his confident front was just a show and a sensitive soul was hiding underneath the brash exterior?

At that moment he looked up. 'I'm just texting Nobby.'

'Oh.' I flushed, caught off-guard, realizing the nervous fiddling was in fact tapping on a mobile. 'Will he be at the party later?' I asked.

Chris didn't bother to look up. 'Yeah, but he's recording the game.'

'Ah.' I nodded. I sensed I should not ask what game this was. This would not be a Cool Question. I imagined a patronizing 'Jesus-you-don't-know-what-game-it-is' roll of the eyes.

I waited patiently for Chris to finish, by pretending to develop an urge to study the room, due to a sudden intense interest in its architecture. Marble columns by reception, hmm, very interesting. A sign for the toilets written in an italic scroll, very nice. A mahogany bar with red velvet-covered bar stools, *fascinating*. Finally he finished and I looked back at him with a startled try at 'Oh, you're still here, silly me I was too engrossed by the decor.' Cool, you see, that's me. Chris placed his mobile on the table and looked at me.

'How was your day?' I piped up.

Dazzling Question Number One, Nicola. However, seeing his face light up like I'd just asked him what he got from Santa made me realize I couldn't have asked Chris a better question.

'Yeah, it was okay, Nicola. Hectic, obviously, always is in an acttttooorr's life. I got headshots done, do you want to see them? He printed me off some contact sheets.'

'Oh, right,' I said, heart sinking as he continued.

'I'm keeping a record of which one people like. Personally I'm a fan of forty-five. I think it says "I'm serious and should break into TV dramas." Don't you?' he asked, thrusting it under my nose.

'Oh yes, it's very um... moody,' I tried.

He laid the sheets out onto the table in front of me. There must have been around two hundred photos of himself, all in black and white, all looking exactly the same as the next. He asked me to pick my favourite five. I sat staring hopelessly at all the mini-Chris heads.

'Um...'

Suddenly the phone was beeping and he dived on it. 'YES, YES, YES!' he cried, punching the air.

'Good news?' I enquired politely, only Chris was involved in another run of frenzied texting. Just to improve my mood, the waitress chose that moment to reappear with the salmon.

'So they did it,' she said laughingly at Chris, while unceremoniously dumping my plate down before me. 'I watched extra time in the kitchen. It was a great goal. Brilliant.'

Chris grinned at her. 'I knew they'd come through.'

'Hmm,' I said, chipping in. 'Great... er...' They both stared at me. 'Great... restaurant. Love the... decor,' I said with a flourish of my fork.

'Well, better get on,' the waitress said. 'I have got other customers, you know,' she added, touching Chris's arm.

Chris nodded at her back.

'Nice girl,' he grinned as she left.

'Very nice,' I nodded. After all the excitement, and the waitress and the game, I was relieved that at least Chris had forgotten he was making me judge his headshots.

'You see, Nic, the important thing is to spend time covering a range of emotions with the photographer. Three and forty-nine are good...'

Oh no.

215

'But I am not sure about eight, or whether I need something for Spotlight that is a little more sixty-seven, or whether I should be going down the matinee idol route that twenty-nine is all about...'

Gah, kill me now.

I tried hard to look interested as he scanned through the prints and, at one point, brought out a small leather book that kept a record of the list of favourite photos that other people had liked. Apparently seven was incredibly popular. 'It's extremely vital to know which look one is trying for and nail it in as few shots as possible. Fabio told me I was a dream to work with. A dream!'

As he spoke, I realized that I was left with few options. It was either option a) gouge my own brain out with the remaining silverware, option b) leave and risk letting James and the company down, or option c) knock back the House White. I decided on the latter and, after a while, everything became much more amusing. Chris's faces were funny. I liked number eleven the best.

Chris was in the middle of an anecdote about skiing with Nobby, when I saw him. James. My stomach lurched. There he was, sitting in the corner of the room, looking earnestly across at a man in a suit sitting opposite him. He was wearing the bottle-green jumper that I liked. He looked tired, stifling a yawn behind his hand as he listened to his companion. He smiled at something, his eyes crinkling in his familiar way, and I had a sudden urge to hide. I didn't want James to see me here with Chris. But it was too late. James turned and stared directly at us both, his mouth open. I tried to smile but, somehow, couldn't.

'All right, babe?' Chris said, smiling at me over the table. 'We best get going to this New Year's Eve party eh?'

'Hmm...' I tipsily dragged my gaze back to him. 'Oh... of course, of course.'

My eyes flicked back without a thought. James had angled his chair so that I could just see him in profile.

My mind was a blur of confusion. Should I go over to James and explain? But explain what? That *he* was the reason I was here? That I'd agreed to go out with Chris because of the agency? I didn't really need to explain, but something in the way he'd just looked at me had made me want to reassure him that there was nothing going on between me and Chris, at all. But as I unsteadily pushed back my chair with a screech and Chris steered me between the tables towards the exit, I realized I couldn't.

Maybe James hadn't actually seen me. Maybe he had been looking over my shoulder at another diner. And anyway, why did it matter that he'd seen me? Why was I worrying? Thalia was probably joining him later. We plunged outside, the cold bringing me to a standstill. I glanced back into the restaurant, searching for his table.

'Nic, come on,' Chris called brightly.

'I'm coming, so sorry,' I said, following him into the taxi.

Standing under the neon disco lights, bopping uncertainly to 'Karma Chameleon' and tugging self-consciously on my new ever-so-short dress, I screamed back at the man standing opposite me. 'AN AGENCY,' I repeated.

I'd assumed his question was in some way work-related, but the chances of me hearing anything over the chorus 'Red, gold and green, red, gold and green' was frankly impossible.

He mouthed something else at me and I caught the word 'Bar' and nodded frantically. A drink. That would help.

The theme was Celebrities and this New Year's Eve party was as 'rocking' as Chris had predicted. The music was blaring and the guests were drinking and laughing. There were a thousand glitzy sequinned ladies, many besuited men, one tennis player, one Elvis and two girls in Kate Middleton masks. Chris had been plying me with compliments and champagne cocktails in between dashing off to talk to newly arrived guests. There were moments where it felt good to be in the centre of things for once, to be out partying normally, without a care. And I needed to get on with Chris. We needed him to stay with the business. James' stressed face swam into view, his ruffled hair, the deepening lines around his eyes after late nights spent buttering up future clients. Chris brought in the money and this date was a small sacrifice to keep him sweet.

He swanned over now, very much the man at the centre of things. One gorgeous blonde in a pair of teeny shorts winked at him as he passed her. He patted her bottom. I smiled nervously at him and bobbed a little more quickly to the music: an effort to show him I was getting into the spirit of things.

I was certainly getting into the spirits as the man who'd been shouting at me returned with another vodka and lime.

'THANKS!' I screeched, nodding at him. I sucked on

the straw, gazing around the room at the other revellers, nodding my head to the beat and trying not to feel too silly and out of place. *This is good for me, character building, character building, have to get out there, have to get out there.* I chanted in my head. Chris put an arm round my waist and introduced me to his friend. 'This is Nicola, isn't she beautiful?' he commented.

I knew I should have been outraged at being patronized, paraded in front of his friend like his show pony, but I felt absurdly flattered. I shook his friend's hand, thanked him again for my drink and decided to relax. I imagined Caroline running into the place to give me a double thumbs up, and smiled at the thought. Parties were great, I mused. You could run away from awkward people, you could leave at a moment's notice, and most importantly of all you could become anyone as no one *really* knew you. This last thought brought on a rush of liberated feelings. I was the mysterious lady on Chris's arm. I was dressed to kill. I was having a good time.

So the evening went on, and after yet another loo visit, I realized I was going to have to strike up conversation with another stranger because Chris was nowhere to be seen. I eyed the semicircle of people at my table and smiled brightly at them. Most just ignored me and one girl with enormous chandelier earrings looked positively startled by my attempt. Raising an eyebrow, she turned to her friend sitting next to her and mentioned something about some lesbian who was around. I couldn't hear the detail, but for some reason the friend was looking right back at me, smirking. It was at that moment a glass came crashing down on the table next to me. Liquid spilled over the sides of the table and splattered my new dress. A man in an Al Capone-style pinstripe suit swayed precariously, then turned to face me, taking a couple of seconds too long to focus on my face.

'This ish my seat where I left it.'

'Um... yes. Well, hello.'

'You're gooorgeous, haven't seen you here before. I'm Seb.' He held out his hand, then slipped and used it to prop himself up on the table.

'I'm Nicola,' I said, willing to overlook the handshake debacle in exchange for someone to talk to.

'What did you say your name was?' he slurred, not quite able to focus entirely on my face, although managing to ogle my boobs quite successfully.

'Um... Nicola,' I said, realizing that my glass was empty again.

'Would you like a drink, Seb?' I asked, spotting Chris across the room, talking to a girl in a pink top and sky-high heels.

'All right, Nikki. But I'm buying,' he said, producing an embarrassing number of notes from a pocket.

'Nicola...' I corrected.

'Erica. I know you said,' he called after me as I left.

I returned moments later with the drinks. Seb hadn't moved an inch. I sat back down.

'So, Anoushka, what do you do?' he said, sniffing a little.

'Well, I work for an actors' agency in town,' I replied,

sipping my drink.

Seb slurped at his beer.

'Interested in acting, are you? I work in PR, give me a call and I can set you up with the right people. It's just a matter of image. You know, Kristen—'

'I'm Nicola.' I patted him on the arm like he was a small child.

'No, you know Kristen?'

'Kristen?' I queried.

'Stewart,' he finished.

'Oh right, of course, Kristen.' I nodded, trying to keep up.

'Yeah, she was a total nobody before she met me and then, whoosh, she went straight to the top, didn't she? Spoke to her last week actually and she said, "Seb. Thank you. You've helped me so much."'

'Oh, right. That's good to hear.' I gulped the rest of my drink.

'So, babe, just get in touch whenever and we'll sort you out.'

'Oh, okay, thanks. I will. Definitely.'

After a few more drinks, Seb turned into a surprisingly amusing guy. I was fairly sure we were enjoying some scintillating conversation. I had a sneaking suspicion we might become best friends. I yanked him onto the dance floor. It might have been down to childhood dance lessons or it might have been the alcohol kicking in, but either way, I suddenly realized I was one of the best dancers in Bristol. I had a talent. A BGT sort-of talent. I was skilful, everything on the beat, moves I didn't even know I had.

I spent the rest of the night snaking round various people on the dance floor. Lucky things. Soon, Chris was on the dance floor (no doubt tempted by my moves) and wrapped himself around me, whispering stuff in my ear. I reckoned we looked good together, writhing around to the beats. I got drink after drink and danced and drank and partied and laughed and drank and danced. This was my new life, the new Nicola.

Then, suddenly, it was the New Year and I was in a SUPER FUN MOOD and I was hugging Chris and joining in the countdown to midnight. Seb had sloped off, which was a shame as we were best friends, but Chris and I had danced a lot together and he WAS nice, I thought.

'Six, five, four, three, two, one... HAPPY NEW YEAR.'

In the midst of all the dancing and embracing, Chris turned to kiss me full on the lips.

'I hope it's a Happy New Year for you,' he said, smiling at me with perfectly straight, white teeth. The moment was only half ruined by a brunette in a figure-hugging midi-dress grabbing him to wish him a Happy New Year too. With her tongue. But before I could react to anything much, I was whisked off my feet by an over-exuberant man in a kilt (he'd come as Mel Gibson) to dance the New Year in and, suddenly, I didn't care two jots who kissed who or where. I didn't need to worry about it all. Mel was an excellent dancer too. There were cocktails and champagne, and Chris, and people laughing. Everything was good.

I can't believe what I'm doing. Chris was right behind me, his hands round my waist, his breath on my neck. He mumbled something about flowers, or super powers, it was hard to tell. What was I up to? This was so unlike me. Dazedly, I headed up to the first-floor landing, Chris still very much in tow. He nearly pulled my dress off on the way up the stairs, and not in a sexy way. He tripped and saved himself by grabbing hold of me. I heard a tearing sound and realized that some part of my blue dress might not have made it.

I got to my door and put the key in. It turned but didn't open. I stared at it, confused, then tried again. Same thing. Then I noticed the frosted window to the side of the door was lit up, the lights were on. That wasn't right. I hadn't left that light on.

I pulled up sharply. 'Oh my God, shhh!' I hissed, inexplicably crouching down on the carpet.

Chris automatically did the same, arms wide, head swivelling left to right.

'Ish this a game?' he asked, his voice slurred. He started giggling.

'Shhh,' I hushed, frantically reaching to put my hand over his mouth and ending up hitting his shoulder, which knocked him backwards onto the floor where he looked like a beetle, his legs still crooked and pointing upwards. Then *I* started giggling. He rolled onto his side and looked at me, his eyes crossing as he tried to focus, cheek against the carpet, face squashed flat.

I stopped laughing. 'It's a burglar,' I explained, mouthing the words and pointing at the window. 'I left the lights off.'

Chris craned his neck to look up at the frosted glass. He didn't sit up.

'What are we going to do?' he whispered.

'He might still be in there,' I said fearfully. 'He's done something to the door so I can't get in. Oh my God. He might still be in there.'

'Let'sh catch him,' Chris said, sitting bolt upright and clapping his hands like a small boy.

'The key doesn't work. I can't get in,' I explained.

'I'll break in, itsh easy,' he whispered, getting up and looking at the door. I joined him, momentarily swaying. Then, clutching his arm, I nodded.

'Do it,' I whispered.

He took his wallet out and fumbled around for a card.

'I've sheen them do this in films all the time,' he whispered confidently, taking time to find the edge of the door. He slid the card down in the gap between the door and the frame, but nothing happened. He tried again, but still nothing happened. I turned away in panic, convinced the burglar would hear us and come and get us with a knife or a gun or something (I'd seen lots of films too). Then, with no prior warning, Chris took a run up, put his shoulder down and smashed through the door. There was a sickening thud as the door came away and Chris staggered in, with me right behind. The living room lights were on.

'Itsh empty,' he announced, spinning round to look at me.

'Shhhh,' I murmured, gesturing over his shoulder. '*He might still be here.*'

I stumbled across the room.

There was a mound on the sofa. The burglar was sleeping? No. But then the burglar started yelling. 'Oh my

God! There's a man in the room! A MAN IN THE ROOM, oh my God.'

It was my brother, not a burglar. I lurched towards him, arms outstretched.

'It's me! Don't worry! I thought *you* were a burglar, Mark, but it'sh you, it'sh not a burglar, it'sh just you, yes, you...' I slurred, going for a hug.

'He'sh my brother, but not a burglar,' I explained to Chris, whilst comforting a terrified Mark. 'We're safe. Everyone is safe.'

The morning light bore down on my eyelids, and a stagnant smell washed over my face. Horrible, horrible morning, and someone was BREATHING on me. I groaned, opened one eye and tried to push the breather away from me. Oh God. Chris. God, why was he here? What the hell was I doing lying next to him? Did something happen last night? I still couldn't move. Another wave of nausea washed over me, my mind a haze of shadowy memories.

I vaguely remembered ordering shots at the bar, but after that, I recalled nothing. I felt like something bad had happened but couldn't quite put my finger on it. Had I done something with Chris? I opened the other eye and noted I was still wearing all my clothes. My dress had twisted round so that one lone breast was poking out, but I didn't have the energy to move. Then my brother appeared in the doorway of my bedroom.

'Mark, what the fuck?' I said, hastily sitting up and trying to cover up the lone breast.

Then I threw up, only just making it to the bathroom in time. When I got back, Mark had disappeared and I flopped back onto the bed. My movements woke Chris. Great. He mumbled something, then groggily opened his eyes. Then closed them. Then opened them really, really wide. Then sat up and shot off the bed, tottered across the room and landed in the armchair opposite me.

'Shit, Nicola, I mean, hi, morning, I mean...' Then he gave up and put his head in his hands. 'My wife is going to kill me.'

I closed my eyes.

Oh God.

CHAPTER TWENTY-SIX

```
Single girl WLTM unmarried
man for quiet nights in.
```

Contact: Box No. 49990

BEFORE CHRISTMAS, James had asked, okay begged, Caroline and I to pop into the office on New Year's Day to deal with an urgent casting the following week. So, after a restorative shower and half a tube of toothpaste I'd dragged my carcass to work where I was now being interrogated by Caroline.

'Chris is married?' she'd repeated in shocked tones after worming the whole sorry story out of me.

'Yes.'

'You know, I think I knew that actually,' said Caroline, sipping at a milkshake.

I gaped at her. 'Something that you could have mentioned before, perhaps?' I suggested.

'Well, I didn't know you were going to go out with him, did I? Anyway, what, Nicola, did you expect of that man? You know I dislike him utterly. Come on, you can't be that surprised? You know he's an arrogant, no-good—'

'Caroline, will you stop talking about me *every* time I leave the office,' said James, emerging in the doorway.

'Ha, ha, ha,' she chuckled as he handed us both tea.

I looked away, not wanting to catch his eye, my face hot as I remembered his surprised expression at the restaurant last night.

'So, who are you ripping to pieces only one day into the New Year?'

'No one,' I said quickly, shooting a warning look in Caroline's direction.

'No one,' she repeated, with a winning smile.

'Hmm... Well, if either of you need me I will be in my office putting up my arrogant, no-good feet and lounging about, of course.'

I watched as he disappeared into his office. He was obviously not going to mention seeing me last night. Maybe he hadn't seen me after all? Maybe he had just been looking over my shoulder at someone else. I really hoped so.

I didn't tell Caroline about seeing James. For some reason, I didn't want to talk to her about it.

Caroline flicked through one of the filing cabinets, emerging with a CV. 'It's Chris's file,' she said, scanning the details.

'Shh,' I scolded, glancing at the door to James' office.

'Oh, look... *married*,' she pointed out helpfully.

I gave her a stony glare.

'Ah, right,' she said, going back to searching his details. 'Hmm, it's as I expected.' She nodded solemnly and put the file back in the cabinet, but not before bending one of Chris's photos and leaving his face horribly creased.

'What is what you expected?'

'His birthday,' she announced. 'It's as I expected.'

'His birthday...?'

'It's in *June*,' she stressed, as if that explained everything perfectly.

'June?'

'Gemini.' She shrugged, smiling widely. 'It explains everything. Chris is a typical Gemini. Typical.'

'Er... this isn't meant to be amusing,' I tutted, annoyed that my life appeared to be an astrological comedy of errors.

'It does explain it, though,' Caroline continued. 'Gemini, the twins, are known to be two-faced, prone to leading a double life. They're interested in everything but can't focus on one thing. Like Trevor in *Brookside* who cheated on his wife.'

'But Chris is nothing like Trevor.'

'No...' she mused. 'But perhaps his moon sign is different?'

'Moon sign?'

'Yes, the sign the moon is in when you are born.'

I looked at her blankly.

'Come on, Nic, don't you read anything? You know you should really take an interest in this stuff. It is fascinating and could save you a lot of trouble. For instance, you're a *Virgo*, so you'd want to find another Earth sign.'

'Like Scorpio?' I said, remembering the ex.

'NOT Scorpio,' she said, halting me with a hand. 'Honestly, Nic. Scorpio is a water sign, like Pisces and Cancer. Scorpio.'

I was really fed up. 'Aquarians are the water-bearers, so I should avoid them, then?' I asked, confused.

'No! They're air, of course.'

Yes, of course. 'Okay, so going back, if I'm a Virgo, what signs should I be looking for?'

'It's not an exact science,' she explained. 'But ideally you would want to look for a Taurus or Capricorn. You wouldn't go far wrong with the Fire signs but do *not* settle for a Sagittarian.'

'Why not?'

'I just wouldn't,' she said, pursing her lips.

'*Why not?*'

'Cheaters,' she stated.

'What, all of them?'

'Yes, all Sagittarians are cheaters,' she said firmly, putting an end to any debate on the matter.

'My mother's a Sagittarian.'

She had the decency to blush.

So it looked like I'd been wasting one sixth of my time. Un-bloody-believable. What was the point of dating people if you were not first armed with this arsenal of facts and potential pitfalls? I logged onto the dating website I'd joined and edited the info. It now stated: 'Geminis and Sagittarians need not apply.'

Three minutes later I received an angry message from user PinkMan687. 'What have you got against Geminis?'

Oh my God. I'm star signist.

I didn't have time to respond to PinkMan687 because James appeared in the doorway to his office. 'Nicola,' he said, not quite meeting my eye as he spoke. 'Could you pop in here and run me through the accounts for the, er...' He mumbled the end of the sentence and I saw a red flush creep up his neck.

'The what, James?' Caroline smirked at him.

'I'm coming,' I said, getting up and self-consciously following him into his office. My palms were a little damp.

James sat at his desk and I sat across from him.

'What did you want me to have a look at?' I asked.

He pushed a piece of paper across to me and my mouth fell open. I had no words. James sat back in his chair and grinned at me.

'I can't accept this,' I said in disbelief.

'What are you talking about, Nicola? You earned it.'

'Nooo, it's too much,' I protested, sliding the cheque with my Christmas bonus back across to him.

'Take it,' he said, gently nudging it towards me. 'You've been fantastic, both of you have, and I've given the same percentage to Caroline. You've both worked hard all year for it.'

'I... thank you,' I said, trying to be graceful.

'Anyway, looks like you'll need it now that you are wining and dining our best client.' He laughed, shuffling papers on his desk. It sounded shorter and louder than his usual laugh.

So he *had* seen me.

'It was just dinner,' I blurted.

'Of course, not for me to judge. I was always under the impression that you weren't a particular fan of Chris, but—'

'I'm not,' I interjected, wondering why I even felt the need to clarify it.

'It's none of my business anyway.' James shrugged casually.

'Quite,' I said, regretting my crisp tone when I saw his face, like I'd said something cruel enough to make the smile fade from his eyes.

My breathing felt loud and my hands were curled tightly around the cheque. James opened and shut his mouth as if he were about to say something else. It never came. I got up to leave.

'Is that everything?' I asked curtly.

'Yes,' he croaked.

'Well, I'll get back to work then,' I said, feeling the burning sensation of tears behind my eyes. 'Thank you, James, for the... just, thanks,' I said, closing the door behind me.

Caroline looked up as I appeared, a frown deepening the lines round her eyes. 'Is something wrong, my lovely?'

I plastered a smile on my face, forcing my mouth to turn up at the edges. 'Fine,' I announced. 'I'm absolutely fine.'

CHAPTER TWENTY-SEVEN

> Single girl WLTM man with
> similar interests. She
> loves: carpentry.
> **Contact: Box No. 5902**

IT WAS the evening of the carpentry class and as I parked the car outside Frenchay College, I took a good long look at myself in the rear-view mirror. The last few days had been quiet in the office and I had barely glimpsed James. Tonight would be a chance to do something different and I was ready to test out my new idea. Rubbing at a dash of mascara that had settled on my eyelid and licking my glossy pink lips, I realized I might have overdone my look. I peered down at the carefully selected outfit. In the full-length mirror in my flat, a lumberjack checked shirt and dungarees had seemed an excellent choice. Now, I realized I looked like a female Bob the Builder, albeit with excellent long lashes and a very pouty smile. Too late now. Taking a breath, I undid my seat belt, stepped out of the car, grabbed my bag and jogged towards the entrance.

I poked my head round the door of Classroom 12B. This was the place. Long, empty tables were arranged in lines down the big room. The strip lighting highlighted a thin layer of orange dust on the surface. Numerous tools were scattered about unattended. The room was empty of people, bar a lone man with his back to me, leaning over what (I would later discover) was called a 'workbench', doing something with a 'tenon saw' and a plank of wood. I coughed lightly, my heart hammering at the prospect of the hour ahead. The sound made the man look up from his work. He frowned momentarily, glanced surreptitiously at the clock just above my head and, finally, broke into a smile.

'You must be Nicola.'

'I'm early, I'm sorry.' I started flapping my hands. 'I can wait outside.' I turned to head back into the corridor.

'Don't be silly! It'll be good to show you the ropes before the rest appear, so you don't feel too at sea on your first day. Just let me finish this. Choose a workbench and pop one of them on over your clothes.'

He pointed to a row of pegs lined with aprons. I unhooked one and approached a workbench in the middle of the room, poking my head through the string on the apron and tying it at the back. I flung my handbag on the floor by the radiator.

The man strolled over, holding out his hand. 'Tom. Thanks for enrolling.'

I took it and shook. He was wearing jeans and a T-shirt underneath an apron that matched mine. He had reddish hair and a thick beard that seemed flecked with sawdust. His hands were enormous and he smelled like hard work and beeswax.

'Now, don't be alarmed, but this class is quite er... male-heavy.'

'That's what I expected,' I said, a little too enthusiastically. I turned red.

'Yes, well, not to worry. I'm sure you will be made to feel welcome. They're a good bunch, mostly beginners and all at varying stages with different projects on the go.'

I nodded along.

'So, what inspired you to take up carpentry, then?' he asked.

I'd practised my answer in the car on the drive over. 'I want to be able to make something, create something from scratch, something, um, beautiful.'

'Sounds good to me. The guys here range from those who want to be able to do basic woodwork without shaming themselves, to Clive who wants to build his own boat. Friendly advice: Do NOT get onto the subject of sailing in front of him unless you have a spare couple of hours to hand.'

I laughed and mentally deleted Clive from my list.

Tom spent five minutes setting me up for the class ahead, fetching the planks and tools I'd need. It looked like a bewildering array of items. I must have looked nervous because Tom reached across and gave my shoulder a squeeze. 'Good luck.'

*

As the rest of the group filed into the room I found myself humming the theme music to *Blind Date* for a moment, expecting Cilla to appear, her great orange bouffant quivering, as she pointed at me and shouted: 'Nicola from Bristol is here to snare a man, so who is going to be the nuts to her bolt?' By the time the last man arrived, I was wondering quite what I'd been thinking when I'd signed up for this class. Of course, I couldn't just pretend to have lots of masculine interests in the hope of finding the man of my dreams. Tom presented me with a plank of wood just a fraction taller than me and I took it hesitantly.

'Some of them have had a good few lessons now, but not to worry, you'll catch up in no time. In fact, Alex will show you how to mark out your wood, won't you, Alex?'

'I'd be delighted,' came the reply. A tall man with curly light brown hair and pronounced dimples turned and smiled at me. A light spattering of grey hair placed him in his thirties and the shirt and tie under the apron suggested he had a respectable job. I looked at him and flashed a smile that I'd also practised in the car on the way over.

'Great.' I was fairly sure my lashes were fluttering.

'First you've got to cut this thing into two,' Alex said kindly. 'I nearly took my hand off with the tenon saw last week so I'll start you off. I could do with the practice.'

'Thanks,' I said, stepping aside so that he could work.

'You slot it into this thing, can't for the life of me remember what it's called but it keeps the wood still. And then you cut it down towards you, it's more effective apparently, and also safer. Well, that's what Tom told me *after* I nearly lost my hand.'

He looked up from the wood and mock-frowned at Tom.

'Right, Nicola, there you go. I'll leave you to do the hard bit, I can't be trusted round this thing.' He indicated the saw. 'When you've done that I'll show you how to mark out your wood for the next bit.'

'Um, thanks.'

Alex moved away, seemingly oblivious to the impact he had made. He had a great arse...

CONCENTRATE, Nicola. You have a tray to make.

As promised, Alex showed me how to mark out the wood. 'If you want to make a line two centimetres from the edge, you do this. Then you can run it up and score a line into the wood. This will show you where your cut will be.'

He pointed at various sections and I used these moments as an excuse to glance at his ring finger. No ring. Feeling encouraged, I spent the rest of the class quietly working, enjoying the logical process, seeing the project coming together in stages. We were doing something with rebate joints when Tom announced that the lesson was over. I headed back to my car, realizing, as I drove away, that I was grinning. I was still smiling as I ate dinner, as I brushed my teeth and as I lay in bed. But it wasn't Alex's face in my happy mind's eye. All I saw were my little planks of wood, all lined up together, my tenon saw resting nearby, my workbench covered in sawdust, and the sound of clapping as the guys in the class congratulated me.

CHAPTER TWENTY-EIGHT

WAKING GROGGILY from an amazing night's sleep, my stomach plummeted as I read the clock with one eye. 8.34 a.m. was NOT A GOOD TIME. My morning routine flew out of the window as I raced round the apartment and then down the stairs and into the street. I was going to be late to the office. Late. I was NEVER late. This didn't happen to me. The small hole in my tights, which I'd made when hoisting them hastily up my legs, had turned into an ugly ladder scarring one calf. With no time to pick up spares – *why* hadn't I remembered to pack them in my handbag? – I pushed open the door to our office and thundered up the stairs.

'I'm sorry, I'm sorry I'm late but I'm... standing alone in the office,' I said, looking round the room and registering the fact that no one else was there. Laughing, I scooped up the post and then noticed the flash of the answerphone. I hit loudspeaker.

'You have six new messages.'

I raised my eyebrows. This was going to be a long day. I could feel it.

Number one was a frantic message from Caroline.

'I'm sorry, I'm sorry, I'm sorry, I'm going to be late. Ben is off school with tonsillitis or some such vile disease...'

'Mummmm...'

'Shh, not now, Benjamin, I'm on the phone... So I'm waiting for the babysitter to turn up. Should be soon, sorry, Nic, call me later...'

Oh dear. Poor Caroline. I pictured Ben milking the situation for all it was worth, hugs, kisses, jelly, lots of cooling ice cream, and smiled.

The second, equally frantic message was from James.

'Good morning-team, I'm heading up to Birmingham today for a last-minute meeting with John from Earpiece Productions. It's a lunch meeting and the man can drink, so I'm taking the train just in case. If I haven't returned by this evening, call all the A & Es round Birmingham as I imagine I'll be having my stomach pumped. Adios, senoritas, don't let the office burn to the ground in my absence. Bye.'

I rolled my eyes and ripped open the first of the post that day. The third answerphone message made me freeze in my tracks. A loud, impatient voice filled the office.

'James, this is Glenn. Where the hell is Lydia? We've set up the shoot and she was given a call time of seven a.m. She better be on her way...'

Christ. Glenn. Glenn was scary. He was the agency's biggest client over at Lime Productions and was shooting a series of adverts for a mobile phone company. He'd been using all our actresses and actors and he was, as Caroline put it, 'the bread on our table', or 'our bread and butter', or, oh, something about bread. Either way he was important. And pissed off.

'*James, for Christ's sake, where is she? We are ready to go, everyone is here, get her down here now.*'

We couldn't lose his business. James had spent weeks, no months, courting Glenn. He'd returned from meeting after meeting drained but exuberant. Glenn was demanding but loyal.

'*James, I don't need to tell you that I am losing my patience. If she isn't here within the hour we will be looking elsewhere. And not just for this job.*'

I'd heard enough. I grabbed the 'Bookings' file and flicked through to today's list. Lydia was meant to be in a town-centre studio an hour and a half ago. I grabbed the phone and dialled 1471. Private number.

'Damn,' I cursed, slamming the phone down.

I could make it. I could go in person and apologize. I could sort this out.

I yanked open the filing cabinet and leafed through to Lydia's CV and details. There she was. I'd ring her on my way. I picked up my keys and raced out of the door.

Huffing, I reached the studio door less than eight minutes later, and then hopped from one foot to another, waiting for someone to buzz me in.

'Hello,' I breathed down the intercom. 'The Sullivan Agency, I'm...' I took a breath, but the buzzer went off and I was in.

I raced to the reception desk. 'Hi, morning, I'm from

240

the Sullivan Agency and I'm—'

'LYDIA,' came a roar from behind me.

A large man dressed in an expensive grey suit was bearing down on me. His nostrils flared as he shouted at me. 'You are nearly two hours late. What the hell are you thinking? We need to shoot this thing now. We're bleeding money, every minute we—'

'Oh no,' I interjected. I'm not Ly—'

'There's no time for apologies or excuses. Follow me,' he bellowed, marching off. He made it three steps before spinning back round. 'I thought you had long hair?' he barked.

'Well, no, you see the thing is—'

'PAUL!' he yelled to a bespectacled man I assumed to be the director (he was sitting in the director's chair looking at a camera). 'I thought you said she had long hair?'

'She did,' Paul said, turning pale as he took me in. He frowned and rubbed his head, 'She... did...'

'I'm not—'

'It doesn't matter now. I think I actually prefer it. Right, get the girl into her clothes and let's get this thing moving. I need to be out of here by lunch, this place costs a damn fortune!' Glenn strode off to yell at some poor runner nearby.

'Um... excuse me,' I said into the ether. Everyone seemed busy, looking at monitors, checking cables or being yelled at by Glenn.

A girl with cropped hair and a tiny nose ring came rushing forward and took my coat and Lydia's CV from me.

'Nice photo,' she smiled, glancing at it briefly. 'You look

younger in the flesh, ooh, you've done a stint on *Casualty*, how exciting,' she said, running off with the CV.

'Oh no, I... I'm not...'

Before I could call after her, I was spun round by an enormous woman with a sizeable chest and tight blonde curls. 'I'm Pauline, wardrobe, you had us worried there. Now, we've got some great outfits for you today so follow me.' She pushed open a nearby door which led to a room lined with racks of clothes. 'MAKE-UP,' she screamed suddenly, making me jump.

'Well, you see, actually —'

'Arms,' she said, signalling that I should raise them.

Uncertainly, I lifted my arms. 'You see, Pauline, I think there might be a little confusion,' I babbled into the material as it was tugged over my face.

'Hmm...' she muttered, rummaging through the clothes rack. 'I thought you were a 36B but those puppies look bigger.'

I crossed my arms over my chest self-consciously. The urge to confess ebbed as I realized I really didn't have an alternative plan. I hadn't even called Lydia. Where was she? Oh God, where was I? What was I doing? It wasn't even nine in the morning and I was semi-naked, being prodded by Pauline and about to pretend to be an actress in an advert I knew nothing about.

Pauline whipped round. 'Your first outfit is a one-piece so take off your trousers and we'll get you into it.'

'Um, right, yes,' I said, not really understanding what she'd just told me, but understanding enough to realize that

I was soon about to be standing in this room dressed only in my bra and pants. The only comforting thought was that they matched.

'Right, we got you these.' She produced a pair of red shoes that seemed so teeny tiny that Tinkerbell herself could have worn them.

'Oh no, I'm a seven,' I explained before anyone tried to jam my feet into them.

'Well, they'll be a tight fit then!'

I bent down and attempted to cram my oversized feet into the delicate little shoes. My heels were hanging over the side. Both my little toes were peeking out at strange angles. Pauline sighed crossly and grabbed her notebook. 'It says here you're a four,' she said, consulting the pages.

'No, they, um, well you see, the thing is—'

'Doesn't matter,' she said whipping them off me. 'I'll get Chloe to find you something out back. CHLOE!' she screamed to the poor runner Glenn was yelling at earlier.

'Yes.' Chloe dashed over.

'Can you go out back and find me something in a seven that would go with the catsuit? Preferably in red? Boots maybe...'

'The what suit?' I gasped, as Chloe raced back off.

'Catsuit,' she repeated as my jaw dropped open.

'Well, what did you expect superheroes to wear?' she asked, smiling for the first time.

'Superheroes? Oh right, okay, right, fine, yup, OKAY,' I babbled, really starting to panic now. Where was Lydia?! What was I doing? This was way out of my job remit!

Glenn appeared in the doorway. My hands flew up and I desperately tried to cover as much of my naked body as I humanly could.

'Pauline, we need her in five,' he barked, oblivious to my humiliation.

'She needs make-up, Glenn,' Pauline said, indicating for me to step into the catsuit she was holding out.

'How long then?' he grumbled.

'Ten,' she called over her shoulder.

'Ten minutes max,' he said, striding out again.

'Rosaline will be doing your make-up,' Pauline said as I squeezed myself into the catsuit. It clung to every single curve of my body. I breathed in as she did up the zip at the back. 'We can straighten your hair, that will be quicker,' she said, smoothing a piece of hair down behind my ear.

Suddenly, the double doors to my left burst open and an older woman with iron-grey hair down to her bottom and dressed in a flowery shirt and navy blue culottes appeared, clapped her hands and stalked over towards me. 'What a beautiful face,' she said, raising my chin.

'No time for that, Rosaline. Glenn wants her asap, we're almost done here,' Pauline said through a mouthful of pins.

'PAULINE!' came Glenn's cry.

'Christ, we're coming,' she whispered, as she plunged a couple of the pins into the back of the Lycra catsuit so that skin-tight was now no longer an accurate description. Second skin was more apt. I looked down in horror, sucking my stomach in a little more.

Rosaline muttered as she pushed her make-up cart

towards a stool and mirror. 'What does that man think I can do in a few short minutes? Magic takes time.' She rubbed foundation between her hands. 'Right, darling, come and sit here. We'll make you look dazzling, asap,' she said, rolling her eyes at Pauline over my head.

I could do little but gulp at her and sit down. I felt sick.

Half an hour later I was waiting nervously off camera, dressed in a bright red skin-tight Lycra catsuit, complete with white go-faster stripes down the left side. My feet were encased in shiny PVC thigh-high boots. My hair was poker-straight and tied into a high ponytail. My face was clear and powdered. My eyebrows were shaped, my eyes were smudged with black eye shadow and thick liner, and I was biting down on my lower lip which was covered in a luscious scarlet-red lipgloss.

Paul, the director, whose cheeks had regained a marginal bit of colour, was explaining my next move. I was to run across to the camera, look left, look right, confidently, bravely. Paul had been great. He clearly knew I wasn't Lydia but seemed intent on continuing with the charade, as keen to avoid losing his job with Glenn as I was to keep Glenn's business. We were partners-in-crime.

The blue screen behind me would apparently be filled with images of a devastated street in some downtown part of a city in America: hastily parked cars, tumbledown buildings, etc., but for now it was just an enormous square of blue. There were yellow crosses marked on the black floor to show me where I needed to run in from, where I should stop and where I should run to. At some point I had to pretend to pick up the back end of a car, but for now it was just a lot of running into shot and out again, looking urgent. In my mind, I was back in the office pretending the fax had broken and that the printer on the other side of the room had started smoking. These dastardly office scenarios were clearly doing the trick as, before long, Glenn was yelling 'Cut!' Rosaline hurried over to powder my nose. 'You are gorgeous, darling. I'm barely earning my money today.'

Six hours later I was out of the catsuit and back in the office, with most of the make-up still on my face. Caroline was bustling about, having managed to rope her mother-in-law into babysitting. 'She tried to claim that she had bridge, but I know they only meet on Wednesdays. Honestly, the *witch*.' She was so distracted, she hadn't asked where I'd been all day and for that I felt grateful. I was not ready to talk about it. Maybe I never would be.

'Poor little lamb. I'm glad I have tomorrow off so I can mother him senseless. That always gets him tearing back to school...'

'Hmm...'

'He's already requested his favourite dinner tonight. McDonald's. But I won't cave. I won't, I... Nic? Nicola?'

'Hmm...' I murmured, distracted.

'Are you all right? You're being strange,' she said, eyebrows meeting in the middle. 'Actually, where have you been? And what's with all the smoky eye make-up?' she added. 'Ooh, have you been dating in your lunchbreak?'

'No.' I laughed. 'No. I, I have to go and see about some office supplies,' I finished.

'That doesn't answer my question about the smoky eyes.' Caroline frowned. 'Oooh, is the receptionist at the office supplies place good-looking? Do you fancy him?'

I ignored her and clicked open my emails.

'Are you seeing someone involved in selling stationery items?' she continued, giggling. 'Are you attracted to a man who knows his compass from his protractor?'

I ignored her again.

There was an email from Lydia. A long and rambling email that explained she'd lost her mobile and hadn't known our phone number and she'd had a big row with her boyfriend, etc., etc. I scrolled down quickly. She had been worried that he was 'going to do something stupid' so she had spent the morning with him, and now – I was *so* relieved to read – 'they had resolved their issues'. Phew.

I hit 'Reply' and assured Lydia that the job had been covered 'by another actress'. Then I deleted 'actress' and replaced it with 'person'. I finished by saying that I doubted we would be using her again as her behaviour had been unprofessional and made the agency look bad.

Moments later, James appeared in the doorway. His jacket was clean, his shirt was smooth, his eyes were not blurry and drunken.

Caroline looked at him. 'You're fine!' she pointed out.

He cheered. 'I survived. It's a first! It's dry January, which is like Lent or something, so we had mineral water,' he explained. 'Incredible.'

He shook his head and walked towards his office. He stopped abruptly at my desk and peered at me. 'Nicola, you look different.' He cocked his head to one side.

'Do I?'

'Hmm... yeah. Oh, um, Caroline,' he said, still staring at me. 'Can you get me the contact info for whoever is in charge of casting at Lime Productions?'

I squirmed in my seat.

'Shall do, boss,' she said, spinning round to search on the desk behind her.

'Good,' James said, walking into his office. He turned back once more and caught my eye.

'I'll help you look,' I called to Caroline, banging my knee on the desk in my haste to stand up.

The day couldn't end a moment too soon, and as the clock's hand clicked round to the '6', I stood up and reached for my bag. James' voice called from the office. 'Nicola, can you get in here please?'

Feeling like I'd been summoned to the headmaster's office, I took a moment to abandon my handbag, straighten my skirt and pull my jumper down.

I pushed open the door to James' office.

'Yes?'

James was at his desk, the usual semicircle of paper surrounded him and he was just putting the phone back in its cradle.

'I've just had Glenn on the phone giving me an earful about today. Apparently Lydia was horribly late.'

'Oh yes, she was, she was very late,' I parroted.

'Late?' James wrinkled his brow.

'Yes, but she got there in the end.'

'She got there in the end?' He narrowed his eyes.

I shifted my weight to my other foot and pushed the nails of one hand into the other palm.

'Yes, it was all fine in the end.'

'So why have I just received a long, emotional email from Lydia begging me not to take her off our books?' He indicated the screen of his computer.

I was suddenly distracted by something out of the window beyond him. 'Oh, look! A... woman. You very rarely see... those kind of women nowadays...'

'So who did you send, Nicola?' he asked. 'Who did the job?'

'The job? The job instead of Lydia?' I said, my voice getting unreasonably loud.

'Yes.' James sighed, raking a hand through his hair.

My chest felt tight. My head felt cloudy. Was this what it felt like to have a heart attack because I might be having one.

'Um... I...' I was flailing. I knew I was. All sorts of answers churned over in my mind, followed by humiliating images of me, making a fool of myself in a bright red, skin-tight catsuit. *Be Brave, Nicola. Brave.*

'Who was it? Glenn loved her...'

This information sank in, slowly, pushed aside the other images in my brain.

Glenn loved her...

'Oh!' I exploded. James started in his chair. 'That's great, GREAT news.'

I turned to leave.

'Wait, Nicola, so who was it?'

'It was... Sam,' I said, spinning back round. 'It was Sam. She's great, just excellent.'

'Right. Well, the agency will be getting the cheque so we'll need to forward it on to this Sam. I don't remember her,' he said, nose wrinkling.

'Oh, she's done some other stuff in the past, small things, you know?' I shrugged, not meeting his eye.

'Well, thank you – you and this Sam have officially saved my day.'

My palms were slippery but I managed to register his comment and smile. 'Not at all. And er... is that everything?' I asked.

'Yes, that's great, thanks, Nic. Not a surprise that you had it all sorted. I can't wait to see the footage, Glenn's going to forward it on after the edit, so let me know when it arrives.'

I froze in the doorway.

There was a pause.

'Will do,' I said, closing my eyes and walking back through to my desk.

CHAPTER TWENTY-NINE

I WASN'T A big drinker but it was days like this when a jug of 'Singapore Sling' really was the only thing for it. I shook the ice cubes into the bottom, grabbed the gin from the bottom of the dresser and poured in a good amount. A good amount if I were having a party and four more guests were arriving at any moment. I took the cherry brandy and poured that on top, shook in some Angostura bitters, squeezed a half of lime and threw it in, and then topped up the jug with ginger ale, which instantly fizzed to the top creating a thin layer of foam.

Seizing a hi-ball glass, and with a slightly shaking hand, I poured in the mixture.

Then I put everything on a tray (I was having steak with fried onions – it had been years), walked through to the living room, switched on the television and perched at the table, simultaneously flicking through channels and drinking the cocktail.

As I was scraping the last onion from the plate, and pouring myself a third glass in about as many minutes, my mobile rang.

'Hey, Mark,' I answered.

'Hey yourself. Long day?'

'You could say that.'

'Anything unusual happen?'

'No, just work... the usual. How about you?' I asked screaming 'deflect, deflect' in my mind.

It worked. We covered: Carol, the possible discovery of a new breed of bat in South America ('Can you imagine, Nic, that guy gets to NAME it!'), and the fact that he had given up drinking for January.

I poured myself a fourth glass. 'James said that his client is having a dry Ja—'

Mark interrupted with a wolf whistle. I instantly went quiet.

'Carry on, sis, what did James say?'

'Nothing,' I snapped.

'No, really, sis, what did he say?'

'Well, he said that his—'

Mark whistled again.

'Mark, stop it.'

'*What?* I'm just happy for you, sis.'

'Well, there is nothing to be happy about so stop whistling.'

'Okay.'

There was a pause.

'But Jaaaaaammeess clearly said something interesting.' He started laughing.

'Mark, stop it, we're not eleven.'

He stopped laughing. 'If I'd been born three days later, I would be.'

'What?'

'It was a leap year.'

'What?'

'So I'd be eleven if I'd been born then.'

'What?'

'I'm just saying.'

'Okay, I'm hanging up on you now, Mark.'

'Oh, fine. So you can go back to Jaaaammm—'

Hanging up the phone, I rested my head back on the cushions. Why was Mark so quick to tease me about James? Had I been speaking about him a lot? I thought back to our conversations at Christmas and in recent weeks. I suppose his name had come up. But surely it was only natural I would talk about him. We worked together every day. We spent a lot of time together. James was with Thalia anyway. I wouldn't ever get in the way of that. *Idiot brother*.

My ex's face swam before me once more. A long, straight nose, thick blonde hair, arms wrapped round someone who wasn't me, someone who I had considered a friend. I blinked as I thought of her now, shiny hair, clothes in bright splashes of colour, a confident laugh, head cocked to one side when I had accused her. Their denials, and then her tears as she admitted everything. That they hadn't been able to help themselves. That he hadn't told her he had asked me to marry him.

I clutched the glass in my hand. I had hated him, hated her too, and now I was scared that I was becoming her. Thinking about someone else's man, someone I had no right to think about. I didn't want to be that girl. Nothing had happened, I told myself. Mark was just making me paranoid. He was teasing.

I flicked through the TV channels and scolded myself for overthinking things. I wasn't that girl. But I'd be more careful from now on.

CHAPTER THIRTY

IT WAS our annual clients' gathering and I'd been running late all day. Racing home, I jumped into the shower, pulled on an outfit and took some straighteners to my hair. Eyeliner, I thought, as I grabbed the pencil. Eyeliner could sort out all problems. I carefully drew the liner across the bottom of my lashes and grabbed some coral lipgloss to complete the effect. It would do. I called a cab and left the apartment building, with a cheery wave at Julio.

An hour and a half later I was standing round a tall circular table crammed with dirty pint glasses and smiling politely at the collection of people in the room. James had been there all evening but I had skirted round him, refusing to be drawn into conversation and carefully ensuring I kept my distance. Thalia had appeared in a rather agitated state halfway through and I'd seen James usher her outside, where they had gesticulated madly under the canopy. Were they arguing? I scolded myself for spying on them and turned back to the guests.

Some of our clients stayed on late and I played hostess, introducing people and making sure no one was left on their own. I'd momentarily panicked when Caroline had left, but they'd all been really friendly and I'd warmed to the role. Later on in the evening, I saw Thalia leaving, James guiding her out with one hand on her back. Catching my eye as he opened the door, I gave him a brief wave. Thalia, fastening up her jacket, followed his gaze and gave me a curt nod.

Then it was just me, in my little black pencil dress and brand-new red heels. A couple of men had attempted to take advantage of my single status earlier in the evening and I was surprised by how unbothered I'd been by the attention. For the last five minutes I'd been answering the questions of a man dressed in jeans and a T-shirt that announced: 'Don't Sweat It, Baby' which, ironically, had large, yellowing sweat patches under each arm. He had very blow-dried hair for a man. He worked in recruitment but played the lute in his free time and liked to dabble in ferret breeding. So, a catch.

I was busy wondering whether to try a Moscow Mule or whether to head home when I thought I heard him say something about the female ferret dying if she didn't mate.

'I'm sorry.' I leant forward, certain I must have misheard.

'Yes, exactly. She dies!' he confirmed.

I realized he actually was talking about ferret sex.

I started to look around worriedly for someone to get me out of this mess. Perhaps a helpful barmaid would show pity on me? No one in the vicinity looked remotely bothered by my predicament and I couldn't think of a polite way to untangle myself from this man. I didn't want to be rude but I also didn't really want the details of—

'—that can then cause bone marrow suppression, and in certain ferrets this can lead to non-regenerative anaemia, and ultimately death.'

Aggghhh.

Then, as if God himself had answered my call, I saw James push back through the doors of the bar. I didn't hesitate.

'James,' I yelped at him, with a half-wave that didn't look unlike the last attempt of a drowning woman.

Sweaty Man stopped mid-sentence, brow furrowed.

'James,' I repeated, nodding at him encouragingly as he approached us.

'James, how *are* you?' I called, my glare getting more insistent. Sweaty Man, realizing he was in no imminent danger, chose that moment to continue his chat.

'So, you see the female actually *dies* if she doesn't mate,' he stressed, a serious glint in his eye and a lingering gaze up and down my body. I shivered.

Then James's voice piped up. 'Oh my God, is that you?'

He moved closer towards me. My shoulders sagged in relief.

He continued, 'I'm sorry I didn't recognize you with that... that...,' he paused, started to flounder. I nodded at him, willing him to continue.

'That um.... Hair,' he said pointing at my head.

Good work.

I smiled at him. 'Oh yes,' I said, patting my hair. 'It's a new look, I decided to... to... clip it back,' I finished triumphantly.

Sweaty Man stared at my hair, then at James and then at me.

'It looks nice,' James continued, leaning in for a hug.

It was my turn to look surprised as we embraced, and he whispered, 'That okay?'

'Oh, I've got so much to tell you, James,' I said, patting him playfully on the chest.

I turned to Sweaty Man. 'I am so sorry but James and I go way back, do you mind?' And with that, Sweaty Man, realizing defeat, turned and left.

'Thank you, thank you, thank you,' I gushed, spinning back to James and smiling madly. 'I'm absurdly grateful.'

'I'm absurdly confused,' he replied. 'Drink?'

'Definitely.'

I turned and saw Sweaty Man standing in the queue at the bar.

I turned back to James. 'Er, maybe not here?'

James took me to a tiny little bar down a side road off Park Street. I removed my coat and looked around the room. The walls were lined with old photographs of musicians, some signed, most in black and white, low glass-topped tables had been placed next to enormous ageing leather sofas, tea lights flickered on every surface, and the murmur of chatter rose in a crescendo as we pushed through to the bar.

He ordered us drinks and insisted on paying. 'Nic, it was a *free bar*, things must have got bad to have left.'

I settled back into the sofa, aware that my dress had inched up to flash a good few inches of thigh. I attempted to smooth the skirt down, with little result.

A man in a trilby hat dragged a stool out from the corner,

set himself next to the microphone and started to gently sing. I sighed, resting my head back on the sofa, and closed my eyes for a second.

'Better?' James laughed.

I opened one eye and nodded at him. 'Much.'

He was wearing a black cashmere jumper over some brown cord trousers, slightly worn at the knee. He sank into the leather seat, looking like a wealthy aristocrat back from walking the hounds. I blinked, realizing I might have been staring.

He leant forward. 'Cheers.' We clinked glasses. 'I'm glad I could rescue you.'

We listened to the music in companionable silence, enjoying the warm atmosphere and the relaxed talk around us. Over in the other corner, a couple laughed, the man reaching across the table, without thinking, to take her hand. I smiled at the moment. James was looking at them too, an unreadable expression on his face. He turned to me. I lifted the straw to my lips, sipping distractedly.

My mind was suddenly fired up with questions. Why had he come back to the party? Where was Thalia? I opened my mouth, then closed it again, not sure whether I should ask, not knowing if I wanted to know. We were just colleagues, I reminded myself. It wasn't any of my business. His private life was private and I couldn't presume anything. He was just being friendly because we worked together. Nothing was happening.

I was brought out of my thoughts by the fact that the singing guy had removed the mike from its stand and was now at our table, holding it out to us.

'Er, James,' I hissed out of the corner of my mouth. 'What's he doing here?'

James looked as alarmed as I felt and hissed back, 'I think it's open mic night.'

The guy nodded encouragingly and thrust the mic towards James. 'Little song, my friend?'

James leaned into the microphone. 'Oh, a song. Right, yes, well.' He paused, hand flying up to loosen a non-existent tie. Then he caught my eye and a slow smile spread across his face. He took the microphone and cleared his throat. 'You'll be pleased to hear that I am with a wonderful amateur actress who I am certain can sing too.' He turned to me with a shrug of his shoulders. I was aghast as James continued. 'But she's shy about her talent and will need some encouragement.'

The couple in the corner started banging their fists on the table, cheering and smiling over at us.

My mouth was agape, my drink wobbled dangerously in my hand.

I made a noise between a yelp and a gurgle.

James turned to me and held out a hand. 'Come on, Nicola. Show the crowd what you can do.'

'But I—'

'Hey, I know you can do it. Glenn sent me the footage of the ad. You looked amaz... you looked good.' He coughed. 'And so confident! I've heard you sing in the office when you make tea.' He stopped, and a hint of red crept up his neck. 'You can do it.'

As if seeing myself from above, I got up, knees shaking, and took the microphone from him. As I moved towards the little raised platform in the corner of the bar, James' words ran right through me. I stepped onto the stage.

I think James must have mentioned my name because people were calling out 'Nicola!' in an encouraging way.

I stood by the microphone and looked at my audience. All eyes swivelled towards me. I leant into the microphone, eyes now down at the floor, expectant bodies around me. I opened my mouth... And no words came out.

I looked with wide eyes over at James who had sat back in the leather sofa and was giggling ridiculously. The sight of his enjoyment gave me a surge of strength. An idea emerged as I saw him clutching his side in mirth. I looked out at my audience, not quite the size of Wembley but to me just as terrifying.

I cleared my throat. 'Tonight is an exciting evening for us all as I am thrilled to announce that I will be performing a rare duet with my equally reluctant singing partner, James.' I then stood back, started to clap, and the room joined in. It was my turn to giggle as James spat a mouthful of his drink back into his glass. I was having fun now. I put a hand on my hip, waggled a finger at him. 'Don't be shy now, James.'

Everyone in the room was clapping as he slowly pulled himself up off the sofa to join me.

'You minx,' he whispered out of reach of the microphone.

'You started it,' I replied out of the corner of my mouth, turning once more to the crowd and giving them an enormous dazzling smile.

'So what are we singing, James?' I held the microphone out to him.

'I think we should sing "Something Stupid", Nicola.'

The music started up, and together, we sang.

Two hours later we were stumbling out of the bar, patted heartily on the back by the host of the open mic night, being nodded and smiled at by perfect strangers and replaying our moment in the limelight. The cute couple walked past, grinning. The man called out, 'Good times!' and slung an arm round his girlfriend, nodding at us they walked away. The street was practically empty, a couple of last-minute stragglers wandering off to the kebab shop on the corner. The windows in the apartments were all dark. The city was sleeping. It felt like we were the only people awake and the thought made me suddenly aware of myself, like the magic had worn off.

'Shall I walk you home?' James asked.

'I'm fine, thank you. I'll jump in a taxi.'

I hailed the first cab I saw, barely glancing at James as I told the driver where I was headed, opened the door and stepped inside. I was sitting on the smooth leather of the taxi seat when I looked back at him. He was standing on the pavement looking straight at me. A question dying on his lips.

Hours later I was still staring at the ceiling of my flat. Kicking off the duvet, I turned over and plumped the pillow for the eighteenth time. Why was I so restless? Images of the evening swam before me every time I closed my eyes and I froze guiltily. It had been nothing more than a friendly drink. I mustn't read too much into it. James was taken, and not even interested in me. We had nothing in common particularly, nothing much at all. I mean, we laughed at the same things, but surely lots of people laughed at things, things could be funny. And I only felt so relaxed around him because I was used to him. It was nothing more and I shouldn't be fretting about it. I should sleep now, I should go to sleep.

'... *And then I go and spoil it all by saying something stupid like I love you...*'

Gah.

Following a night of broken dreams, I woke up extra early and headed into work. I squeaked a hello at James who was so completely *normal* with me it only served to show how right I had been about there being nothing between us. I needed to get on and meet other people, and keep on track with the search.

In a flurry of activity that afternoon, I booked some things to do, activities where I could meet a good man. Valentine's Day was approaching fast and I wanted to ensure I had a date on that day. I needed an entire day of masculine-type activities. Man Stuff. I noted the nearby greasy spoon cafe opening times and found a golf course. It was a start.

CHAPTER THIRTY-ONE

THE DAY of Doing Man Stuff dawned and, as if in celebration, it was sunny. First, I was heading to the cafe for a full fry-up, which I would eat whilst reading the sports pages. Then I was going to the driving range, where I would hit some balls, then I would head to the supermarket to hang around the Car Magazine section and then, if all that failed, I would head to a sports-themed pub for a pint and some pork scratchings. This plan was foolproof. I looked for holes. I could think of none. I would ensnare a man, I would entrap a bloke, I would capture a member of the male species, I would—

'Weird mantra, sis.'

A head popped round the bathroom door and I realized I had said those last bits aloud.

'Get out, Mark,' I said to his reflection in the mirror.

'Righty ho.' The head disappeared.

A call came from down the corridor. 'I hope you are successful at entrapping a bloke, or that a member of the male species is captured.'

On a mission, I felt energized as I pushed into the greasy cafe at the end of my road. The windows had steamed up and the whole place smelt like bacon. I approached the coffee-stained counter and ordered a Full English Breakfast. Sliding into one of the wooden booths, I wondered why I had never been here before.

I pulled the paper from my bag and pretended to read, really surreptitiously searching the cafe for potential victims. I mean men. My fellow diners were a varied bunch: girl in hoodie, couple holding hands over waffles (they looked too close for siblings, so he was obviously taken), single man with back to me (it was broad. Broad might have been a polite way of putting it – but he went on the list) and two guys on stools, chatting by the counter. It was hard to get a good look at them without drawing attention to myself but I deduced that one of them had long red hair tied into a ponytail and the one facing me had a large tattoo on his face. I returned my focus to the broad-shouldered man in the booth opposite, willing his tanned, potentially gorgeous visage to turn towards me. He shifted in his seat and I hastily looked down at the paper, only then realizing it was upside down. I turned it over and started to read something about the football Champions League. Something had gone badly for Chelsea. I was not sure if that was a bad or good thing but felt I should probably have an opinion if I was reading about it. I decided I was sad about it and put on my best sad face.

It was like a magnetic pull: the broad man turned round at me and smiled, nodding at the paper. I nodded back as my fry-up appeared. Wow. My stomach rumbled at the sight of two gorgeous yellow fried eggs, bacon covered in grease, two plump sausages and a side of beans and toast. I tucked in, groaning in an embarrassing way as I loaded another forkful into my mouth. When I finished I realized there were no men left in the cafe. The breakfast had completely distracted me from my mission.

I headed to the driving range, spirits lifting with every mile I drove, and parked outside a lonely-looking shed buffeted by the wind. I saw fields stretching beyond as far as the eye could see, a neat manicured golf course in the other direction. I breathed in the air, the cold stinging my face and whipping strands of hair in every direction. Feeling refreshed, I opened the boot and pulled out a club with the number 7 on it, like a She-Warrior drawing her sword. I practically ran back to the shed screaming a battle cry.

Walking through the entrance, the noise of the wind faded and I was faced with a vending machine standing on a cold, concrete floor. I realized that this was where I needed to get the golf balls from. I queued politely behind a boy of no more than ten who was tugging on the sleeve of his dad's arm. (Single father? Widowed young? Just him and his son against the world?) Then a woman dressed in top-to-toe diamond-patterned stuff cooed from a nearby bench. 'Get fifty, darling, I am feeling good about this today.'

'Darling' muttered something and then jabbed at the machine. I listened as balls rattled into a wire basket below. The pair wandered away, carrying their precious load.

Fifty must be what I should get if I felt good. And I did.

I had watched a bit of golf on the television. It was sort of like hockey, but with a slightly smaller club, and although I wasn't the best at hockey (horrendous flashbacks of 1994 and that situation with Emily Green and those braces threatened to overwhelm me), I hadn't been completely dreadful. I confidently pressed the '50' button and looked on in horror as fifty golf balls spat all over the concrete floor.

'Wire basket, you need a wire basket!'

A man behind me started laughing, stopping some of the escaped balls in their tracks and scooping them into a basket he was holding.

'Oh God, oh no, oh God!' I scrabbled about hopelessly, collecting the balls into a makeshift pouch in my jumper.

'Here, let me,' said the man, holding out the basket so I could pour the balls into it.

I stopped the moment I heard his words, and looked up to see James standing there, a huge grin on his face.

'Didn't know you were a golfer, Nicola,' he said.

'I, um, I... thought I'd, you know, give it a go,' I mumbled.

Five minutes later, and with the entire range staring at us, we'd finished collecting the balls. I suspected my face was the same shade as James' red jumper.

'Thank you,' I said, taking the basket of balls from him.

'Not at all.'

I waited, not sure what to do next. He pointed to the machine behind me and turned to pick up another wire basket. 'Well, I should...'

'Oh God, sorry! Yes, of course,' I babbled, picking up my club and moving towards the sectioned-off areas of the range. I looked back over my shoulder at him. He was pressing '50'.

I turned into the third, empty section, trying not to think too much about James being here. Placing the wire basket down, I reached for my first ball and balanced it on the bright orange rubber tee that was jutting through a hole in the green square. I took the club, held it with both hands at the top, looked down at the ball, swung through and gazed into the field beyond, shielding my eyes with my hand for good measure. I heard a little laugh behind me. Looking down, I realized the ball had not left the little green square and that James had seen everything.

'Always happens to me on my first swing,' he said kindly.

I nodded, fiddling with the ring on my right hand.

Then I looked down, concentrating doubly hard, and swung. It connected. The ball flew alarmingly off to the left but I made a triumphant little yelp of victory. This was progress.

'Better.' He smiled. The sunlight streaked across his face, highlighting the day-old stubble on his jaw.

'Thanks.'

'You might want to stand a little further back on it. It won't pull like that.'

'Thanks for the tip,' I said, shuffling back a few inches.

I could feel him watching me from his side of the fence.

I looked up. 'Sorry, do you mind, it's hard to...' I indicated the ball and he laughed and popped back over to his side.

I swung through the ball and watched as it lurched forward about thirty feet. It went in a straight line. Much better. I popped my head over to James' side and watched as he missed his own ball.

'Well, that will show me.' He laughed.

The next half an hour was spent hitting balls into the green field. Most of mine ended up diving sharply off to the left or right, and one even flew straight into the tin roof, making all the golfers gasp, turn and stare in unison. I decided to call it a day on that one and noticed that James had started packing up too, even though there were a few balls left in his basket. Something flipped in my stomach. I inwardly told myself off. *Leave the building, Nicola.* I headed to the exit, dropping the wire basket back in the pile. I mumbled a goodbye in James' direction.

'Nicola, wait.'

He jogged over towards me. 'I would offer to take you for a round of golf but I'm not sure either of us is quite "there" yet. How would you fancy coming for a drink with me? Have you got time for some food?'

'I can't. I've got my carpentry class tonight,' I said, putting my lone club back in the boot of the car. 'And I'm sure you are busy too,' I said, before he could ask anything more.

'Well, I am busy, but I want to,' he said, waiting for my response.

I thought of the purpose of the day and realized how ridiculous it was that I had ended up here with James after all my efforts. I looked at his face and was so tempted to say yes, to follow him anywhere for a drink and to sit in the warmth of a pub with someone who seemed to know me. Then I pictured Thalia and shook my head, an excuse spilling out before I could say yes. 'I really do need to get back, prep for my class.' I walked round to open the driver's door. 'I'm so behind,' I lied.

He took a step forward and went to speak but I ducked into my car. I needed to get out of there. Maybe James had just meant it all in a casual, friendly way but I knew what it was like to be the girl left behind.

'See you in the office,' I called brightly, turning the key in the ignition and reversing out of the space.

I left him standing in the car park, his clubs resting by his side, his face in a frown as he watched me drive off.

CHAPTER THIRTY-TWO

I TOOK EXTRA care over my outfit for the second of my carpentry classes that evening. As I jumped out of the shower and padded through to my bedroom, my mind briefly flickered to Alex, his easy smile, and quick laugh. My stomach did a tiny flip and I was pleased that I was excited. I wondered whether the anticipation of seeing him again, or whether the class itself was firing me up. I hoped it was Alex. He seemed nice and I wanted to like him. I wanted to like someone available.

I sat in front of the mirror in my room and piled my hair on top of my head, securing it with some kirby grips. I'd decided on three-quarter-length black trousers and a pink T-shirt, in an attempt to work a sort of Sexy-Peter-Pan look. Grabbing my keys, I raced down the stairs and smiled at Julio as he called goodbye.

Shifting gear and slowing to turn into the car park, I smiled at myself in the rear-view mirror, looking forward to the class. Today I was finishing my tray, or so I'd been promised, and I couldn't wait to get in there and see my handiwork from last week. I wasn't the first to arrive this time and I waved a quick greeting at Tom, who nodded hello while talking to another member of the class. I grabbed an apron from the hooks. My tray rested on the workbench and next to it lay a sheet, no bigger than A5, of bright yellow sandpaper and a small black rectangular block. I set my bag down and looked proudly at the tray, running a hand down the edge, marvelling that it had been made by my fair hands.

I jumped as a voice at my side stated: 'Ah, the first piece. You have broken your carpentry virginity, m'lady.'

Alex grinned at me from behind his safety goggles as he reached over the workbench and pulled his creation towards him. 'A much better effort than this old thing.'

Before I could ask him what he was constructing, Tom bustled over to fill me in on what he had planned. As I pushed my neck through the hole of my apron and tied it up at the back, he wrapped the sandpaper round the block and showed me how to run it along the tray to smooth off the edges and get the surface ready for painting or varnishing.

'You'll have time to sand and varnish today. It will dry pretty quickly with the stuff we use and you can take it home today if you like.'

'Oh, I would!' I burst out, grinning at him.

He laughed. 'Ah, the passionate response of a first-timer.'

I was absurdly overexcited about the prospect, imagining piling the tray with a vintage teapot and delicate little saucers and teacups (note to self: buy vintage teapot and delicate little saucers and teacups) and carrying it out to admiring tea-party guests and saying, 'Oh, this old thing.

It's nothing, just something I made!' (followed by a light tinkly, humble laugh). I set to work immediately, chatting to Alex as I sanded and he measured up a length of slats, cursing every now and again under his breath as he checked the length with a metre ruler.

Concentrating on rubbing down the tray's surface, it was a moment before I realized Alex had thrown his ruler down on the workbench and was grimacing at his creation, hands curled into fists by his side.

'What is it?' I asked.

'I can't do it,' he announced dramatically.

'Of course you can do it,' I said in my most encouraging tone. 'Um... what is it?' I asked.

'See, you can't even tell what it is,' he said hopelessly.

'Oh, of course I can! It's a, well, it's something you, it's...' I started to panic. 'It's a sledge?'

'It is not a sledge,' he wailed. 'It's meant to be the makings of a cot for our firstborn.' His shoulders sagged as he rested his palms flat on the workbench.

I was too distracted by his words to respond. A cot? For a baby? For his baby? I probed my own feelings as I stood there watching him have his meltdown. Was my stomach churning? Did I feel sad? Disappointed? He had certainly been the most promising man I'd met in recent weeks. He picked up two slats and stared at them. I was surprised to realize I didn't actually feel anything. Not a whiff of disappointment. My eyes widened in surprise.

Alex took this as a bad sign. 'You don't think I can do it either,' he stated.

'Hmm?' I focused on him and then burst into life. 'Oh no, not at all, I was thinking about something else. Of course you can do it. What do you need to do?' I asked.

'Make these wooden slats all the same length and slot them into these holes, but I've made the holes too small.'

'Ah,' I stated, my beginner's brain befuddled by the prospect.

'So, I'm not sure I can make the holes bigger without splitting the wood.'

'I see.' I nodded. (I didn't.) 'So your first child!' I smiled, attempting to distract him from gloomy thoughts.

Alex nodded. 'We went to the second scan yesterday. I need to have things ready soon.' His voice rose again.

'Boy or girl?' I stepped in.

'We're not finding out. But I have less than four months until he or she needs to sleep in something and this is not going to be finished, and my wife will give me that look she gives me – the one she gives me when I flick through the TV channels and select *You've Been Framed*, and I will have failed.'

He put his head in his hands as I started laughing. 'You're being a drama queen!' I pointed out.

'I'm allowed,' he mumbled from the workbench, head now resting in his folded arms.

'No, you need to get a grip. Ask Tom for help and get back to work,' I said in my most businesslike voice.

Alex slowly raised his head. 'You're right.'

Tom soon appeared and took over, showing Alex what to do and getting him back on track. I started to varnish the surface of my tray. With every stroke it turned a rich mahogany brown. Like antique furniture, like warm melted chocolate. I was mesmerized and worked in peaceful silence for the next hour. The room had a warm buzz, everyone focused on their projects, some light talk, some manoeuvring and intermittent sawing. An elderly man in front of me had brought tea in a flask and was handing round plastic cups of sweet Earl Grey. His neighbour, Brian, was here because four years ago his wife had dared him to make her a present. He had come to the class ever since. His wife was now the proud owner of three bowls, two trays, a spice rack and a sleigh bed.

Alex was now back in the groove, cradle panic over.

'So do you have kids?' he asked in an off-the-cuff way as we returned to work.

'No,' I answered promptly.

He didn't probe further but the silence wasn't uncomfortable.

At the end of the class I saw a woman smiling at Alex through the square window in the door.

'Is that your wife?' I asked, bobbing my head towards her.

Alex's face glowed as he replied, moving instinctively towards the door. 'That's her.'

She was petite, hair cut to her shoulders and slightly curled, wearing a pink sundress over the world's most delicate bump. She looked like a pregnant extra from a production of *A Midsummer's Night Dream*.

She pushed into the room and seeing the pile of wood on the bench, she raised an eyebrow. 'Er, very promising, darling,' she said.

I smiled at her comment. She caught my eye and we giggled.

Alex turned to her. 'Oi, stop it you two. Fran, this is Nicola, Nicola, my ever-trusting and loving wife, Fran.'

I shook her hand. 'It's nice to meet you, and congratulations,' I said, indicating her bump.

'Thank you,' she replied, moving closer to inspect my work. 'Now this I can get on board with,' she said, examining my recently varnished tray. It did look good. The varnish had dried and the wood looked smoky and rich. 'But Alex is ambitious, imagines he will be able to build us a house soon.'

'You bet on it,' he said, one hand patting the slats. 'This will look wonderful when it's put together, just you see.'

Another arched eyebrow and Fran smiled at me. 'Remind him the baby is due in less than sixteen weeks, won't you, Nicola. Don't let him get involved in any intricate engraving or anything like that. Just a cot. And I'll cancel the order I put into Mothercare.'

'You've ordered one from Mothercare?' Alex asked, aghast.

'Of course not, darling,' she said quickly, winking at me as he turned back to clear away the slats of wood.

I giggled again. 'See you next week, Alex, and lovely to meet you, Fran,' I said, hanging my apron up.

'You too.'

Waving a goodbye to Tom, I picked up the two ends of the newspaper my tray was resting on and pushed backwards through the door, holding it out carefully in front of me as I manoeuvred down the corridor and out into the car park.

I would take it into work. We needed something with which to carry our endless cups of tea.

Fran and Alex emerged as I was driving out. Alex had stopped, one hand resting gently on the belly of his wife as he pulled her, laughing, towards him for a kiss. I wanted that, I thought as I drove past. Briefly, a face flashed across my mind. My stomach twisted and I distracted myself by turning on the car radio and accelerating away.

CHAPTER THIRTY-THREE

'**W**HY ARE we whispering?'

'I'm not sure, it just feels like a whispering moment.'

'I agree.'

Mark and I went back to gazing up at the stars scattered above our heads. He'd got us into the planetarium after work. It was amazing really. Lying back in my seat, it really was as if there were no edges to it all. I really felt like it was just tiny me and the universe.

'So, did you have intercourse with New Year's Eve Man?' This was already a creepy question from Mark, but seemed worse because he whispered it.

'Mark.' I sat up with a frown.

'What? It's a perfectly sensible question.'

'Do you have to call it *intercourse*?' I craned my neck to look at him. He'd rolled his leather jacket to create a makeshift pillow and was staring at Orion's Belt or the Saucepan. Or something.

'That's what it's called.' He shrugged.

I rolled my eyes.

'Fine,' he muttered. 'Nicola, did you make sweet love on your date?'

I lay back down. 'No, Mark, I did not make sweet love. In fact I didn't make anything.'

'Was that James?' he asked.

'What? No, it wasn't. James is my boss and nothing is happening with James, and why do you keep bringing him up anyway?'

'Boss? Is that a euphemism?'

'What?'

Mark was shaking with quiet laughter.

'You're a Prick Face. How's it going with Carol?' I asked, swiftly changing the subject.

The ensuing silence made me sit up again. 'Is everything all right with you two?'

Mark sat up. 'Well, actually, Nic... I was going to say...'

I looked agog. 'Mark Brown, tell me you have not broken up with a girl who is utterly perfect for you in every way. A woman who loves disgusting rodents, who's super fun and who has a figure that rivals Jessica Rabbit...' I realized I was huffing.

'Nic, Nic...' Mark reached out and punched my arm.

'Ow,' I yelped.

'Sorry, I was just trying to shut you up. I have to tell you something.'

'You could go for the traditional: "Sister, I have to tell you something."'

'Whatever, Nic. This is important. Carol and I haven't broken up. In fact...'

If it wasn't so dark in the observatory, I'd swear my brother was blushing.

'...I wanted to ask, whether, and I want your honest opinion, Nic, whether you think I should ask her to move in with me?'

There was a perfect silence and over our heads a star streaked across the sky.

I sat up slowly, blinked a few times and looked at my lovely brother.

'That is a brilliant idea. Yes, you definitely should.'

And then, grinning, I threw myself into a hug and punched his arm so hard that he swore. I knew my brother had found the one person who could make him happy. And that made me happy too.

On the way home my feet became heavier and, climbing the stairs to the flat, I felt weary. The excitement of Mark's news had worn off slightly by the time I closed the door on the outside world, and instead I felt lonely and tired.

As I poured myself a glass of wine I ranted inwardly at myself. What kind of person did this make me? My brother was having an epic romance and here I was feeling sorry for myself. I was ashamed of myself. I should have dragged him back to the flat and pulled out a bottle of champagne so we could toast this lovely moment in his life. I should have forced him to sit on the sofa and fed him lots of sisterly advice.

Maybe that was my problem. Who was I to advise him? What did I really know about relationships? Here I was, sitting in my pristine flat, alone, again. I'd spent the last two months on useless dates with hopeless men and had nothing to show for it.

The image of Alex with his wife popped into my head along with my brother's face when he talked about Carol — they were incredibly lucky. What an amazing thing to have, to know that kind of love was possible.

I sighed lightly and a little flame of hope stirred within. I had to keep up the search. It was worth it. I'd seen proof.

CHAPTER THIRTY-FOUR

STRUGGLING INTO the office just past eight-thirty the next day, I was surprised to see the door ajar and Caroline, who normally wafted into the office just after nine o'clock, rearranging the furniture and scattering any spare surface with shiny confetti pieces shaped like tiny balloons. She turned, mouth half-open, before putting a hand to her chest.

'Nic! Oh good, you can help. I thought you were James arriving early.'

I put my bag down on my chair. 'What are you doing?'

'It's James' birthday! I thought we should make a fuss of him.' She threw me a pack of unopened balloons. 'Get to work.'

'You know it's not even nine o'clock and I've had no caffeine as yet.'

She rolled her eyes and walking towards the office kitchen, said, 'Coming right up, your majesty.' She bowed in the doorway and I laughed, tearing open the bag and taking out a balloon in an alarming shade of yellow. By the time Caroline returned with a mug (that said 'I Love Leeds' for no discernible reason), I was surrounded by an assortment of balloons in varying sizes and had the onset of earache.

Caroline tapped at her computer and Lesley Gore's 'It's My Party' started up.

'Just getting us in the groove,' she called over the chorus.

I looked to the heavens in mock exasperation and reached for the mug.

The music was still blaring when James appeared. He laughed as he walked through the office. 'You *have* been busy,' he chuckled, looking round the room.

Caroline walked over and folded him into an enormous hug. He laughed again and kissed her on the cheek. 'You're both brilliant.'

He leant down to kiss me on the cheek. Our eyes met. 'Thank you.'

I felt my whole face get hot. I looked away hurriedly, my insides screeching.

We ate *Ben 10* chocolate cake for breakfast off kitchen roll, crumbs scattered over the CVs on my desk, and drank tea with a drop of whisky. ('It's a special day,' Caroline argued, pouring in a sizeable amount.) She was making us both laugh with her tales from the weekend. Apparently Ben had decided that clothes really inhibited people and he wanted to be 'like Adam in the garden'. The trouble was that he decided to become Adam in the garden at one of her husband's work dinner parties.

James was sitting on the floor, head resting against the wall, long legs stretched out. His tie had come loose and he clearly hadn't shaved that morning. He would have looked devilishly attractive if Caroline hadn't forced him into a cone-shaped hat emblazoned with 'Birthday Boy' in big cartoon letters.

A Meatloaf track played, and as I leant against the wall laughing at something Caroline said, James' hand brushed against mine. My stomach lurched. I felt as if I were fourteen years old. Before I could look at him there was a cough from the doorway. There, dressed in an immaculate navy-blue pencil skirt and silk cream blouse, stood Thalia. I snatched my hand away from James' like I'd touched the hob. James struggled to his feet as Thalia tottered into the room, looking down at us, her height made more impressive by four-inch Louboutins.

'Cosy,' she sniffed.

I laughed, one 'ha': horribly forced. James had taken off his hat and I hastily brushed confetti pieces off my jumper into my hand, feeling foolish, seeing the scene through her eyes. Caroline remained sitting on her cushion, openly put out that the party appeared to have had its moment. She offered Thalia some cake.

Thalia replied, 'Wheat free,' and tapped her stomach, which made Caroline place a hand on hers protectively.

'Er, this is a surprise,' James cut across.

'I just came to wish you a happy birthday.' She smiled: it didn't reach her eyes. 'Shall we?' She motioned with her head to his office and James took a moment to follow her train of thought.

'Yes, okay.' He turned round. 'Caroline, Nic, thank you

for the impromptu birthday party.' He dabbed at the corner of his mouth, missing a chocolate smear that Thalia then reached out and wiped for him with her forefinger. James took a step back. The intimate gesture made the edges of my mouth turn down. They disappeared into his office. Caroline looked at me, head on one side as she searched my face. She didn't say anything, just got up and started to clear away the empty mugs. I busily flicked the crumbs from my skirt with a piece of kitchen roll, feeling foolish that there was a lump in my throat.

Thalia left shortly after she arrived, a brief grunt of goodbye at Caroline, who rolled her eyes a fraction at me as we listened to her descending the stairs outside the office. Too kind to comment, Caroline continued to help me arrange auditions for a new voiceover campaign, sending over clips to the company and ensuring our artists were booked in and given all the right details. It was busy and the bustle and action worked as a distraction. Then Caroline received a call that made her face fall. She spoke into the phone. 'No, well, you better, no, it'll be too late for that, no, no he's working now. I'll come, they can wait here for me. No, that's fine. Okay, okay, thanks.'

She groaned as she put the receiver back. 'Childminders are the bane of my life,' she tutted. 'Nic, would you mind? I've got two abandoned children this afternoon and a whole heap of work to get through. Can we bring them in here? They'll be good. I'll promise them McDonald's and doughnuts for dinner.'

I waved a hand. 'Of course,' I said, pressing 'Send' on

an email and looking back to the screen. 'It'll be fine. Don't worry.'

Caroline grabbed her keys from her desk. 'Great, I'll go and get them now. Could you tell James? He's less likely to shout at you.'

'I'm less likely to do what?' A voice came from the office. 'Who is using my name in vain, Caroline Harper?'

'Nic will explain,' she called back to him, zipping out of the office door and down the stairs before I had a chance to refuse.

I sighed and got up, pushing open the door to James' office. 'She's had a babysitter crisis and is bringing the kids in,' I explained, turning to leave.

'Nic... Nicola,' he called after me. I looked back at him. He had a pen mark on his left cheek and his hair was a little dishevelled. 'Thank you for this morning. It was sweet of you both and I'm sorry that, well, I'm sor—'

I cut him off. 'It was Caroline,' I explained, voice abrupt. I regretted the tone the moment I saw his face fall a fraction.

'Yes, right. Anyway, it was a lovely thought and I just wanted to thank you.'

I replied in a quieter tone. 'That's fine, of course. Happy Birthday.'

He lifted a little out of his seat as if he was going to come over to me, but just as quickly seemed to change his mind.

'You know, Nicola, I think you might have the wrong idea about Tha—'

'I need to get on and work,' I said, feeling silly, trying to regain the upper hand, behave professionally.

'Yes, right. I have lots of work,' he said, shuffling papers about.

I nodded at him curtly. 'Best get on.'

Ben and Alice arrived in a whirlwind half an hour later. Caroline, climbing the stairs outside, called instructions of 'calm' as they rushed ahead. Ben ran over to my desk, grinning at me, and held something towards me.

Caroline appeared in the doorway, puffing and dabbing at her forehead as she entered the room. 'Oh, this is going to be chaos, isn't it?'

Alice was already upending the wastepaper basket. Caroline scooped her up and plonked her on her office chair to spin.

'Come on, monkey,' she said, making Alice squeal as the chair spun.

Ben was still holding up a little wooden item, a hexagonal-shaped piece of wood with legs.

'He wanted to show you his cake stand,' Caroline explained, laughing. 'He made it at school and I told him you'd been doing carpentry too.' She turned to Ben. 'What did I tell you Nic made us in her class?'

'A tray,' Ben half-shouted.

'Don't shout, Ben. Do you want to see it?' she asked.

'Yee harrrrrr,' he replied, which Caroline took to mean 'Yes, Mother.'

'I'll get it,' I laughed, pushing back my chair and already feeling a million times lighter as I took Ben's stand from him and examined it. 'Ben, this is really good,' I said. 'I love the way you've nailed the legs on.'

Ben grinned like he might burst.

I brought back the tray and he took hold of it with both hands, really carefully, like it might fall to pieces. 'Cool,' he said. Then he put it on the floor, loaded all his cars onto it and carried it round the room, nose in the air, like a butler.

Alice suddenly appeared at my side and was holding both her hands up to me.

'She wants you to pick her up, Nic,' said Caroline, looking at me a little nervously.

'Oh,' I said, startled. Then, without really thinking, bent down and picked Alice up, returning to my desk to sit with her on my lap. She was lighter than I expected and up close her skin was so smooth I nearly asked her what moisturizer she used. Then I remembered she was three years old and that was the answer. I'd never liked being around children before but this was easy. It was nice. Alice sat quietly on my lap and I tapped out an email, talking her through the very boring job I was doing. She seemed happy to sit there and Caroline and I actually managed to achieve something, if only for a few minutes. Ben rolled his cars round the floor, seeming very focused on lining them all up into 'one long traffic jam'.

'That's nice,' Caroline muttered in response. 'It looks just like the M5, darling, well done.'

Ben beamed and proceeded to make the queue longer.

Alice got bored and turned to look at me. She put both hands on either side of my face and squashed together. I puffed my cheeks out.

'You're very pretty,' she announced.

I felt my cheeks getting hot under her little hands before she released them. 'Thank you, Alice. You're very pretty too,' I said.

'Can you brush my hair?' she asked, running to grab a small hairbrush from Caroline's bag.

'I suppose so,' I replied, taking the brush from her and slowly dragging it through her fine, strawberry-blonde hair.

James emerged from the office at just that moment and practically tripped over the M5 tailback. 'Whoa there,' he said, bending down to look at what Ben was doing.

'It's a traffic jam.' Ben grinned proudly.

'It certainly is,' agreed James. 'Like on a Bank Holiday.'

Ben nodded.

James gave him a high-five and then stood up, looking over at me with Alice on my lap.

'She's pretty,' Alice repeated, pointing at me and looking at James.

'She is, isn't she,' agreed James.

I squirmed in my seat but couldn't turn away as I was pinned down by Alice. *Focus on the hair brushing*, I thought, feeling my whole body get hotter under the scrutiny. When I took a peek back up, James was still looking right at me, a small smile on his face.

CHAPTER THIRTY-FIVE

WALKING HOME at the end of the day, I thought about dinner. Lightly buttered asparagus with some Parma ham, a hot slab of ciabatta, maybe some melted Camembert for dipping. Before I started salivating onto the pavement, I fished in my bag for a stick of chewing gum, rooting around past stray receipts, loose coins and kirby grips. When did my handbag get this messy? How had I not noticed? My hand lighted on the gum and I pulled it out triumphantly. I was about to put it into my mouth when I felt a hand on my shoulder. I yelped and spun round, holding the gum out like a weapon. My attacker looked at me coolly and I nearly dropped the gum in surprise.

'Thalia,' I said, the shock apparent in my voice.

'It's Nicola, isn't it?'

I frowned, questions swimming around my mind. 'Can I help?' I asked, noticing her usually tanned face looked paler than usual, and that her eyes, normally carefully ringed with kohl, were a little red-rimmed. 'Are you okay?'

'I wanted to talk to you,' she stated.

'Okay.'

'There's no need to be sarcastic,' she snapped.

My mouth clamped up. I hadn't meant to sound sarcastic. I felt a stirring of annoyance. What did she want? Couldn't she take her glossy, Armani-clad body off and get out of here? I had lightly buttered asparagus to eat. I was definitely going to have the Camembert. I waited for her to say something else, both of us standing on the street as commuters steered round us.

'I wanted to ask that you leave him alone.'

I didn't need to ask her who she meant by 'him'.

I felt the blood rush to my face. 'I'm not, I don't...'

'I know all about girls like you,' she announced, eyes narrowing. 'And I won't let you make trouble for me. I hear what he says about you. Oh, it's all very cosy up in that office, isn't it?' She stressed the word 'cosy', drawing it out so that I grimaced with every letter.

What had he said about me? What about our office? I fought the urge to ask, a little bubble of, what was it – hope? – suddenly sparking in my stomach.

'Thalia, I'm not doing anything,' I said, gesturing with my arms.

'You know what you're doing.'

'I'm not doing anything,' I repeated.

She scoffed quickly, her eyes glinting.

Was I doing anything? Was I causing trouble? I tried to look at it from her point of view. The woman in the office, the birthday party, the brief moments when we'd shared a laugh or a joke. That look... Hadn't I had a few thoughts like

291

this in recent weeks? Hadn't I considered... I shook my head, I hadn't *done* anything, though.

Something gnawed at me. Colleagues were close, they shared some funny times, they spent time together, that's all it was. And she couldn't know what I felt. I felt tears sting the back of my eyes. I brushed at my face, feeling suddenly angry. I would not stand here and let this woman see me cry.

I focused on the space above her head and talked to the air. 'You have nothing to worry about.'

'Oh, I know that.' She laughed, a high, mean little noise.

'Well then,' I said quietly, head dropping.

'I just wanted to be crystal clear about things, Nicola. I wanted to tell you that I know what you're doing and I wanted to spell out what I think about it, what I've seen. And don't you dare think of talking to James about this, because I'll deny we spoke. And you'll look even more pathetic with those little doe eyes following him around. It's pitiful.'

Was it? Was I pitiful? The tears threatened to spill over. I swallowed, trying to recover myself.

She was done with me. She smiled widely. 'I'm glad we talked.' She spun round, long glossy hair flying out behind her, one hand on her black leather handbag, the other hailing a nearby taxi.

I stood on the street looking after her, all purpose forgotten, utterly miserable. I wanted to throw up. I shuffled slowly over to a bench just up the hill, sank onto it, the little stick of gum, hot from me squeezing it, dropping to the floor as I sat.

CHAPTER THIRTY-SIX

```
Single girl WLTM unattached
man who she doesn't work
with and who doesn't
have a nasty supermodel
girlfriend with great
clothes.
```
Contact: Box No. 5790

DRAGGING MYSELF back to my feet, I realized I had left all the notes for my meeting tomorrow back in the office. I would need something to take my mind off things that evening and so I trudged back down Park Street to fetch them. Believing everyone to have gone home, I was alarmed to hear a voice and realized that James was talking on the phone. I was in no hurry to see him and walked quickly over to my desk to scoop up the notes and get out of there. The door to his office was open and I was relieved to hear him tell whoever it was that he was going away over the next couple of days, 'working' (if you could call your hot supermodel-type girlfriend wrapping her legs and Louboutin-encased feet around you in some kind of spa hotel 'work'). I was just about to escape when I heard him click down the phone. 'Is that you, Nicola?' he called through.

Damn.

Frozen to the spot, I closed my eyes. Could I simply creep out? Pretend I wasn't here? Why couldn't I have just gone straight home?

He stepped out of his office.

'I thought it was you,' he said, one hand through his hair, a hint of a smile on his face. 'I thought I saw you outside just now.'

I nodded. I desperately wanted to flee the scene, magic myself home.

'That was Chris on the phone,' James said. 'He's renewed his contract with us, so thank you for er... well, whatever you did to persuade him, I'm grateful.'

I bristled with the suggestion. 'I didn't *do* anything.'

'I know. I'm sorry, that isn't what I meant.' He took a step towards me. 'So, why are you back here, Nicola?'

'I was just popping back for some notes,' I claimed, shuffling the papers on my desk.

'Was that Thalia I saw you talking to in the street just now?'

'Yes,' I replied.

I didn't need him to say anything more. I wanted to get out of there, to get home and hide under a duvet and block the world out. I shoved the notes in my bag and left the office without another word.

Maybe Thalia was right and I *was* trying to capture

James' attention at work, trying to muscle in with him, forge a closeness with somebody. Had Thalia seen me for what I was? The guilty party? I walked down the street and cringed as I thought of the New Year's Eve and my behaviour with Chris, a married man – something I had always said I would never do. And fine, I hadn't known he was married but maybe I *was* that girl, a girl that didn't care about others, just selfishly going about doing whatever she liked and stampeding over the relationships of other people. All these efforts to bag a man in time for Valentine's Day had simply done one thing – highlighted how much I wanted to find a match, someone I could laugh with at the same stupid things, be myself with and not be afraid to show the ugly bits or worry they'd be put off if I was just me. I wanted the nights in together mooching about cooking food, watching films and planning trips away. More than that I wanted to make plans with someone else, travel with them, share a flat with them. I wanted my life to change.

Valentine's Day is round the corner and I've lost the dare, I haven't managed it. I'm going to be alone again.

My mobile trilled. 'Sis,' came Mark's voice. 'That was quick.'

'Hey.'

'You normally force me to leave you voicemail, I—'

'I'm on my way home,' I interrupted him.

'You okay?'

I made a noise somewhere between a 'Huh' and a 'No'.

Mark lowered his voice. 'I'll pop over for an hour.'

I could feel the tears threaten again.

I gulped and whispered a quiet 'Thanks' and hung up.

Wrapping my coat around me, I traipsed back to my empty flat. I felt so tired, like I'd been running for ages. I needed to sit down.

Mark came over as promised and I let him in with a smile, already feeling lighter just looking at him, beloved helmet under his left arm, leather jacket slung over his right.

'You worried me, sis. It's not like you to sound so down,' he announced, drawing me in for a one-armed hug.

'I'm all right,' I said, giving him a small smile and walking through to the kitchen. 'Let me get you some tea on.'

'Hey, sis,' he said as I poured the boiling water into a mug.

'Yeah?'

Mark looked shyly at his toes. 'Carol agreed to move in with me,' he said, not able to keep from grinning.

'That's *brilliant* news,' I said, butting him affectionately with my hip.

'Hey, you know you'll work it all out too,' he said.

'I hope so,' I admitted, handing him his tea and pouring myself a glass of milk.

'You will. You'll meet someone perfect for you. You're a cracking girl. Although,' he paused, 'you do currently have a milk moustache.'

I swiped at my face and gave Mark a push for good measure when I heard the flat buzzer going. Frowning at Mark, I hurried through to the living room and pushed down on the intercom to hear James' voice crackling over the line.

'I work with her...' he was saying in an insistent voice.

The unmistakeable Portuguese reply was clear. 'I've not seen you here before.'

'It's okay, Julio,' I called into the intercom. 'I know him.'

Without a moment to compose myself, and hastily wiping at my face for any last traces of milk, I watched in slow motion as James walked up the stairwell. He was wearing the camel-coloured winter coat that I loved and seemed flustered when he appeared at the top of the stairs.

Catching my perplexed expression as I stood in the doorway, he glanced behind him. 'You have quite a bouncer downstairs,' he laughed. 'I had to prove my honour or he wouldn't let me pass.'

I smiled in a slightly stunned way, questions buzzing around my head. 'That's Julio,' I said, in an oddly high voice.

James started to thrust objects awkwardly into my arms. 'I thought you looked a bit pale earlier. I thought you might be ill. I brought you some get-well gifts,' he explained.

'Oh, thank you,' I said, feeling redness creep up my neck, embarrassed that he was bringing me presents when I was perfectly fine, just feeling upset after being confronted by his girlfriend.

A chisel and a box of Maltesers.

'I know you've taken up carpentry so I assumed you might find some use for it, the chisel that is, the Maltesers are just for eating.' He gave a quick laugh and put a hand up to the back of his neck. If I hadn't known better I would have guessed he was embarrassed too. Why couldn't I be better in these situations? Why couldn't I put him at ease?

'Thank you, that's very kind,' I said, smiling. Despite

myself, I felt some of my earlier happiness returning. James had come to see me, he'd brought me gifts.

'Look, Nicola,' he started. 'I know you spoke to Thalia. And the thing is, I wanted to be clear with you that—'

Just then Mark's voice called out, 'Tea or coffee?'

James took a step backwards. 'I'm so sorry, I'm interrupting, you have company already, of course you do, I'll go,' he said, turning round to leave.

'No, it's fine, come in and have tea,' I said, concerned I sounded pathetic. 'He's just—'

'No, I should've thought, just bursting in on you.' He looked at me, his face fixed in a frown. 'I misunderstood.' He started back down the stairs.

Mark appeared in the doorway, looping an arm round my shoulders.

'Hey,' he said, looking at James.

James paused in his descent, turned back to see Mark and I in the doorway, and continued quickly down the stairs, muttering a last apology as he went.

'James—' I called, but he'd already gone.

'What was that all about?' asked Mark, eyeing me as I clutched my chisel and chocolate.

I swallowed heavily, my throat dry. 'Nothing. It was nothing,' I said, pushing the door firmly closed.

Later that evening when Mark had gone and the Maltesers had been eaten, I admitted defeat. Tomorrow was Valentine's Day and I had not been able to find the perfect man. My stomach churned, and in a flurry of activity I grabbed my laptop and typed something into Google. I wouldn't be alone on Valentine's Day. I couldn't face it. I needed to take drastic action. In a rash click of buttons, the uploading of my payment details, and a gulp, I had done it: I was going on a singles holiday.

I picked up the phone and dialled Caroline's number, explaining to her voicemail that I wouldn't be in work after all tomorrow. Then, in a babble, I recounted my latest hasty holiday-booking action. I wanted her to know that I hadn't given up. I wanted her to know that the dare had changed me. Had coloured in my life. As I made a quick goodbye on her machine and hung up, I wondered briefly whether I would continue in that job. I loved it, but how on earth would I cope with seeing him every day?

I shook myself to rid my head of the thought and pulled down my suitcase. Sliding the door of the wardrobe across, I stared at my clothes. Right. What outfit would best suit a girl on a singles holiday?

CHAPTER THIRTY-SEVEN

THE SLOW, steady patter of rain seemed to reflect the bleak mood I found myself in as I took a cab to the airport the next morning and lugged my suitcase into the 'Departures' area. My heart felt as heavy as the bag I was struggling with as I looked around the terminal at all the couples and families leaving on their holidays. How had it come to this? Could anyone be this depressed on their way to a holiday in Crete? Should I turn back? Immediately, I pictured work and James' face and realized I couldn't.

The queue to the check-in desk seemed to snake round the entire building and I stood listlessly as we moved forward inch by inch. A tap on the shoulder and I was acquainted with a girl wearing an orange vest-top and pink patent stilettos.

'You going too, eh?'

My head must have nodded because she replied, 'Sick! Me too!' and then pointed at her luggage. 'Packing light as ever. Ha ha.'

I zoned out while the queue moved forward, offering vague responses as Overly Bright Airport Girl continued to try and make conversation. I attempted to cheer myself up with the thought that I was off on a holiday. *Come on, Nicola, there will be sunshine and loungers.*

'You know, I've been on three of these holidays and I've *always* pulled.' She paused to stretch a bit of the gum out before rolling it back in her mouth. 'Shagged one guy for the whole week last time and then he got picked up at the airport by his *wife*. Awks.'

She smiled at me. It was my line.

'That's *terrible*,' I said.

'Yeah, whatevs. I 'spose it just wasn't meant to be. Better than the 2011 guy who was super clingy. I had to be all, like, "Hellooo, back off, I am totes not into back hair."'

Me again: 'Er...'

'Soooo, you hoping to meet a fella?'

I opened my mouth to speak, but the words stuck in my throat. I wondered again what I was doing in this queue of people: how had my life come to this?

'Your first time?' Her head cocked to one side.

'Yes,' I confirmed, as the gorgeously tanned woman behind the check-in desk beckoned me over. I approached and slid my passport over the counter. Overly Bright Airport Girl stayed fixed at my shoulder. I waited for Check-In Woman to shoo her back into the queue, but it was clearly assumed we were travelling together because Check-In Woman took her passport too. I turned to Overly Bright Airport Girl and said with a gulp: 'It's... my first singles holiday.'

She squeaked at my announcement, her glossy pink mouth a big 'Ooh' of pleasure. A tall man in the queue next door sniggered.

I coughed and continued. 'Yes. I am a single woman who is deliberately going on this holiday with the hope of meeting someone who will love me.'

Check-In Woman looped a sticker through the handle of my suitcase and raised one neatly pencilled eyebrow. Arms wide, I turned to the rest of the airport. 'It is my first ever, *ever* time on a singles holiday,' I cried. 'I booked it last night because it seemed like the right thing to do. I just needed to... I wanted to, you know... um...' I trailed off idiotically, watching as my suitcase juddered along the luggage belt and out of sight.

In the distance I thought I heard someone calling my name and in that moment my heart soared. I whipped round – hair flicking across my face in my haste – and scanned the crowds hopefully...

Nope.

Nothing.

I'd imagined it. My stomach lurched.

Overly Bright Airport Girl slung her meaty arm round my shoulders.

'We should totes sit together on the flight. I'll show you my holiday pictures from last year. I've got them all on my phone. All of them.'

I sniffed, nodded once. 'Great.'

Nicola Brown, how the hell did you end up here?

The sticker was on and the suitcase was about to make its bumpy journey out of sight when, once more, I thought I heard a voice call my name. I frowned and looked over my shoulder but saw only Overly Bright Airport Girl. I was just about to burst into tears, when I heard my name again, closer this time, and from the corner of my eye noticed someone waving. A man, a tall man, a man I recognized, waving at me and yelling my name repeatedly. It was James. Warmth flooded through me, and with my mouth hanging open, I did a half-wave back.

'Sorry, hold on, I, well, I...'

Suddenly, I seized my bag and hauled it off the scales, wheeled it round and pushed backwards through the queue of people. There was swearing and Check-In Woman was calling something after me, but all I knew was that I had to get out of that line. My heart lifted in hopeful anticipation. It was a long way to travel to the airport, and he'd have had to go through the business of parking and walking to 'Departures', which was a long way from the car park and, well, he wouldn't do that if he didn't really, really want to see me, would he?

I stopped in my tracks. Maybe he was just taking a business flight somewhere and caught sight of me and waved hello? Worse, maybe he and Thalia were off on some kind of week-long sex trip in the sun. I looked up, scanning the crowds for James again. It occurred to me then that maybe I was hallucinating him. Was I so desperate that I'd conjured him up, in the airport, waving at me, just like in a scene out of *Love Actually*? Oh my God, how foolish. I was running towards a mirage, like a thirsty woman in a desert. I buried my head into my hands.

'Nicola.'

I looked up, and he was definitely there, waving at me.

I tried to compose myself, tried to look nonchalant and as if this situation was normal. I failed completely. As he pushed through the crowds and drew up right by me I guessed that I resembled a startled rabbit in the headlights; staring eyes, frozen and unable to move. James reached out a hand to me, before pulling it back.

'Don't go,' he said.

I didn't know what to say, so I stood there dumbly.

'It's not, I need to explain,' James continued. 'The thing is...'

I'd never seen him like this, tongue-tied, awkward. I felt my insides growing warm and then admonished myself internally, reminding my brain that he was going out with Thalia and had no interest in me whatsoever.

'Thalia should never have said those things,' he said.

'How do you know what she said?' I frowned.

'I asked her.'

He was here to apologize for her rudeness?

I nodded. 'Well, thank you. But I can look after myself.'

'No, I know that, Nic. But, you see, she shouldn't have said those things because they are totally untrue. Thalia and I haven't been seeing each other for months. She became so difficult before Christmas, pretending her mother was ill so she could stay on in the apartment, lying to me again and again about things. Turning up uninvited. It's completely over.'

James took a step closer. He took my hand.

'So... you're free?' I checked.

'That's what I came to tell you yesterday, in case, well,

in case you were interested. And then I saw the man – who Caroline has since told me was your brother, but who, at the time, I thought was... you know... your boyfriend, or...'

I looked up into James' face. His lovely, kind, open face. And I smiled fully, deeply, for the first time in a while.

'So, you came to tell me that you're not seeing anyone, in case I was interested?' I asked.

'Exactly. Caroline told me what you were doing and I just couldn't let you go without telling you, so I... I made a mad dash for the airport. And here I am.'

'To tell me you are currently available?' I clarified.

'Well, actually, I was hoping to go on holiday with my new girlfriend,' he said, drawing me closer towards him.

'Oh, really!' I laughed, my whole body feeling light and ridiculous, like if he let me go I would soar towards the ceiling.

'We *are* at the airport.' He shrugged. 'It would be rude not to.' He steered me round to face the Departures Board. 'So, where do you fancy?'

I leant back into him and his arms encircled me.

'I've never been to Florence before.'

'Neither have I.'

He took my hand and walked me over to the tickets desk. 'Two tickets to Florence, please.' He slid a credit card across. 'And we'd like to travel first class.'

As the tickets printed, James grinned at me like a child. He squeezed me close. I snuggled into him.

'Hey.' He pulled back and grinned at me. 'You know it's Valentine's Day tomorrow?'

'I do.'

He nodded. 'Well, I did want to wait until we got somewhere a little more, well, private, but I just can't help myself.'

And, ever so slowly, he leant his head down to me. As my arms wrapped around his neck, our lips met and we had our first amazing kiss.

ACKNOWLEDGEMENTS

THIS IS going to get gushy. I can tell.

Firstly to some lovely ladies who agreed to read early drafts of the book and give me some invaluable feedback – Rachel Hawes and Amanda Murphy – thank you for your time and generosity. And to Richard Campbell, my new writing buddy, for an inspiring edit sesh over Skype. Another thank you to some friends who shall remain anonymous (Olivia Solon) for their disastrous date stories. We feel your pain and can comfort you with the thought that at least they make great book fodder.

It has been an absolute blast to be part of Novelicious Books and I don't think I could have enjoyed the process more. Thank you to Louise for her eagle eye and her encouraging edit notes. To Jade for proofreading so well (I was going to leave out an 'o' and make a proofreading joke but I imagine she would be tempted to fix it). And of course to Kerry for being a total pleasure to work with and for getting me into cool magazines and blogs yo.

An enormous squishy hug-style thank you to Kirsty at Novelicious for first believing in this book. For her hilarious emails, edit notes and energy. And to Edd for his incredible work on the original cover, website and all things super techie.

A huge thanks to the whole team at Darley Anderson for the support – it is such a fantastic agency. Particular thanks to Mary for her enthusiasm and time in drumming up foreign rights interest, for Sheila David for trying to land me a movie deal (*chants 'GO SHEILA YOU CAN DO IT I BELIEVE IN YOU'*) and, of course, to my amazing agent Clare who has simply been the best agent I could have wished for. She would have corrected that sentence.

This book is dedicated to my parents for always making me believe anything is possible. For Daddy – I hope there aren't too many split infinitives – and to my own Ma 'Basia' for reading eighteen versions of the manuscript, and who is as chirpy as her namesake in the novel. To my sisters and brother for the bants – well done, team, I hope you LOL big time – and finally to my ever-patient husband, Ben. It is really not easy living with someone with a full-time job and a full-time obsession, and he is brilliant at not getting at me when the house hasn't been unpacked and there is no food in the fridge. Or any of the cupboards. Love you all big time. Huge.

And of course lastly to the many book bloggers, other authors and readers who have contacted me or tweeted me, retweeted me and generally roused such enthusiasm. My online buddies have been fantastic – you really are an incredible bunch of bighearted, bookish nerds.